Loving a
Borrego Brother

Loving a Borrego Brother

Johnni Sherri

URBAN Renaissance

www.urbanbooks.net

Urban Books, LLC
300 Farmingdale Road, NY-Route 109
Farmingdale, NY 11735

Loving a Borrego Brother
Copyright © 2019 Johnni Sherri

ISBN 13: 978-1-64556-042-5
ISBN 10: 1-64556-042-2

First Mass Market Printing April 2020
First Trade Paperback Printing November 2019
Printed in the United States of America

10 9 8 7 6 5 4 3 2 1

*This is a work of fiction. Any references or similar-
ities to actual events, real people, living or dead,
or to real locales are intended to give the novel a
sense of reality. Any similarity in other names,
characters, places, and incidents is entirely coin-
cidental.*

Distributed by Kensington Publishing Corp.
Submit Orders to:
Customer Service
400 Hahn Road
Westminster, MD 21157-4627
Phone: 1-800-733-3000
Fax: 1-800-659-2436

Chapter 1

Risa

As the hot water rained down onto my body, I silently cringed from the burning sensation I felt in places coated with open wounds. The areas appeared to be mostly welts and deep bruises from what I could see. While I stood in the shower, I closed my eyes and unwillingly allowed my mind to relive the horrific events of the night before.

I stood in the kitchen, making Zo's favorite spaghetti and meatballs for dinner. While humming softly to myself, I suddenly received a text from Vick. Vick was one of Zo's workers, and he was also one of his closest friends. He was asking where Zo was because he'd apparently been hitting his line all day for an urgent matter and Zo hadn't been answering. I sent him a quick and innocent reply, stating that I'd get Zo to give him a call.

As soon as the next text came through from Vick, saying, Cool, Zo was walking in the kitchen. Without saying a single word to me, he aggressively snatched the phone out of my hand and looked down at the screen.

"Fuck Vick texting you for?" he asked, already wearing a scowl on his face.

Vick and I had also been friends since high school. As a matter of fact, I'd known him longer than I'd known my boyfriend Zo. So the mere facts that I had his number in my phone and he had mine were normal.

"He was looking for you," I said, staring back at him with confusion.

"That nigga don't need to be texting you at all!"

He then paused, allowing negative thoughts to slowly seep into his mind. I watched the expression on his face gradually change from irritation to rage.

"And what the fuck were you texting him back for? You wanna fuck that nigga or som'?" he began to accuse with his finger pointing in my face. Then his left eyebrow raised, almost as if he had just had this big epiphany or something.

"No! Of course not," I quickly answered, shaking my head.

Zo and I had been dating since junior year of high school, so I could always tell when he was about to snap. There was a certain crazy look in his eyes and something about his tone of voice that was always a dead giveaway for me. This night was no different.

"Then why the fuck you texting that nigga?" he roared with spit flying out of his mouth.

"Zo'mire, please calm down. He was just looking for you. That's all!" I pleaded, holding my hands up to his chest in hopes that he would calm down and be rational.

But as always, that didn't happen. He forcefully grabbed me by the hair and threw me down on the cool tile floor, causing me to shriek out in pain. Although I was used to his abuse, I was still scared shitless each and every time. As a matter of fact, there was never a time he'd put his hands on me when I felt prepared. Zo never hit me in the face though, because he didn't want anyone to see the bruises on me. To state it plainly, he was a coward. He once told me that I was too pretty to have bruises on my face. As if having bruises everywhere else on my body was acceptable.

Immediately after forcing me down onto the floor, he began kicking me hard in the stomach and on my arms from where I tried to block him. His boots stomping onto me repeatedly left me lying on my back, defenseless. As Zo's rhythmic arms went up, his foot came crashing down with more and more force each time. The only words I could manage in between my pain-filled cries were, "Please stop."

"You wanna be a ho, huh? You wanna fuck my niggas and shit behind my back, bitch? Well, I'ma treat yo' ass like a ho," he spat, unbuckling his black leather belt from his waist.

His dreads were now swinging wildly across his head as spit continued to fly from his mouth. With full-on rage, he repeatedly pounded his foot down onto my body.

"Please, Zo, stop. Pleeaaase!" I begged.

I was already in so much pain from him stomping me in the stomach that I didn't know if I could take much more. After tightly gripping the belt buckle in his right hand, he reached up and violently brought it back down onto my flesh. Whap. Whap. He proceeded to beat me like I was his child. As I wore only a thin tank top and boy shorts, the leather lashings against my skin stung and burned.

As he continuously whipped me, calling me every bitch and whore in the book, I could only cry and pray: cry for the hurt while praying for it all to end. My body remained curled into *a fetal position until he grew tired and the beating was ultimately over.*

Finally, through labored breathing as if he'd just finished running a marathon, he said, "And don't you ever, in yo' muthafuckin' life, lemme catch you texting anotha nigga. I don't give a fuck who he is! Now get the fuck up and finish my goddamn dinner."

With the back of his hand, he wiped the slobber from the corners of his mouth before pushing back a few loose locks that were dangling in his face. When he left the kitchen and stormed back down the hall to the bedroom we shared, I could still hear him fussing under his breath. My face, while unharmed, was covered in tears from the pain I had endured. All I could do was remain on the cold tile floor, crying my heart out.

I had sustained his abuse for the past four and a half years, and I was finally fed up. No one ever knew that Zo put his hands on me—not even my three sisters, who were pretty much my only friends—other than Sabrina. I hid it well from everyone because that was one of his requirements. I was dating a well-respected dope boy, and he didn't need the additional label of a woman beater. The expectation was for me to always look and play the part.

Not that I was conceited, but I certainly knew I was a beautiful woman. I had a deep brown complexion, with long, silky, straight black hair, similar to that of an Indian or a Spanish woman. Often I was told that my dark, sleepy brown eyes were seductive. And to top it off, I had been blessed with my mother's deep dimples. At five foot five and 147 pounds, I was considered a bad bitch, although I really didn't care for that term. I was even finishing up my junior year at Spelman for a degree in political science because I wanted to become a lawyer just like my daddy.

Daddy wasn't my real father, though. He was, however, the man who raised me from birth, adopted me when I was just a toddler, and had even given me his last name. Still, I always knew that I wasn't his biological child. Although my parents never kept that a secret from me, they also never mentioned who my real father was. In fact, at 20 years old, I still didn't know my real father's name.

Often as a young child, I would eavesdrop on my mother's private conversations with Grandma to perhaps catch his name or hear any mention of him at all, but there was never any. When I'd ask her his name and who he was, she'd simply say, "Your daddy is Bradley Thomas Brimmage, and that's all you need to know." Eventually, as

I got older, I stopped asking because it was true, Bradley was my daddy, and I knew for a fact that he loved me. Yet the curiosity of who my biological father was never really wavered and would forever remain in the back of my mind.

I remembered one summer day when I was about 9 or 10 years old, my mother had fallen asleep on the sofa watching the *The Price is Right*. While my sisters were merely a few houses down at a neighbor's house playing, I allowed curiosity to get the best of me. I knew my mother kept a brown leather trunk pushed to the back of her closet, hidden behind her long dresses. On this particular day, I badly wanted to know what was in that trunk. I secretly hoped that there was something, anything, in there that would tell me who my real father was.

After five or ten minutes of rifling through my mother's belongings, which included old family portraits, my sisters' birth certificates, tax documents, and other important papers, I'd found a picture of her in the hospital. My mother's young, bright face beamed as she held two sleeping newborn babies in her arms. The hand of a dark-skinned man rested on her shoulder, but his face was out of view. And on the back of the picture, beautifully written in blue ink, was the date: August 4, 1995, my birthday. I could never tell Mama that I'd seen that picture that day, because then she would know I was snooping through her things. However, that image was something I would never forget.

From the outside, it appeared that I had it all. I was a pretty girl from a wealthy, two-parent home getting her college degree. Yet what people didn't know was that deep down I had this yearning for a sense of belonging. I wanted to belong to someone and namely a man. I could only guess that this was how I ended up with Zo. Each day I was living in fear for my life. I never knew what mood he might be in or what little thing might tick him off. He was always on edge, and finally, I was at my limit.

I was emotionally drained, sitting in my old dorm room. My parents still paid for the place even though I was barely there. With Zo still asleep in bed this morning, I sneaked out of the apartment and headed to class, still sore from the night before. I had final exams this week, and then I was headed home to Greensboro for the summer. My only prayer at this point was that Zo would let me go in peace, because Lord knows that's exactly what I needed: some peace.

While I sat on the edge of my bed applying lotion to my legs, with my towel still wrapped around me, I felt my phone suddenly vibrate beside me. It was a text from my youngest sister, Raina, who we all affectionately referred to as Baby Girl.

Baby Girl: Just six more days. Good luck on finals.

Me: Thanks. Can't wait 2C U guys.

Baby Girl: Can't wait 2C U either. Love ya.

Me: Love ya.

No matter what I was going through, I could always count on my sisters to lift my spirits. Keeping one of the darkest secrets of my life from them was the hardest thing I had ever done. However, I already knew that if I'd told them about Zo beating me, they would try to intervene, which would cause Zo to hurt them or, even worse, have them killed.

Taking me out of my thoughts, there was a sudden knock at my door that startled me. Since I'd left Zo early in the morning and hadn't called him at all, I dreadfully looked out of the peephole. When I saw that it was only my girl Sabrina, I quickly opened the door to let her in.

"Hey, babe, you done for today?" she asked, plopping down in my desk chair.

"Yeah, I'm done. What about you?"

"Girl, yes. I have two more exams this week, then a bitch is outta this camp," she sang.

"I've got three more, and then I'm headed back home."

"You not staying here with Zo this summer?" she questioned.

Although not always by choice, Zo and I were pretty much inseparable. It was a key indicator that something was wrong between the two of us when I said that I was going home for the summer.

"No, I need to go home and be with my family for a while. I'm not really feeling Zo like that right now."

"Hey, what happened to your leg?" she asked, pointing to my exposed calf.

"Oh, it's nothing. I just fell down the stairs outside of Zo's apartment last night," I lied.

"Oh," she said, still appearing concerned. "Well, since you're not feeling that nigga right now, let's go out tonight. The frats are having a party at Club Nixx, and you already know it's going to be lit."

"It's been so long since I've been out. I probably won't even know how to act," I whined.

"That shit is like riding a bike. You'll be fine. Matter of fact, let me see how you gon' twerk it," she said, standing up to dance. We both fell out laughing as she began shaking her behind stripper style.

"All right, what time do I need to be ready?" I asked halfheartedly.

"Bitch, you're driving. So you tell me, shit!"

"Fine. I'll be to your room by eleven," I said, shaking my head. My body was still a little sore from the night before, but I decided that I could really use some fun in my life, if only for one night.

Later that evening, around a quarter to ten, I hopped out of the shower for the second time that day. Usually, I would just wrap a towel around my body, but due to my bruises, I wore my full purple robe that I knew would only expose my lower legs. Most of my clothes were still at Zo's house, so I didn't even know what I was going to wear.

While humming the melody to Jeremih's "Oui," which was booming from my Beats Pill in my room, I skimmed through my sparse closet. Not having much to choose from, I decided on a cream-colored jumpsuit from Bebe. It had a deep V in the front with three-quarter-length sleeves, which was sexy but also helped cover up my body. I paired it with nude Louboutins and gold accessories. I wore my hair in a high, messy bun, and I kept my makeup light with soft pink lip gloss.

I thought it was a bit unusual that I still hadn't heard from Zo all day, but I'd rationalized that it wasn't all that uncommon for him to leave me alone and give me a little space after whooping my ass. After grabbing my cell and gold clutch off my desk, I headed out the door to scoop up Sabrina. When I knocked on her door, she was prepared to go and looking cute as always. She was light skinned and short at five foot two inches. Since she weighed about 145 pounds, Sabrina was super thick, but she always maintained a small waist and a flat stomach. She kept her hair in a long, freshly trimmed bob that had a purplish tint to it, and on this night, she wore a black bandage dress, diamond choker, and black Manolo heels.

"Yaas, bitch!" she said, smacking me on the ass.

"Ugh! You look nice too, and you know I don't play that gay shit, Brina!" I said, giving her a look.

"Let me grab my clutch so we can go," she exclaimed.

When we finally arrived at Club Nixx, there was a long line wrapped around the building. We pranced past everyone and headed straight for the door because Sabrina's latest boy toy said that he could get us on the VIP list. While several girls in the line gave us hateful stares, Sabrina smugly grabbed my hand and led the way to this big *The Green Mile*–looking dude who was barricading the door with a clipboard in his hand.

"Names?" was all he said in a deep voice.

"Sabrina Mallette and Risa Brimmage," she replied with a smile. Without any expression on his ugly face, he simply nodded before allowing us inside.

When we walked into the two-story club, it was packed and filled to capacity. While colorful strobe lights flickered throughout, Young Dro's "We In Da City" could be heard. I bounced my body a little to the music as we made our way through the thick crowd and up the stairs to the VIP lounge. Somehow, I could feel the eyes of multiple people on us as we approached the roped area. Through the thick cloud of smoke, I could see that it was designed very chic, with all-white leather sofas, sheer white drapes, and white pub tables.

After taking my seat, I quickly noticed that there were three guys sitting on the other side of the VIP lounge. Being with Zo for so long, I could tell they were most likely dope boys because they all looked like money. They had diamonds in their ears, around their necks, and

even on their wrists. Plus they were all wearing
Gucci. Being into fashion, I could easily spot
the latest and most expensive pieces from a
mile away. They were all attractive from what I
could see, but I wasn't pressed nor was I trying
to impress anyone on this night. Tonight was
about me getting out of the house and somehow
mentally escaping the terror of the night before.

While Sabrina was ordering us a bottle of
peach Cîroc from the cocktail waitress, we heard
the DJ ask for all the bad bitches in the building
to hit the dance floor. In that moment, sounds of
one of my favorite club jams, "Where The Ladies
At" by Crooklyn Clan featuring Fatman Scoop,
blared throughout the club. I didn't know what
it was about that song, but it always put me in
the mood to shake my ass. As expected, Sabrina
immediately grabbed my hand and led me back
downstairs toward the dance floor. Of course, we
considered ourselves bad bitches. While I wasn't
big on dancing, especially without drinks in me,
that was my song, so I happily followed her.

As we made our way down the stairs, I noticed
a guy walking past me, heading up the steps. The
scent of his Jean Paul Gaultier tickled my nose
when our paths crossed. He was tall and dark
skinned with coal black wavy hair and dark eyes.
He also had a pretty, little black beauty mark sit-

ting right underneath his left eye, which stood out to me for whatever reason. Straightaway, he emerged from the crowd in his all-white attire. I could tell he had a nice, hard body by the way his white Gucci shirt slightly clung to his muscular physique. His big diamonds gleamed in each ear, and he wore even more diamonds around his wrist. To say that he was fine would have been an understatement. The man was a god, and he had all eyes on him.

Not wanting to appear thirsty, I took a quick glance back at him as he passed by me. However, to my surprise, our eyes met because he was checking me out as well. I quickly looked away and continued down the steps with my girl.

When Sabrina and I got to the dance floor, we made our way through to the center of the crowd. We instantly began dancing because we didn't want the song to end before we got our chance to twerk. Sabrina loved to be the center of attention, so she began throwing her ass in a circle, while I just kept cool. I closed my eyes with my hands held high in the air and allowed my hips to naturally rock to the beat.

"Check it out. 'Where the ladies at,'" I sang.

As the DJ said, "'Go down, baby,'" I snaked my hips in a circular motion and dropped all the way down to the floor. Rhythmically, I popped

my booty just a bit with my lips pursed for effect.
I loved that part of the song. Sabrina looked over
at me, laughing because she knew that was my
shit. Then she bent over with her hands on her
knees to begin twerking to the beat. She was
always over the top, but that's what I truly loved
about her. I always knew I could count on her to
show me a good time because she was wild, and
I was the complete opposite.

When I stood up and opened my eyes, I
glanced up at the VIP balcony that overlooked
the dance floor. The handsome man in all white
was looking directly at me. We matched gazes
again for what felt like minutes when, suddenly,
Sabrina leaned in my ear and said, "Do you
know that nigga?"

I shook my head to answer.

"Girl, that nigga can't keep his eyes off you. He
fine as fuck though," she said. I just shrugged
and let out a small laugh.

The DJ yelled out into the microphone, "The
Borrego Brothers in the muthafuckin' building
tonight, y'all! Ladies, show them niggas some
love." The DJ then pointed toward the VIP area.
The girls on the dance floor swooned and hollered out for them, while the frats began doing
their call. To my surprise, the three guys in the
VIP section, including the guy in white, all stood

up. They held up their hands, making a sign, and let out the same fraternity call. I assumed then that they were in frats too. It was odd because I could usually spot a dope boy from a mile away, or at least I thought I could.

Chapter 2

Micah

"Shawty in the cream pantsuit was bad as fuck last night," my brother Dre stated groggily with a yawn. He was still partially hung over from the night before.

"Nigga was sitting there drooling over her ass all damn night. Yo, you didn't even get at her," said my baby brother, Damien, or Dame as we called him.

"I ain't got time, bruh. Baby mama already too much. I gotta keep my head in this business. Later for all that other shit, ya feel me?" I said with a slight nod before getting up from the couch and heading into the kitchen for another biscuit.

It was the day after the party, and my brothers and I were all just chilling in my condo, eating breakfast and talking shit like usual. We had just moved back to Georgia from Miami four months

ago to help Pops head up another hotel in the
Atlanta area. My father owned an international
luxury hotel chain that spanned from New York,
D.C., Miami, Los Angeles, and Las Vegas all the
way to Paris, Italy, and even Hong Kong. He was
born and raised in Cuba, while my mother
was originally from Haiti. Growing up in Cuba,
my father and his brother, Raul, were heavy into
the drug game. While my father later used his
money to come over to the states to start a legit-
imate family business, my Uncle Raul stayed behind in Cuba and continued his drug trade.

We lived in Atlanta from the time I was 10
years old up until I graduated from high school.
Even though I spent the first ten years of my life
in Cuba, Atlanta had quickly become my home.
So when we later moved to Florida, because Pops
decided to open up his fourth hotel in Miami, I
attended FAMU on a football scholarship. The
only thing I hated was that I had to leave my ace
Timo behind in Atlanta.

Timo and I had been tight since the sixth
grade. You'd never see one of us without the
other. We even played Pop Warner together. In
fact, I remember in high school, we called ourselves trying to be dope boys and shit. Well, that
was up until my father found out and kicked my
ass. While I went back to playing football and

focusing on school, Timo kept grinding in the streets and eventually made a name for himself within the East Atlanta area. It's crazy because even though Timo's name was well respected in the streets of Atlanta, our family name carried more weight, not just in Atlanta but in every city and state we traveled. Whether it was because of Pops and Uncle Raul's drug dealings back in the day, my father's hotel chain, or maybe even a combination of the two, I was never really sure. It had been three weeks since Timo had been locked up with Fed charges, and I needed to talk with my nigga to see what was good.

"You talk to that nigga Timo yet?" Melo asked, sealing up his morning blunt with a lick of his tongue. I just shook my head as I rubbed my hand down my face.

Melo was my brother from another mother. Well, actually he was my first cousin, or double cousin as some may say. He was Uncle Raul's son, but his mother was also my mother's twin sister. Mom and Pops ended up raising him from the time he was 5 years old, right after Melo's mother took her own life. She blew her brains out right in front of him. Uncle Raul couldn't cope after Aunt Kizzi died, and he expressed that Melo needed to be raised by a woman.

I knew seeing his mother take her own life did something to him because Melo never talked much growing up, or even now for that matter. Plus that nigga had a short fuse. Melo was the big, quiet nigga nobody wanted to fuck with. Although on the surface he was this light, bright, pretty nigga with hazel eyes, his demeanor could sometimes be that of a stone-cold killer. He just didn't give a fuck. Despite his ways, Melo was a computer geek. He was completing his sophomore year at Clark in pursuit of a degree in information technology, and currently, he had a 3.9 GPA with employers already trying to recruit him. He, however, was training to become the future chief information officer of Pop's hotel industry.

"Yeah, I'ma try to get up with that nigga today though," I said, propping my feet up on the leather ottoman.

Looking over at Dame, I couldn't do anything but shake my head as he sat up to surf through the channels. He was still in high school, yet his hardheaded ass just had to come to Atlanta for the party last night.

"Yo, ain't your ass supposed to be in school, li'l nigga? I thought you were going back home early this morning," I said sternly.

He knew I didn't play that shit when it came to school. Our parents had a big-ass mansion on the outskirts of Greensboro where he stayed and went to school, while Dre and Melo stayed in the frat house near campus here in Atlanta. All of us traveled back and forth to Greensboro though and had rooms at Moms and Pop's crib.

"Yeah, I'm about to head out now 'cause you know I got practice and shit. I'll probably make fourth period, though."

"You fucking up, li'l nigga. How's your calculus class going?" I asked.

"Pshh!" he responded before running his hand down his face.

"Get you a tutor, nigga!"

"A tutor! Fuck I look like? I can probably just get a girl to do my homework and shit."

"What about tests? And what about when you get to college and have to go through all of the same bullshit with calculus again? You supposed to be our money nigga, making sure shit always add up. How you gon' do that if you can't even pass your math class?" I fussed, pushing my index finger into his forehead.

Dame had always been an A student when it came to his math classes, which was why Pops was training him to be the next CFO of his hotel business. So why he was fucking up now was beyond me.

"A'ight, Micah, I hear you. Damn! I'm gonna get a tutor and get my shit straight," he declared before standing up to stretch his arms out wide, cracking the muscles in his back and chest. This was something all four of us habitually did.

"Anyway, I'm 'bout to be out," he said, dapping up Dre and Melo before pulling me in for a hug. I didn't play when it came to my baby bro, and everybody knew that shit.

Later that day, I was taking a nap on my sofa when I got a collect call from Timo.

"I'll accept," I said in a groggy tone.

"Yeah, what's up, bruh?" Timo asked.

"Ain't shit. Need to be asking you what's up," I replied while sitting up and rubbing the sleep out of my eyes.

"They ain't got shit, but they prolonging my bail hearing to keep me in here. You know how that shit goes. The hearing is supposed to be this week, so I'm just praying they grant a nigga bail at this point," he explained.

"So, is there anything you need while you in there?" I asked before getting up and heading toward the bathroom.

"I'm glad you asked, my nigga. Get up with my little brother, Zo. He got some information for you."

"A'ight, bruh, I got you," was all I said before killing the line. I knew that he couldn't go further into detail on the phone.

At this point, I knew the streets were drying up and niggas weren't eating, so that was most likely what Zo needed to talk to me about. Over the years, I never really fucked with Zo because he always appeared to be sneaky, but that was my man's little brother, and I respected it. Timo put Zo on when he was still in high school, so what he wanted to talk about had me perplexed. If anything, Zo needed to be out handling shit while Timo was down, but I was willing to hear him out on the strength of Timo.

Thinking I was going to get me a little nap in before heading into work, I lazily lay back down on the couch. No more than five minutes after I closed my eyes, my iPhone started to vibrate. I looked down at the screen and saw that it was my baby's mom, Keesha. I took a deep breath before answering on my Bluetooth to prepare myself for any bullshit.

"Yo."

"Hey, baby daddy, where you at?"

"I'm handling business, Keesh. What's good? What you need?" I asked tiredly and irritated altogether.

"I was just checking to see if you had made any moves yet to get me and Zari up there with y'all?"

I only sighed, getting a little annoyed with her persistence, but then I said, "Nah, not yet, but I'll let you know something soon. How's my baby, anyway?"

"She's doing good. Sleeping right now, though."

"All right, well, give her a kiss for me, and I'll hit you later."

"All right, daddy. I love you."

I hung up without responding, then closed my eyes again. I loved my baby Zaria. I even had love for her mother, but I wasn't in love with her. She kept trying to keep us in a relationship that she knew was dead. Keesha was nothing more than a bad-ass stripper in Miami I slipped up and fucked raw one drunken night about three years ago. She had a pretty face, brown skin, a small waist, and a fat ass. You know the type. She pretty much trapped a nigga, but I still did what I had to do as a man to make sure she and my baby were taken care of financially.

I moved her into a luxury condo and gave her enough money every week so that she could quit stripping. I even tried to work it out with her and officially make her my girl. However, that relationship was temporary, because everybody knows you can't turn a ho into a house-wife. Besides the infidelities on both our parts, we were completely dysfunctional together. We couldn't even be around each other for more than an hour before I got the urge to choke the life out of her. I told her that I was going to move her and Zaria with me so that I could be closer to my baby, but knowing the bullshit I'd have to put up with prolonged me from making it a reality.

As bad as I wanted to holla at ol' girl in Club Nixx last night, I had too much shit to deal with between the hotel business, Timo, and now Keesha. I could tell with just one look at her that it wouldn't just be about me fucking. So if I was going to step to her, I wanted to come correct. At the rate things were going in my life, I didn't know when that would be. I had plenty of women I could call when I needed a quick nut, but that's all it was for me. I never went out on dates, I never brought women back to my home, and I never brought them around my family. The last girl who met my family was Keesha, and even that encounter was by default because of Zaria.

"Muthafuckaaa!" I groaned at the sound of my phone vibrating again. They wouldn't let me sleep for shit. I grabbed my phone and saw that it was Dame.

Dame: Whaddup?

Me: Nigga, did you make it to school?

Dame: Yeah, Micah.
Me: What period, li'l nigga?
Dame: Fourth
Me: And calculus?
Dame: I got a plan in motion.
Me: A'ight, one love.
Dame: One love.

I couldn't help but smile at that li'l nigga. I loved all my brothers, Melo included, but Dame was my heart. He was seven years younger than me, and even when we were growing up, he would follow me around and imitate my every move. When I was in high school, I took that li'l nigga everywhere with me. I'm talking football games, basketball games, the mall, wherever. Girls thought it was sweet that I always wanted him around me, but I didn't do it for the attention or the affection of girls. I did it because that was my li'l man, my heart. Now that this nigga was 18, I tried to stay on him about school just like Pops did me. I even tried to school him about the ways of women, but he always claimed he was straight in that area.

Shaking my head as I thought about him, I lay back on my couch once more and closed my eyes again.

Chapter 3

Raina

"Yo, I got an oldie but goodie for y'all out there, a'ight? I'm taking it all the way back to da nineties. For all those who remember this, hit me up. This ya boy KDO on Hot 95.5, leggo!" DJ KDO shouted just before I heard Lauryn Hill singing "Killing Me Softly" in my ears.

It was the end of another long and ordinary day of high school for me as I stood at my locker, pulling out my earbuds and gathering up my things to go home. I began to think about the fact that this Saturday was my school's spring formal, another school dance that I wouldn't be attending. No one had asked me to go, and truthfully, I wasn't even surprised. Between my schoolwork and dance practice, I didn't have much of a social life. I knew a few friends of mine who were going solo, but I really wasn't in the mood.

Just as I shut my locker and turned around, I saw none other than Damien Borrego, the school's star point guard. *Damn.* He wore a basic black tee, a black and red Braves fitted cap worn to the back, and a gold Cuban link chain around his neck. His black stonewashed jeans sagged just a little, and he rocked black and red Jays on his feet. He had this certain swagger about him that screamed, "Look at me!"

Damien was that guy. He was brown skinned, six feet three inches, and was clean-cut with coal black wavy hair. The thin layer of hair above his upper lip was always neatly trimmed, and his body was that of a true athlete, lean but muscular. Damien also had the most beautiful set of straight white teeth. It was like he was fully aware of it, too, because he was known for always laughing and smiling. Ever since he'd transferred to the same school a few months prior, I had secretly thought he was cute, but we never hung in the same circles. He was instantly Mr. Popular, and I wasn't. Never had been.

"What's up, Raina?" he inquired with a nod, smiling and flashing that pretty set of white teeth before walking past me. Astonished that he even knew my name, I felt my heart instantly racing.

"Ah, hey, Damien," I stuttered to the back of his head, smelling the fresh cologne he wore as it floated past my nose.

As the youngest of the four Brimmage sisters, I was 16 years old and a junior in high school with a 4.3 GPA. While I was doing my thing academically, my social life was pretty much nonexistent. I had been chubby all my life, and throughout my elementary and middle school years, my breasts had always been larger than those of the other girls my age. Up until the eighth grade, I wore glasses on my face and metal braces on my teeth. For those reasons, growing up, I constantly got teased, and it resulted in me staying to myself. Although some considered me to be somewhat of a bombshell these days because of my long, silky black hair, bright caramel-colored skin, light brown eyes, and Coca-Cola-bottle figure, I still wasn't confident. I certainly felt awkward around someone like Damien Borrego.

I did have a handful of friends, though. I was even the captain of the majorettes for the best high school band in all of Georgia. Strangely enough, dancing on the field in front of a big crowd was where I felt most comfortable, front and center. When I danced, it was like I didn't care what anyone thought about me. I loved the feeling of the wind whipping through my hair and the crunch of grass beneath my feet. There was something about the sound of the beating drums blending in with the loud, blaring cheers from the crowd that did it for me. Hands down, I was the school's best majorette, and even though I exuded poise and grace out on the field when I danced, I knew I lacked that same confidence off the field. In fact, I'd never even had a boyfriend or experienced my first kiss. Not that guys didn't try to talk to me, but like I said, I pretty much kept my nose in the books and never showed any interest.

As I rode home from school in the front seat of the bus, I stared out of the window, thinking of Damien. Chatter and the sounds of laughter could be heard behind me. There was also a strong smell of feet lingering in the air from the family-sized bag of Cheetos that was being passed around. As I lightly bounced up and down in my seat every so often from the bumps in the road, I could see spitballs periodically fly past my peripheral vision. Naturally, I assumed they were aimed at the bus driver. Even with all the chaos that surrounded me, all I could think was, *he actually spoke to me.*

Damien could have any girl in the school he wanted, even outside of school for that matter. He was the guy who made everyone laugh. The type of guy who was invited to all the parties, had mad game on the court, and did I mention this nigga was fine? He had only been at our school for going on four months because he transferred midyear. I presumed he was there to play ball, but either way, he had already made a name for himself.

He had this bad boy side of him that attracted most of the girls. For instance, he would sometimes wear grills on the bottom row of his teeth just to make a fashion statement, or he would practice in the gym with no shirt on, exposing all the muscles in his arms and chest. For Damien to only be eighteen, it was unusual that his upper body was covered in tattoos. On several occasions, I'd even seen him go toe-to-toe with some of the biggest niggas on our rival basketball teams. In the end, he'd always come out on top. The fact that he could fight only added to his appeal.

As I continued gazing out of the bus window, so many questions filled my mind, like how did he even know my name, why did he speak to me, and did he think I was pretty? The thoughts of him were overwhelming me, and he'd only said, "What's up." When the bus finally came to a halt, I realized that it was my stop and instantly got up from my seat to start for the steps. The same unwavering chatter and laughter continued in the background when a spitball came flying and landed directly on the side of my face. My nose turned up in disgust as I flicked it off and continued down the steps and onto the sidewalk. I could hear the entire bus erupt in amusement before pulling off.

After checking my mailbox, I immediately ran inside the house. I could hardly contain my excitement. I needed to tell my older sister, Raquel, that Damien actually spoke to me. Raquel had just turned 18 a month ago and was also a senior in the same high school. However, she probably had the most boring life among me and my other sisters. Although she was highly intelligent, kindhearted, and naturally beautiful with her flawless brown skin, hazel eyes, and long, silky chestnut-colored hair, she mostly stayed to herself. She only rocked with me and my sisters, so people usually mistook that for her being stuck-up. You know how that goes. Raquel always had her nose in a book or her fingers on the piano.

Just like me, I knew, Raquel had never experienced being in love. She called herself having a boyfriend at one point in time a couple of years ago, but that was short-lived. Raquel could sometimes have a bad attitude and a smart-ass mouth. In addition to that, she wasn't into all that hugging and kissing, lovey-dovey stuff, so guys just didn't know how to take her. She said that she didn't want to change who she was for some nigga. She'd say that if he couldn't handle her attitude and her smart-ass mouth, then that was his problem.

As soon as I entered Raquel's room, which was neatly decorated in navy blue, pink, and white, I saw her sitting up in the bed. "Guess you're feeling better, huh?" I asked.

"Yeah, I am."

"You will never guess who spoke to me today," I mentioned with excitement.

"Who?" she asked with her eyebrows raised, yet her eyes never left the television.

"Guess."

"I don't know, Raina. Just tell me," Raquel retorted with a little attitude.

"Damien!"

"*Damien* Damien?" Raquel emphasized as her hazel eyes grew wide, finally landing on me.

"Yup, the one and only," I gloated with a smirk.

"What did he want with you?" she asked with a tinge of envy that I could hear in her voice.

"He just said, 'What's up, Raina,'" I explained, trying to imitate his deep tone and the nod he gave me. "I mean, I didn't even know the boy

knew my name," I finished, tossing my book bag
to the floor.

"Hmm. Well, isn't that nice?" Raquel rolled
her eyes.

I figured that my sister was probably a little
jealous, being that she and Damien were both seniors and he had never spoken to her. I decided
to let the subject go because a *Cosby Show* rerun
was on and had caught my attention. Man, we
could watch those episodes over and over again.
After slipping out of my shoes, I stretched across
the foot of Raquel's bed to watch the show. Both
Raquel and I fell out laughing at Theo trying to
hide his ear piercing from his dad.

"Hey, what are y'all watching?" my other sister
Romi asked, standing in the doorway.

Romi was the third eldest Brimmage sister
at 19 years of age. She was considered by most
people to be the most attractive of us four sisters.
The problem was that, unlike Raquel and myself,
she knew how beautiful she was and wasn't
afraid to flaunt it. She had smooth, buttery skin,
long black shiny hair, and large breasts. With her
wide hips, round booty, and a twenty-four-inch
waist all sitting on a five foot six inch frame, she
was a total knockout. Romi even had beautiful
green eyes that complemented her light skin
tone. She was the only one out of the four of us
to inherit Mama's green eyes.

Our parents were so disappointed when she didn't go to college last year after she graduated. She claimed that she needed a year or two off to figure out what she wanted to do with her life, but I knew that would get old to Mama and Daddy soon. Romi was forever sleeping in until noon, and coming in the house past midnight.

"You'll never guess who spoke to Raina today at school," Raquel said to Romi.

"Who?"

"Damien."

"Y'all still talking about that nigga," Romi replied with her nose scrunched up, looking down at her nails, which were painted a very pretty shade of pink.

Romi couldn't relate to me and Raquel. She had always been a part of the in crowd during her high school years. She was the cheerleader captain, the SGA president, and the homecoming queen. One might think that her popularity would have trickled down to us, but that didn't happen.

"Really, Romi?" I asked with my head cocked to the side and lips pursed for effect. "He's just the finest nigga at Greene County, that's all," I stated matter-of-factly.

"You girls have a lot to learn about niggas. Long as they know you checking for 'em, they won't give your ass the time of day. But show 'em that he ain't nobody special, you know, that he's no big deal, and he'll be all over your ass. Trust!" Romi schooled us.

I watched Romi smile as if she was recalling the days in high school where she could have had any boy she wanted. Then we suddenly heard Mama call us downstairs for dinner.

"Girls, get washed up for dinner," she shouted.

"Anyway, do you think I should speak to him if I see him tomorrow or just play it cool?" I asked, getting up from the bed. I knew I was probably making a big deal out of nothing, but guys like Damien didn't talk to me on a regular basis, so I needed some help in that department.

"Just play it cool. It may not have meant anything," Raquel said, pushing her way past Romi to head downstairs.

I shrugged my shoulders at Raquel's last remark, then turned to Romi for a better answer, but Romi just nodded to agree with her.

Moments later, we were all downstairs for dinner. Our mother, Ernie, had made Cajun fried chicken, baked macaroni and cheese, collard greens with shrimp, candied sweet potatoes, dirty rice, corn bread, and an apple pie for dinner. Mama was Creole with fair skin, long, fine, silky black hair, and green eyes just like Romi.

She was born and raised right in New Orleans, so everything she cooked was shrimp this and Cajun that.

"This looks great, Mama," I complimented her.

"Sure does," Raquel agreed, licking her lips and rubbing her hands together.

"Y'all girls go ahead and set the table while I run up here and try to do something with this head of mine," Mama said, patting her hair.

"Yes, ma'am," we spoke in unison before beginning to set the table.

Suddenly, there was a knock at the front door.

"I'll get it," I shouted before looking out to see who it was.

It was Mr. Charles, our daddy's best friend of twenty years. Mr. Charles was 39 years old and a deacon at our church. He was married to Mrs. Evelyn, and they had an 8-year-old daughter named Marie. Daddy and Mr. Charles went to Morehouse College together and had even pledged to a fraternity together.

Mr. Charles was a six foot four inch, clean-cut, dark-skinned man with a chipped front tooth. For some odd reason, that tooth only added to his attractiveness. He was the kind of man who always looked good in a suit. Not too muscular, but in excellent shape for his age. Although he was fine for an older man, he was also a little arrogant.

"What's up, Baby Girl? Your daddy home?"

"Hey, Mr. Charles. No, he's not home yet, but he should be here in a few minutes. Mama has us setting the table for dinner."

"Oh, Ernie's here. You mind if I come in and wait for him, then?"

"Sure, come in," I welcomed him inside.

As we walked into the kitchen, both Raquel and Romi said, "Hey, Mr. Charles."

Romi walked over to give Mr. Charles a hug and asked, "Do you want me to make you a plate, or are you staying for dinner?"

"Maybe a plate to go," he replied with a smile.

For some reason, Mr. Charles and Romi were acting way too friendly for my liking. Hmmm. Maybe it was just my imagination. I hoped it was, because he was practically an uncle to us.

Chapter 4

Romi

I suppose you could have guessed it, but Charles and I had been screwing for the past month. I knew he was married, and I also knew that he was twenty years older than me, but for some reason, I just couldn't stop. So for that, I'd taken the title of the ho sister. I had fallen in love for the first time with someone other than Charles about three and a half months ago, and that nigga broke my heart something terrible. The aftermath was me doing anything and everything I could to fill that void. With Charles, it was just supposed to be a one-time thing after our so-called slip-up, but then he kept calling and texting, wanting to see me again. This was how it all began.

One evening, Mama invited most of the deacons and their families over to the house for Sunday dinner. After Daddy said the blessing, we all released hands and lifted our heads in anticipation over the magnificent feast laid before us.

"Ernie, you sure have outdone yourself," Charles said.

"Amen to that," Daddy agreed as he turned to Mama and gave her a wink.

"Ernie, you sure have some gorgeous girls. They've grown up so beautifully," Ms. Evelyn said, looking at me and my sisters.

"Thanks, Evelyn. Are you two done with having children?" Mama asked, looking at both her and Charles.

"Well, I don't know," she replied, looking coyly over to Charles.

For some reason, I was watching him like a hawk, waiting for him to respond. I really didn't even know why. Maybe because after hearing Mama talk about how doggish he was, it intrigued me to see what his answer would be. However, Charles kept quiet with his head low, shoveling food into his mouth.

"Charles, do you want any more children?" Mama insisted.

He choked a little on his chicken breast, which made me chuckle. "No, I think we're done," he finally said with a little cough and a closed-lip smile.

Ms. Evelyn looked surprised by the response Charles gave. I recalled a few years prior, she and Charles were talking about trying for a baby boy, saying how nice it would be to have a little Charles Jr. running around the house. However, I thought Ms. Evelyn knew that this was neither the time nor place to bring that up. Instead, she fidgeted in her seat a little before switching subjects.

"So, Romi, have you thought any more on what college you want to attend?"

She caught me off guard with that one and pissed me off in the process trying to call me out.

"I haven't really given it too much thought lately," I nonchalantly answered.

"Well, you had better start thinking about it, and I mean soon, young lady," Daddy chimed in with a stern voice.

At that point, I was irritated, so I excused myself from the table and went to begin cleaning up the kitchen.

"What about you, Raina? Do you know what you want to do after high school?" I could hear Ms. Evelyn ask while I was cleaning up.

"I really want to go to Clark or Spelman. Or maybe even Hampton University. I don't know."

"Oh, really? What exactly would you study?" I could hear Ms. Evelyn asking.

Moments later, Mama entered the kitchen and asked if I could take some of the boxes she'd packed down to the basement. It was some of the old china and things of my grandmother's that no longer fit in our china cabinet.

"Here, let me help you with that," Charles walked in and said.

"Cool. Thanks, Mr. Charles."

We went down into the basement with the boxes and began neatly stacking them against the wall.

"So, you and the missus don't agree on whether to have any more kids, huh?" I asked knowingly with a smirk.

"I mean, I'm damn near forty. What the fuck do I look like with a newborn, ya know?"

It was crazy because I had never heard Mr. Charles cuss before, and I felt by the way he was talking that he was more my age than Daddy's. He seemed pretty cool.

"Yeah, I get it. But I know when I find Mr. Right, I want me lots of babies to have running around the house. I want these hips spread nice and wide," I stated flirtatiously, rubbing my hands down my hips and thighs for emphasis. Yeah, I knew I was toying with Mr. Charles, but I was a flirt by nature.

"They already spread pretty nice if you ask me," he mumbled.

I looked over to see him smirking and seductively looking me up and down. He licked his lower lip a little before rubbing his hand down his beard. What could I say? Mr. Charles was straight turning me on, and in that moment, I no longer saw him as Uncle Charles or Daddy's best friend. He was just some old-ass nigga looking good as fuck. I just laughed though and quickly waved him off before turning around to finish stacking some more boxes. As I was bent over, I could suddenly feel his hardness on my booty and his hands holding on to my hips.

"I've always thought you were beautiful, Romi," he mentioned in a low tone behind me.

I turned around with an attitude like "this nigga has done lost his old-ass mind." Before I could even open my mouth to say anything, he pressed his lips against mine and forced his tongue inside. In my heart, I knew it was wrong, but my panties were getting more soaked by the second, and I could feel the thump of my clit all the way up in my throat. After he pushed my skirt up and slid my lace panties to the side, I felt two of his fingers slip inside of me, causing a low moan to escape my lips.

"Feel good, baby?" he asked with his mouth still hovering over mine.

"Uhmm, yes," I whined in pleasure.

I wasn't ashamed to admit that I was a straight-up freak. Quickly I began unbuttoning his pants, wanting more than just those two fingers he was offering. The next thing I knew, he lifted me up off the basement floor and wrapped my legs around his waist. I could feel the basement wall pressed against my back before he gently slid me down onto his long pole. Slowly he began pumping in and out of me.

"Young pussy. Mmmm, damn," he muttered before tightening his grip on my ass.

I'd admit that he felt so good inside of me that I didn't want him to stop. I arched my back a little and tightened my legs around his waist, which caused him to go deeper inside of me.

"Wait, Charles, uumm," I moaned, feeling my orgasm rise.

"Ahh, shit!" he groaned, pumping quicker and deeper.

The sounds of our wet bodies slapping against each other only turned me on more. Between panting and breathing, we continued to kiss and moan nastily into each other's mouths until we both came simultaneously. All in all, it was only about a good five minutes, but my body was completely satisfied.

I told him that it would be our little secret and that we'd never do it again, but a whole month later, I was having a full-blown affair with this old-ass nigga.

As I started making his plate, Daddy walked in the house.

"What's up, Charles? What are you doing over here, man?"

"Well, you know our next homecoming is coming up in October, and a few of the frats are already booking rooms and getting tickets to the party at the Hilton downtown. You and Ernie rolling with us?"

"You already know I'm going. Is Evelyn going with you?"

"I doubt it. She needs to stay home with Marie, but don't make Ernie miss out on all the fun just 'cause she's not going. The other wives are coming too, so she'll be fine," Charles explained.

"Ernie!" Daddy called upstairs.

"Hey, baby," Mama said before greeting Daddy with a kiss once she made it down the stairs.

"Hey. Charles wants to know if we're going to homecoming this year. There's a party at the Hilton downtown. We can go to the game, then come back and chill at the hotel before heading to the party downstairs at the Hilton. Whatchu think, baby?"

"That sounds good. Is Ev going, Charles?" Mama asked.

"Nah, she ain't going, but Antwan's wife Mickey and Kenny's wife Brenda will be there. Didn't y'all pledge together?"

"Yeah, we did. Okay, cool, I'll call them and let them know I'm going even though it's still early. October, right?" she inquired.

"Yeah, October, but you know they start booking everything early," Daddy informed her.

"All right, Brad, I need three hundred and fifty dollars from you. Two hundred for the football tickets and a hundred fifty for the party at the Hilton. I'll let you and Ernie make your own hotel reservations."

"Who's tailgating this year? Not Ronnie and them again, I hope," Daddy said, shaking his head while pulling out his wallet.

"It's going to be all of us, so be prepared to hit the stores when you get up there. If you got room to haul your grill, bring that, too. If not, you already know we can pick up some small ones when we get there. But, man, we got plenty of time. We'll talk."

"All right, man, let me get in here and eat this dinner my baby done made for us," Daddy said, dapping him up and giving him the $350.

"Let me use your restroom real quick before I leave," he said before making his way down the hall to the half bathroom.

While Mama and Daddy headed for the kitchen, I sneaked down the hall. I lightly tapped on the bathroom door with a special beat so that he'd know it was me. Knowingly, he unlocked the door, and when I opened it, he was standing there with a wide smile on his face. Only a few seconds passed before he reached out and pulled me into him.

We were straight bold with it, all up in Mama and Daddy's house, but I was like fuck it. This was the kind of stuff that turned me on. I looked down at Charles, and he already had his pants dropped to his ankles with his long, hard member waiting for me. We immediately began kissing while I stroked him up and down with my hand. He pushed my leggings down to my knees and started rubbing in between my legs.

"I need to feel you," I moaned.

He quickly sat on the toilet with the seat closed and pulled me down onto his lap with my back facing him.

"Ahh," I moaned, feeling all of him inside of me.

He grabbed me by my waist, but I pushed his hands away and started circling my hips to grind onto him. As I closed my eyes and began catching a rhythm, his hand found its way back to my waist. The gentle and rapid plucks he placed to my clit made my body feel like the strings to his musical guitar. With his finger still in motion, he gently nibbled on my neck, and I could feel a massive orgasm building. I let my head fall back onto his shoulder and continued gyrating my hips, relishing the sensation.

"Fuck," he groaned, grabbing my waist again to try to control my movements.

He slowly lifted me up off his dick and repeatedly brought me back down onto him. Each time he pushed my body back down onto him, I moaned quietly, enjoying the feeling.

"Go ahead and cum for daddy Charles," he whispered in my ear.

"Ahhhh, fuck! I'm cumming," I muttered, reaching my peak.

After I came, he lifted us up from the toilet into a standing position. He pushed both of my hands up against the wall, and naturally, I tooted my ass up, allowing him full access to stroke me from behind. With one hand grabbing my hip and the other gripping my shoulder, he forcefully rammed himself in and out of me. Although my body was tired, the feeling of him inside of me still felt good. I could feel him beginning to swell within me before he reached underneath my shirt and firmly grabbed my breasts.

"Unnghhh!" he groaned, releasing inside of me.

After quickly cleaning ourselves off, we quietly exited the bathroom one after the other. I casually strolled into the kitchen while Charles headed toward the front door.

"All right, B. I'll talk to you later, man," he hollered back.

"Later, man," I heard Daddy call out from the dining room.

I calmly made my plate as if nothing had ever happened, then went to join everyone at the dining room table. That night, I was unusually quiet at dinner. I was thinking about the countless times Charles had told me that he would leave his wife for me. I wasn't a fool by a long shot, nor was I naive enough to think that this nigga would leave his wife of thirteen years for me. I'd lost my virginity at 14 years old, and I had run through enough niggas to know the game. I was just using him to fill time and the empty space Dre left in my heart. Unfortunately, the shit wasn't working.

Chapter 5

Raina

I tried to get myself together for school the next morning, but I couldn't believe what I had heard the night before. How could Romi be having an affair with Daddy's best friend? Hearing them in the bathroom right under all our noses disgusted me. The fact that Mr. Charles was twice her age was even more grotesque. Just as I was heading downstairs to catch the school bus, I walked past Romi in the hallway.

"Baby Girl, we need to talk," she said.

I ignored her and ran down the stairs and out the door to catch the bus. Sitting next to Raquel on the bus, I stared out of the window trying to figure out what I was going to do, or if I was going to do anything at all about Romi and Mr. Charles.

"Is everything okay?" Raquel asked.

"Yeah, everything is fine. I'm just thinking," I said.

"You're still thinking about Damien, huh?" Raquel asked with a smile.

"No," I stated promptly.

As soon as we arrived at school, I went to my locker to unload my fourth-period books. I did a quick makeup check in my locker mirror, although I didn't wear anything but mascara and lip gloss. Suddenly I felt a light tap on my shoulder.

"Damien?" I exclaimed, surprised, when I turned around.

"I just wanted to say wassup, beautiful," he said, licking his lips, which were slowly forming into a smile as he looked me up and down. I knew that I was just supposed to play it cool like Romi and Raquel told me to, but I was such a dork and couldn't control myself. A huge, goofy grin came over my face no matter how hard I tried to hold it back.

"Thank you," I said, twirling a piece of my hair. As Damien walked on to class, I felt so embarrassed at how I had acted.

"Thaank yoouu," I quietly mocked, teasing my own damn self. I slammed my locker door shut, then headed to class. With everything going on with Romi and Charles and now with Damien, I knew I wasn't going to be able to concentrate.

Later that day, I was walking down the hall with my girl KeKe on our way to lunch. She was a pretty, brown-skinned girl with straight, black, shoulder-length hair. We'd been friends since the sixth grade. While I was getting teased for being fat and wearing glasses and braces, she was constantly getting teased for being too skinny. So we were just a natural pair. I had lost the baby fat, the glasses, and the braces, but poor KeKe was still a hundred pounds soaking wet. Nonetheless, she was my girl.

As we walked, I instantly spotted Damien and a group of his friends hanging in the hallway outside of the cafeteria. He leaned against the wall with one of his feet propped up against it, laughing and smiling that big, bright smile while the others crowded around him, hanging on to his every word. I didn't know if he would speak to me now that he was in front of all his friends, or if I should speak to him for that matter. Instead of risking the embarrassment, I decided that I was just going to play it cool and only speak to him if he spoke to me.

When he finally spotted me and made eye contact, I instantly grew nervous. My stomach felt extremely queasy. Then I saw him lean over and whisper something to one of his friends. He was a tall, dark-skinned guy on the basketball team who sported a high-top fade that was dyed blond at the top. He was freakishly tall at about six foot seven and thin, weighing somewhere around 180 pounds or so. They both looked over at me and burst out laughing. Now I was irritated, because I knew that whatever he said was about me. I decided to keep it moving to the cafeteria, but just as KeKe and I walked past him and his crew, he said, "Hey, Raina, let me holla at you for a minute, beautiful," grinning with those damn grills in the bottom of his mouth.

Lord, why does he have to be so damn fine?

"Okay," I responded, a little unsure as I turned to KeKe. "You can just go get us a seat, and I'll be right there," I told her.

Damien began to walk with me a little down the hallway, away from his friends. "We've been running into each other a lot lately, huh?" he asked.

"Yeah, I was surprised you even knew my name when you spoke to me the other day," I admitted.

"Well, you knew my name, didn't you? So why wouldn't I know yours, beautiful?"

I loved it that he called me beautiful like it was my first name.

I didn't want to come right out and tell him that I was a nobody at school while everybody knew who he was, so instead, I just changed the subject. "So, what's up?" I asked, suggesting that he get to the point.

"I think you're taking calculus this semester, right? Word around is that you nerdy as fuck, so I was wondering if you would tutor me or maybe do a nigga homework and shit?" he said, smiling like he was doing me a big-ass favor.

I snapped my head back, giving him a look that said, "Nigga, you done lost yo' mind."

He must have caught my attitude, because he said, "But for real, shawty, I got a scholarship on the line for next year, and I can't afford to fuck up and fail that class."

Hearing him talk about his scholarship made me ease up a little, so I just sighed heavily, thinking about it.

"So, shawty, you gon' help a nigga out or not?" he snapped impatiently, waiting for me to respond.

What happened to him calling me beautiful?

I was the only junior in Mrs. Waters's calculus class. All her other students were seniors, so Damien must have taken that class during a different period than I.

"Yeah, I guess I can do that, but I'm not doing your homework. When do you want to get together?"

"Get together? Shawty, I just asked you to tutor me. If you wanna fuck, that's a different conversation," he mentioned cockily, giving a sexy smirk.

I felt myself getting so red with embarrassment, but before I could even respond, he looked me up and down while licking his lips and said, "Don't let me find out you hot in the ass, shawty."

At this point, I was too through with his arrogant ass.

"Well, to rephrase my question, when do you want to get together to study?" I said, emphasizing the word "study."

"Well, I know you be dancing and shit, 'cause I see you after basketball practice, so how 'bout we study tomorrow after practice?" After all he had just said, I was stuck on the fact he'd actually noticed me.

"Okay, tomorrow is cool. So where we going? To the library, my house, yours?" I questioned with my hands out and shoulders shrugged.

"Wherever is fine. You just let me know."

"Well, can you come over to my house? That way, my parents will know what I'm doing and who I'm doing it with."

Fuck! I regretted those words as soon as they left my lips.

"Who you doing it with?" he teased. "Shawty, don't lemme find out you hot in the ass now," he said again, shaking his index finger at me and giving me a wink.

Damn, why does he have to be so cute?

"Damien, you know what I meant," I whined, giving him a little attitude.

He simply laughed at me. "Nah, I know what-chu meant, shawty. I'll meet you at your locker after practice tomorrow, and I can take you home. Bet?"

"Okay, that will work."

I tightly pursed my lips to keep my smile hidden as I walked back down the hall, passing by his group of friends to go into the cafeteria. Before I entered the cafeteria door, I looked back at him to see that he already had his arm draped around Tina, the cheerleader captain. Finally, I realized what Damien wanted with me. I guessed I'd be riding home in his car tomorrow.

Again, because neither one of us had a social life, I couldn't wait to tell Raquel. I wondered what Romi would say. As soon as I thought about Romi, I felt upset all over again from what I had heard last night. She'd exited the bathroom and saw me standing not too far from the door with a look of disgust on my face. I certainly needed to talk with her to clear things up, because there had to be an explanation of how something like this could even be happening.

Later that day after school, I was about to burst from withholding everything that happened with Damien. So I decided that I couldn't wait any longer for Romi to get home and that I was just going to tell Raquel. Even though I was upset with Romi over the thing with her and Mr. Charles, she was my sister, and we were all close. There wasn't much I didn't tell one without telling the other. She was really the only one who kept secrets.

I walked into Raquel's room and flopped down on her bed while she sat by the window at her desk, studying. "Hey, I finally found out what Damien wanted," I stated with anticipation.

"Oh, good," Raquel replied sarcastically, rolling her eyes.

She knew damn well how excited I was to tell her all about Damien, but the truth was, deep down she was a little envious. Hell, I would be too if I were her.

"Well, don't you want to know what he wants?" I asked, searching for just a shred of excitement from her.

"What did he want, Raina?" Raquel asked dryly, still reading her book.

"He just wants me to tutor him in calculus. He's coming over tomorrow after school."

"Oh, okay. Did you tell Mama?"

"Yeah, she said it was fine. I even told her that he was driving me home after practice." I figured that would get her attention.

"Oh, so he's going to drive you home?" she said, finally looking up.

"Yup!"

"Bitch!" She laughed. "Well, ask him if I can get a ride too."

"Well, we're leaving after practice, and you know you leave right after school so . . ."

"Uh-huh, I see what it is. You're trying to have some one-on-one time with your man," she teased with a curled-lip smirk.

"Shut up, Raquel. He's not my man. In fact, he was all hugged up with Tina today during lunch period."

"Ugh, Tina? It is so typical for him to be with someone like her," she retorted.

Tina Thompson was one of the most beautiful girls at Greene County High. She was precisely five foot seven inches tall, with dark brown skin, gray eyes, and a perfect body. She always wore the perfect clothes, had perfect white teeth, and had the most beautiful, curly, shoulder-length hair. She was exactly like Romi with a darker complexion, perfect looking. Unlike me, she was also a senior this year. Tina was the captain of the cheerleading squad and had been on the homecoming court all four years. I knew that if Damien had Tina, then there was no chance he'd ever be interested in someone like me. I figured, at best, maybe I could steal a few glances of his fine ass while we studied, get a break from riding that damn bus home from school every day, and possibly end up with a new friend. Who knew?

Chapter 6

Romi

It was eight o'clock on the dot when I stepped out of my red Toyota Camry in the Plaza Hotel's parking garage. Entering through the elevator doors, I quickly pushed the number five and released a slow breath. When I got off, I gave myself a once-over in the hallway mirror and smoothed my hair, which flowed down my back. For some reason, I always wanted to look perfect for Charles. I had never been rejected up until my last relationship with Dre, so I seemed to be overdoing it with my appearance these days. I was hoping to never feel that type of rejection from a man again.

I wore a black bodycon dress with a deep V-neck to show a little cleavage, and black red-bottom stilettos to accentuate my perfectly shaped calves. Shit, I was hot, and everybody knew it, including me. And although I wanted to talk to Charles about getting this whole mess straight with Raina, I wanted nothing more than to first feel him inside of me.

"Knock, knock," I announced as I knocked on the door.

Charles opened the door for me. My old-ass nigga was looking good. He must have just gotten off from work, because he still had on his shirt and tie.

"Come in, baby. Let me look at you," he said while taking off my jacket and checking out my ass.

He stepped back and licked his lips as if he was thinking of all the nasty things he wanted to do to me. He said, "Umph uh hmm," like old niggas did.

Then he grabbed me by the waist and twirled me around to further inspect me before planting a deep, wet kiss on my lips. I submitted to his touch and kissed him right back. He was so excited that he jumped right to it by reaching up my dress and pulling down my red lace panties. I always wore the sexiest red lace underwear because it was Dre's favorite color. They were an exact match to the shade of my lipstick.

After unbuttoning Charles's pants and lowering them to the ground, I realized how happy he was to see me. He picked me up by palming each of my cheeks and lowered me onto himself. My eyes instantly closed in anticipation of his girth. Gently, he pushed my back up against the wall to brace himself before slowly grinding in and out of me. This position was his favorite, but I had to admit, I liked it too. The sounds of our moist bodies colliding filled the room while my pussy throbbed, awaiting its gratification.

"Ooh, Charles," I whispered directly into his ear.

Hearing my voice must have lit something in him, because his dick began to lash my insides faster and faster until I shouted out with orgasmic pleasure.

"Ahhh, shitt!" I wailed.

When my muscles tightened around him, I could feel my legs trembling and growing weak. Suddenly, he dropped me to the floor and quickly spun me around. As he led me over to the bed, I could tell how badly he wanted me from behind from feeling his hard dick pressed against my butt. With a forceful push, he bent me over before penetrating me once more.

"Damn, girl," he groaned.

Charles's strokes grew quicker and deeper until he finally released inside of me. After we were through with our lovemaking session, we lay in bed together with him spooning me from behind.

He planted soft kisses on the back of my neck while gently caressing my arm. Closing my eyes, I wondered if he was like that with Evelyn.

"Babe, what are we going to tell Raina?" I asked.

"I've been thinking about this all day long. Hopefully, she hasn't said anything to your parents."

"I don't think she would."

"Tell her that we kissed that one time and that we thought about being together but decided against it."

"She probably overheard us fucking, Charles. She's not stupid!"

"Well, what's your idea?" he replied with frustration.

"I don't know. I can tell her that we had been flirting and that night was our first night fooling around in the heat of the moment. But now we've realized that it was just a mistake. I'll tell her that it's never going to happen again, and then I'll swear her to secrecy. What do you think?"

"If you think that will work. I mean, she's your sister."

"Well, I don't know of any other way to explain it to her other than to just flat-out tell her the truth."

"No, no, no, we don't want that. Lord, your father would kill me," Charles said while sitting up in the bed. For the next few minutes, we sat there quietly, both thinking about what would happen if my parents found out.

"Baby, do you and Evelyn still have sex?" I asked, breaking the silence.

"That's my wife. Why the fuck would you ask me something so personal like that, Romi?" he spat dramatically.

I quickly sat up, realizing that this nigga had just lost his mind. I cocked my head to the side and said, "Well, it's no longer personal, nigga, because I don't wanna share no fucking more."

I got up from the bed and immediately started putting my clothes back on. The audacity of him to tell me it was personal had my emotions fucked up as shit. Fuck him!

"Romi, don't leave. We have the room all night, babe, and I'm not even going home to her tonight."

"Charles, I'm not feeling this anymore. If you're not going to leave her, just let me go. Please."

"I'm gonna leave her. Just give me more time," he begged.

"Do you still love her?" I asked, looking him square in his eyes.

After a few seconds of silence, he took a deep breath and said, "Romi, she's my wife. What do you want me to say?"

I stood there deep in thought for a moment, carefully deciding what my next words would be.

"I don't want you to do anything but leave me the fuck alone. If you call or text me again, I can promise your ass that I'm telling my daddy *and* that little wife of yours."

I tried to keep it together, but I just couldn't hold back the tears. Without another word between us, I finished slipping on my clothes and shoes, then grabbed my Hermes bag off the chair. As I headed for the door, I looked back at him for what I knew would be the last time.

"Now, stay the fuck away from me, nigga!" I yelled, slamming the door behind me.

It was 10:30 that night when I found myself driving home alone with tears streaming my cheeks. I hated that I let that fuck nigga see me cry, let alone fuck the shit out of me for a whole month. But hey, you live and you learn. So even though I was a little sad, a bitch wasn't going to be down for long. I knew I really didn't love Charles, but I didn't like being alone either. Above everything, I wanted to rush the mending of this broken heart that Dre had left me with. The saying wasn't true: the fastest way to get over a man wasn't to get under another.

I used to ooze confidence from the top of my head to the bottom of my feet, but now I was slowly starting to feel insecure. I was beginning to feel like I wasn't worthy of a real relationship or real love. All I wanted was someone to really want me, all of me, and the only one I truly wanted that from was Dre.

As I walked up the stairs and inside of our house that night, I could faintly hear both Raina's and Raquel's voices. They must have still been up talking, so I instantly went into Raquel's room.

"What are y'all doing up?" I asked, standing in the doorway, taking off my heels.

"Raina was telling me that her man Damien is driving her home from school tomorrow," Raquel replied before sticking her tongue out at Raina in a teasing manner.

"No, it's not really like that. Damien just wants me to tutor him in calculus, so he's coming over tomorrow to study. That's all."

"Well, I know you like him, so just play it cool like I told you, okay?" I said with a wink.

With my hand, I quietly motioned for Raina to come talk to me outside of Raquel's room. So Raquel wouldn't know what was going on, Raina got up from the bed and stretched, adding a little yawn.

"Well, let me go pick out what I'm going to wear to school tomorrow. It's getting late, so I need to be getting ready for bed," she explained.

Raina and I walked out into the hallway before disappearing into my room.

"Raina, I need to talk to you about what you may have heard last night. It's not what you think. Well, it's not exactly what you think."

"Are you sure? Because it sounded to me like you and Mr. Charles were getting it on. Eww, Romi! That's gross," she said, shivering with disgust.

"Well, first it started off real innocent, you know, just flirting. Then it just ended up being more," I said, not really wanting to disclose the full details of my sex life to my baby sister.

"So does he want to be with you? Is he leaving Ms. Evelyn for you?" Raina naively asked.

"No. I just broke it off with him. So you don't even have to worry about it anymore. I just realized that he was a mistake and a waste of my fucking time. Can you promise me to just let this go and not tell anyone?"

I could look at Raina and tell that she really didn't want to promise me, but because we were sisters, she did.

"I promise," she replied.

I gave her such a tight hug because I was happy and relieved that she was going to keep my secret. "Now let's go pick out a sexy outfit for tomorrow, because I know you want to look good for Damien," I said, pulling back from our embrace.

We walked over to Raina's room and picked out a pair of white skinny jeans that were ripped and holey, and we paired them with a form-fitting V-neck tunic that had peach, aqua, and white print. I looked in her closet and grabbed a pair of nude peep-toed wedges that I saw. On Raina, this outfit was enough to make any man weak. My sister was hot. She just didn't know it. I even told her to come and wake me in the morning if she wanted me to do her hair and makeup, but she declined. She said that she didn't want to overdo it, and she was right. There was no need for her to be looking all thirsty.

As I eased my way back down the hall and into my bedroom, I quickly began to undress. I still couldn't believe that I had let that old-ass man play me out like that. So here I was, rejected once again. It was funny, because I was always the one who ran game on niggas, not the other way around, but I guessed this was just my first time dealing with an old-school nigga.

"Ha," I laughed with a little snort at the thought.

As I lay down in my bed, I pulled the pillow over the top of my head and thought, *I gotta get my fucking life together*.

Chapter 7

Damien

It was around five o'clock after basketball practice, and I was waiting for Raina by her locker like I told her I would. I really wished shawty would go ahead and just do a nigga's homework. That would be one less thing I had to worry about. I already had so much on my plate with my other classes and basketball, not to mention Tina's needy ass. I was tired as fuck. Did I really want to go back to this girl's house to study? Hell no. I told Raina that I had a scholarship on the line, but the truth was Pops and Micah were just strict when it came to school for whatever reason. I didn't need a scholarship to pay for school because my family had enough money to buy a damn college if that was what we needed to do. I just assumed she might've agreed to help a nigga out if I laid it on a little thick. I already had a 3.8 GPA, so I wasn't worried about getting into Clark Atlanta. Hell, I had already been accepted. I just didn't want to disappoint Micah or my pops if I came home with an F in calculus. The way things were going right now, I was definitely getting an F if I didn't start turning things around soon.

I looked at my G-Shock on my wrist because it was getting late and I knew damn well shawty didn't stand me up. When I looked up, I saw her finally walking toward me.

"Hey, Damien, sorry I'm late. I just wanted to shower and change back into some real clothes," she said.

While she was all dressed up and looking pretty as hell, I only had on a basic white tee with the sleeves cut off, black basketball shorts, and black-on-black Jays. Since I had just gotten out of practice, I didn't give a fuck. Looking her over, I had to admit that she was looking good. I could see her smooth, caramel-colored skin through all the holes in the jeans that she was wearing. *If she were my girl, I'd make her throw them shits away,* I thought.

"So, beautiful, you ready?" I asked, watching her struggle to get her book bag zipped. I grabbed it and carried it for her. It was the least I could do since she was helping me out. She must have stuffed every damn textbook and notebook she owned in this book bag, because it was heavy as fuck and damn near busting at the seams.

"Yo, what you got in here, a body, shawty?" I joked.

She laughed with that pretty-ass smile of hers. "No. After we get through with calculus, I have homework in all of my other classes," she explained as we walked outside.

"Yo, this me right here," I said, pointing to my black-on-black Charger.

Like the true gentleman nigga I proclaimed to be, I opened the door for her. She plugged her address into my GPS, and we took off, riding in silence for most of the way. During the time that we were stopped at the traffic lights, I stole glances of her and took notice of how truly beautiful she was. She had some pretty-ass toes that were peeping through her shoes. Her titties were sitting perfectly in the shirt she wore, and all of that long, silky black hair that swung around to one side exposed her pretty neck.

Although shawty was stunning, she was young as fuck. Outside of Tina, the chicks I usually fucked with were at least 21. When I transferred to this school a few months ago, it didn't take long to realize that Tina was the bad bitch of the school. With me being who I was, I made sure that she was the one on my arm. However, she wasn't the type I would ever make wifey. She knew she was my main girl, and she was satisfied with that.

"Yo, I meant to tell you that you look real nice today, Raina," I complimented her, breaking the awkward silence in the car.

"Wow, you actually know my name?"

"Whatchu mean?" I asked, confused. Waiting for her response, I leaned back into my seat with one hand on the steering wheel and kept my eyes on the road.

"Well, usually it's shawty this or shawty that," she said before laughing.

"Oh, you got jokes, shawty," I said, laughing too.

"Nah, I'm just playing. Thank you for the compliment though," she said with a smile.

When we pulled up to her community, I instantly noticed that she stayed in a nice-ass neighborhood. "Oh, so you're a rich girl, huh?" I smiled.

Lake Oconee was one of the most prestigious areas in all of Greensboro, where the all-brick homes ranged from 4,000 to 6,000 square feet and had a view of the lake.

"Rich?" she quizzed, looking confused.

"What do your parents do?" I asked.

"Well, my father is a lawyer, and Mom stays at home."

"A lawyer, huh? Yup, rich like I said," I replied jokingly. I mean, you could tell they had money, just not the kind of money my family and I had.

"Well, what do your parents do for a living?" she asked.

"My pops runs his own business, and my moms, well, she stays at home just like yours."

"Oh, okay." Raina nodded. "Do you have any brothers or sisters?"

"Yeah, I have two brothers and my cousin, who my parents raised as their own. So, really I have three brothers. What about you?" I asked.

"Yes, I have three sisters. My oldest sister, Risa, is in college at Spelman. She's going to be a lawyer like my father. Then, there is Romi, who's nineteen. She's not in college. Doing nothing, actually." She rolled her eyes at that. "Then there's Raquel. You know Raquel, right?"

"Nah. Who the fuck is Raquel?" I asked.

"Oh, well, she goes to school with us. She's a senior like you. And then there's me, Baby Girl!"

"Baby Girl, huh? Are all yo' sisters as beautiful as you?" I asked, knowing I shouldn't even be fucking with her young ass, but hey, I was telling the truth.

"Yes, they are all beautiful. A lot more beautiful than me," she said, blushing.

"Pshh, I seriously doubt that shit," I replied, shaking my head. Then I thought about it for a minute. "You said Romi? Romi Brimmage, yo, that's your sister?"

"Yeah." She nodded.

"Ohhh! I know her. You're right, y'all are beautiful." I smiled. Romi was fine as fuck with those green eyes, no lie. I could tell that Raina didn't know what to make of my last remark. It was almost like she didn't know whether to be jealous or proud.

"Yo, her and my brother Dre used to fuck around some months back. That's how I know her," I said, trying to clear shit up.

"You sure do curse a whole lot. Do you think you can tone all that down when we go up in my house?" she questioned with a little attitude. I only shrugged and laughed. I liked how her young ass was low-key putting me in check.

As we entered the house, Raina called out to her mom.

"I'm in the kitchen, Baby Girl," her mother responded. Raina motioned for me to follow her into the kitchen.

"Baby Girl," I whispered in her ear just to tease her while pulling at her love handle. She quickly batted my hand down.

"Hey, Mama," she said, kissing her mother on the cheek. "This is Damien. I'm tutoring him today, remember?"

"Yes, I remember," her mama said, reaching out to hug me. I had to admit that her mama was fine too, looking like Vanessa Williams. I'm just saying.

I hugged her back and said, "Nice to meet you, ma'am," trying to sound all proper and shit.

"You two need to go into the dining room to study," her mama said while eyeing Raina.

I guessed Mama was no fool. She probably noticed my swagger and my Charger parked out front, figuring I was a street nigga, even though I wasn't.

"Okay. Come on," she told me, pulling me by the hand toward the dining room.

"Your house is real nice, Baby Girl," I complimented her as I looked around, admiring the beautiful hardwood floors, coffered ceilings, and fancy artwork hanging on the walls. Our house was twice as big, but I could tell that her pops was definitely doing great things.

Shortly after, we sat down at the table, and she started pulling out her calculus book. "So where do we start, Baby Girl?" I asked with my notebook and pencil in front of me.

"Are you going to start calling me Baby Girl now? You call me everything but my name," she said, shaking her head.

I laughed, knowing she was right.

"First it's beautiful, then it's shawty, and now you're calling me Baby Girl," she quipped with a cute little attitude, flipping through the pages of her book.

After turning in my seat toward her and resting my arm behind her on the chair, I looked directly into her eyes. "Shawty, it just doesn't feel right for me to call you Raina. So out of the names you just said, which one do you want me to call you?"

"I don't know." She smiled coyly, trying to avoid eye contact. After a few moments of her giving it some thought, she looked up at me and said, "I liked it when you called me beautiful."

She quickly returned her gaze to her book.

"Why do you like when I call you beautiful?" I asked, lifting her chin with my finger so that I could look into her beautiful light brown eyes. I knew I was fucking with this young girl while I was supposed to be over here studying and shit, but there was something about her that I was drawn to.

"Outside of family, I don't know if I've ever been called beautiful," she quietly confessed.

And just like that, something instantly came over me. I looked at her, and she had that pretty-ass neck exposed again with all her long hair flipped to the other shoulder. Without another thought, I lightly kissed her neck, allowing my tongue to slightly graze her skin. She didn't resist. In fact, I could have sworn that I heard a slight moan seep through her lips.

I grabbed her chin again and looked her directly in her eyes and told her, "Shawty, you're beautiful as fuck, and don't you ever believe anything different. Now let's get this studying done 'cause a nigga tired and huuungry."

She shook her head and giggled. "I'm thinking we just need to do today's homework assignment. Did you understand today's lesson at all?" she asked.

"I never understand that shit Mrs. Waters be talking 'bout. That's half the problem right there."

Raina laughed, knowing where I was coming from. Mrs. Waters could be a little confusing at times.

"Well, I understood today's lesson pretty well, so I can review that with you as we do the assignment. Okay?"

I nodded.

"And we have a test next Friday on the last three chapters, so we're going to need to get together a few more times next week to study for it."

I nodded again, then reached out and softly grabbed her hand. I tried staring right into her eyes again, but shawty wasn't having it. She kept her eyes down in the book.

"Thank you, beautiful. You don't know how much this means to me," I said as I softly caressed the back of her hand with my thumb.

She gazed down at her textbook for a few moments, allowing her hand to still rest in mine. Then she gently pulled it away. I guessed things were getting too awkward for her.

"All right, problem number one . . ." she said, changing the subject.

I laughed to myself while shaking my head. I could already see that shawty was different.

Chapter 8

Raquel

While I was upstairs, I heard Raina and Damien come in the house. So of course, what did I do? I went downstairs to be nosy.

"Hey, Mama, where's Raina?" I asked.

"They are in the dining room studying." She pointed with a smirk, already knowing my motives.

I headed straight for the dining room but decided to listen in a little before entering.

"So, the absolute value, in this case, would be twenty," Damien said.

"Yes. You got it!" Raina replied with excitement.

"A'ight, beautiful, let's try one mo'."

Did he just call her beautiful?

After hearing that they were actually studying, I decided not to disturb them. Instead, I went in the living room and finished reading my book.

Raina would tell me all the juicy details when he left anyway.

About an hour or so later, I heard him and Raina walking toward the kitchen. I adjusted in my seat, pulling my feet from underneath me, and glanced up at the clock on the wall. It was seven o'clock, and time for us to eat dinner. I could smell Mama's cooking, and my stomach had started to growl.

"Hey, Damien, did you want to stay for dinner?" Raina asked him.

"Sorry, beautiful, but my moms is expecting me back home soon. Maybe next time, shawty," he mentioned while rattling his car keys in his hand.

"Oh, okay," Raina replied.

Somehow, I managed to see the disappointment in her eyes although she tried hard to disguise it. When they finally made it to the front door, Raina looked back at me.

"Oh, this is my sister Raquel I was telling you about."

"Hey, how are you?" I said with a little attitude.

"I'm good, shawty, just trying to get this calculus shit straight. But I holla at you," he replied. "Come walk a nigga to the car, shawty," he told Raina, nodding toward the door.

I grabbed my book and got up from the couch to go look out the window as they walked toward his car. *The rumors about his family must be true,* I thought as I looked out at his Charger. I mean, shit, we were only in high school. Who drives a brand-new black Charger with black rims and illegal tint in high school?

As I watched them continuing their conversation, he leaned against his car with her standing in front of him on the curb. I couldn't hear what they were saying, but suddenly he reached out and pulled her close for a tight hug. She was so short compared to him that she literally had to stand on her tippy toes.

I was even more surprised by what I saw next. This nigga leaned down and kissed her right on the neck. Yup, I was calling her ass out as soon as she walked in the house because this little hussy didn't even flinch or pull away. I had to admit that he was fine though, so I probably wouldn't have pulled away either.

A few moments later, she walked in the house, and I was right on her heels. "Umm-hmm. I saw that."

"Saw what?" she asked, playing stupid.

"I just saw that nigga kiss your neck, Raina. What's up with that?"

She laughed and waved me off before heading up to her room. I followed closely behind her and figured that she probably didn't want to talk downstairs with Mama being in the next room. When we finally reached her room, I plopped down on her bed and got comfortable.

"Spill it, bitch!" I said.

She only started laughing, but then she looked at me, realizing that I was as serious as a heart attack. There was no shame in my game. I wanted all the tea.

"I guess it was just a friendly kiss," she said with a shrug.

I could tell she really didn't know what to make of it. "Oh, and I heard that nigga in there calling you beautiful while y'all were supposed to be studying. What's up with that?" I asked, shaking my head and laughing.

"That's his nickname for me," she said, smiling ear to ear.

She began filling me in on their whole study session. I could tell my sister really liked him. I just hoped he liked her back the same way, and if he truly did, I hoped he would protect her heart at all costs, because that was Baby Girl.

"So, what were y'all talking about outside?" I asked, looking down in my book.

"He was just thanking me for my help and told me that he actually understands it a little more now. We exchanged numbers so that we could set up our next study session. Oh, and then he said that after he saw you, he recognized you from school. He said you always stay to yourself, though."

"Well, that's true," I admitted with a shrug. I knew it sounded crazy, but I really didn't like people. Shit, my sisters were all the friends I needed.

"And after seeing you, he said that he wanted to hook you up with his brother who is really his cousin. He said that he's twenty and they all know Romi somehow. Do you know a Melo Borrego?" she asked me.

"No, I don't know a Melo, but how does he know Romi?"

"He said she used to deal with his other brother, Dre," she explained, shrugging her shoulders with a questioning look. "Oh, and he also thought you were pretty."

"Uh hmm, whatever," I said with a little attitude. I was trying to downplay his compliment even though I was blushing on the inside.

"So are you interested?" she asked, looking in her closet for something to wear to school tomorrow.

"I don't know. You know I don't like people like that, Raina. What this nigga even look like?" I asked.

"Yeah, you're right! You don't like people, but I know you eventually want a man to find love, right?" she questioned with emphasis on the word "man" as if she was asking me if I was gay.

I only laughed. "Of course I eventually want a man, Raina. What kinda question is that?"

"I'm just asking."

"When is Mr. Matchmaker trying to do this hookup? And you didn't answer my question, Raina. What this nigga look like?" I asked again, curling my lips to the side.

"I don't know. I'm going to text him to see if he'll shoot me a pic. He did tell me that he and his brothers are throwing a party Saturday night after the dance. He said for us to roll through and holler at him," she said while texting.

"It's whatever. If you want to go, I'll go," I retorted nonchalantly.

"Thank you, Raquel!" she squealed with excitement while performing a little celebratory dance.

She gave me a quick and playful kiss on the cheek. I rubbed her kiss off, because she knew I didn't play that mushy stuff.

I didn't know who this Melo guy was, but if he was half as fine as Damien, then I would consider giving him some of my time. And trust me when I say I didn't give anybody any of my time.

There were guys in school who tried to hit on me, but when word got around that I didn't give out my number, I didn't have sex, and I barely even talked, nobody wanted to approach me, which was exactly how I liked it. I just wanted to play my piano, sing, read my books, and graduate. In that order.

Suddenly, I heard a text message come through her iPhone. "Did he send the pic?" I asked, feeling nervous for some reason.

"He did, and this nigga is fine, Raquel. Oh, my Gawd!" she shouted while smiling and looking down at her phone.

"Let me see," I said, quickly snatching the phone out of her hand.

I looked down at the picture, and she was right, at least from what I could see. Although he was pretty, his face was emotionless. He was kinda light-skinned, more so caramel, and he had piercing light brown eyes, or maybe even hazel. They sat below the most beautiful dark, long eyelashes and reminded me of how people talked about mine. People would usually tell me that my hazel eyes stood out more because I didn't have light skin like Romi or Raina. I didn't want to stare too long at the picture and get all geeked up over this nigga. All I wanted to do was graduate in June and head to Clark Atlanta in the fall where I would pursue a degree in music.

"Oh, okay," I said disinterestedly, passing her back the phone.

"That's it? Will you at least talk to him if we go?" she asked in disbelief that I wasn't drooling over his ass.

I shrugged in response and returned to my book.

Raina and I went back downstairs for dinner and asked Mama if we could go to the party. Of course, she told us to "go ask your Daddy," which meant that she really didn't want us to go, but she didn't want to be the bad guy and tell us no.

"Daddy, can we go to Damien's party this Saturday? It's after the dance from nine to midnight, and his parents will be there along with other people from school," Raina asked, giving Daddy those puppy dog eyes.

"Only if Romi goes and drives you two," he said.

"Yes!" Raina said excitedly, already assuming Romi would go.

"Where is Romi?" I asked, noticing that she was missing.

"Oh, she's out with her friends. I guess she'll be home a little later this evening," Mama replied.

"How did the tutoring go, Baby Girl?" Daddy asked with a raised eyebrow and a smirk. He knew how pretty his daughters were and that we were all teenagers. Any time a young man came to the house, he always suspected that there was a little something going on.

"It went well," Raina answered, shoveling a forkful of spaghetti in her mouth.

Daddy rolled his eyes and mumbled something under his breath. Raina and I both knew exactly where Daddy was going with all of this.

"It's not like that Daddy, really. He just needs help in calculus. He's even going to the dance with Tina on Saturday," she said. She was a little bothered, but only I could tell.

"He is? And are you okay with that?" I asked. She definitely left that part out when she was telling me about their study session.

"I'm not his girlfriend, so it doesn't bother me at all," Raina said, lying her butt off.

"Well, let's just keep it to tutoring, okay?" Daddy teased, giving Raina a wink.

"Okay, Daddy," she said with a small laugh.

After we finished, Raina and I stayed behind to clean the kitchen. Raina would always wash while I dried and put the dishes away.

"You didn't even tell me that he was taking Tina to the dance," I said. Tina was a popular little black Barbie doll with nothing but a head full of air. I wondered if that bitch could even hold a conversation. Yes, I was hating on her a little bit, because she was dating my sister's soon-to-be man.

"It's no biggie. He's not my man," she said, trying to sell me.

"Umm-hmm," I replied, giving her a "yeah, right" sort of look.

"I mean, he's cool and all, don't get me wrong. He's real down to earth and a really good guy, I think. At least that's how he came off today," she said, staring off, thinking about Damien.

"Was he like a dumb jock when you were trying to tutor him?" I joked.

"No. He's more like a smart thug than a dumb jock to me. And he actually picked up on the material pretty quickly. I guess he just needed some one-on-one help and maybe someone to explain it to him in a different way. You know how Ms. Waters teaches?"

"Yeah, I know how she teaches. How did you find out he was going to the dance with Tina?"

"I asked if he wanted to study tomorrow."

"On a Friday?" I shouted. I mean, yeah, I was a nerd and all, but even I knew the answer to that question.

"Yes, I know," she said with her hands up in surrender. "But anyway, he told me no because he had to get ready for the dance. He asked me if I was going, and I said no. Then I just came out and asked him who he was going with. He said Tina, his 'buddy,'" she explained, using air quotes and with her mouth twisted to the side, as if to say, "Yeah, right, nigga."

"What are you trying to say? You think they are more than friends?" I asked. I had no life of my own, so when something like this happened, I dug in deep with interest.

"Yeah, don't you? I mean, look at her. If you were a guy, could you only be friends with her?"

"I guess you're right, but you know she's as dumb as a bag of rocks, right?" I said, laughing. "Okay, tell me this: do you like him? Are you jealous that he is going to the dance with Tina?" I asked with a sly grin as if I didn't already know the truth.

"I don't know about all of that. I was just saying that I think there is more to him and Tina than he's willing to admit to me right now. And yeah, from what I know about him so far, I like him."

"When are you and Damien studying again?"

"He said we'd 'chop it up' over the weekend," she said, using air quotes again and making fun of Damien's street lingo. "My guess would be next week sometime. If he knows like I know, he'd better want to hit the books before the big test next week," she said.

Just as we finished up the dishes, Romi walked through the front door, wearing a tight-fitting red dress that stopped about six inches above the knee and hung low enough to see one and a half inches of her cleavage.

"Of course you would stroll in now that all the work is done," I said, giving her a hard time. Raina and I cleaned the kitchen after dinner practically every night, so this was nothing new.

"Sorry, I had dinner with Sherry downtown tonight. How'd it go with Damien?" Romi asked.

"Fine, I guess. We just did some studying, like I said."

"Damien told her that he's going to the spring dance with Tina this Saturday, and now she's all bent out of shape," I chimed in.

"I'm not bent out of shape. I don't give a shit," Raina snapped, which was unlike her. Romi and I were usually the ones with the slick mouths, so I knew she was in her feelings.

"Tina who? Tina Thompson?" Romi asked.

"Yes," Raina replied, rolling her eyes.

"She's not all that, Raina. Just play it cool. The only thing she has over you is confidence. You are prettier than her, smarter than her, and most importantly, you are the little sister of Romi Brimmage. And trust there ain't a bitch out there who can top that," Romi said, bouncing her eyebrows as we all fell out laughing.

I could tell that Romi instantly made Raina feel better. She was right. Tina didn't have anything on Raina except for confidence, and everyone knew confidence was key.

"Well, Damien did invite us to a party at his house this Saturday. Daddy said if you go with us, then we can go. Plleeasse!" Raina begged, giving Romi those same puppy dog eyes that usually worked like a charm.

However, Romi was tougher than Daddy. She didn't give two shits about Raina's sad eyes. "Nah, I got plans Saturday night. Sorry, Baby Girl," she said, walking out of the kitchen.

"Oh, and he said that his brother Dre was going to be there too. He said you two know each other?" Raina questioned, following her up the stairs.

"Oh, really?" Romi quizzed, stopping in her tracks and turning around with a smile. "Yeah, I was low-key in love with that nigga not that long ago."

"How were you in love with someone we never even knew about?" I asked, making my way up the stairs behind her.

"Because he didn't want to be with me like that. By the time I realized I'd fell for him and wanted to be in a committed relationship, he ended things. There was no need bringing him around y'all if I knew he wasn't going to stick around, ya know?" she explained in a serious tone.

I could almost see a sudden sadness in her green eyes.

"Yeah, I get it. Did you sleep with him?" I asked.

"Now you getting too personal, little girl," she sassed, rolling her eyes, which of course I took as a yes.

"And if we go, Damien's supposed to be hooking Raquel up with his cousin Melo," Raina said, showing Romi the picture of him on her phone.

"Yeah, I know Melo, too. That nigga too much for you though," she said, looking at me with a smirk. "But hey, now you've got me interested. I'll have to go pop up on Dre's ass and see what that nigga's been up to."

It was looking like we were rolling to the party Saturday night. I just wondered what Romi meant by Melo being too much for me. I guessed I'd just have to wait and see.

Chapter 9

Damien

It was about 11:00 that night when we finally entered the gates to my home and drove up the circular driveway. I could already see several cars that I recognized parked out front. The sounds of Gucci Mane's "No Sleep" could be heard thumping from inside my house. It was good that our property sat on about ten acres of land and the nearest neighbor was about a half mile away, because the music was loud as fuck. I looked over at Tina and had to admit that she looked good tonight on my arm in her red strapless dress and Louboutins.

I wasn't really into going to school dances and shit, but the whole basketball and football teams had gone. Those were my niggas, so I had to go show some love. Now several of them were pulling up in the driveway behind me, ready to get the real party started. As I slid out of my leather seat, I looked down to make sure my Louboutins were still clean. Exposing the grills in the bottom of my mouth, I smiled in anticipation of the fun night I was about to have. I had a fresh, crisp haircut with my deep waves on swim, and I wore an all-black Tom Ford suit. I even had my Tom Ford shades on just for the hell of it, diamond studs in each ear, and a diamond-encrusted Cartier watch on my wrist.

As Tina and I entered my crib, I dapped up several of my niggas from school and from around the way. I searched to find the location of my brothers, which would unofficially be the VIP area of tonight. There had to be about 200 people in my house already, and the night was still young. We even had the pool and the hot tub open out back. A lot of people were out there dancing around the pool half naked or sipping drinks in the hot tub. Our formal living room and the adjacent den area had been cleared of all furniture for the night. In there we had the DJ set up, and it was completely transformed into a dance floor. Throwing a house party was certainly one thing my brothers and I knew how to do.

On the dance floor, I could see half-dressed girls twerking and some of my niggas throwing their hands in the air, holding up either a blunt or a red cup. I looked over to my left in the kitchen and saw that our marble island was fully stocked with several bottles of Hennessy, Rémy, Cîroc, Patrón, Ace, and several other types of premium liquors and beers. To my right were the double doors that led to our game room. There was a thick cloud of smoke rolling out of it. I knew then that it had to lead to my brothers in the VIP area. I smiled, anticipating the blunt that I was getting ready to smoke. While Tina went out back to talk to some of the other cheerleaders by the pool, I went into the game room to see my crew.

"What's up, bruh!" I said, touching hands with my oldest brother, Micah, before pulling him in for a half hug. Micah was 25 and next in line to take over Pop's empire. He was what we all considered the true definition of a boss. Out of all of us, Micah was the most focused on the family business and the most responsible.

"What's up, li'l nigga? How was your li'l school dance and shit?" he asked, eyeing the suit I was wearing.

"Ha-ha, you got jokes. Shit was straight for real though," I said, plopping down on the leather sofa and taking off my jacket.

"Where yo' girl at?" he asked, referring to Tina.

I nodded toward the back of the house.

"I can't believe you brought her back here with all this pussy running around."

"Fuck was I supposed to do? Invite the whole school except for her?" I questioned and laughed while firing up my blunt. "She'll be straight though. She knows we not like that," I explained.

"Pshh! Yeah, a'ight, li'l nigga, keep telling yo'self that shit," Micah said, unconvinced. "I don't know a woman alive who won't show out if you ain't claiming her as your only bitch after she done came up off the pussy."

"What's up, bruh?" I said, nodding to both Melo and Dre, who were sitting at the other end of the couch. Dre and Melo were both finishing up their sophomore years at Clark Atlanta. While they were in school, they also helped Micah a little with the business when they could. They were both in frats, and next year I also planned on pledging, to follow in my brother's footsteps. My father didn't play when it came to our education, even Micah had an MBA from FAMU. Most people didn't know how to take us, because we were educated, but given our family legacy, we were also highly respected in the streets.

"How's everything at school?" I shouted to Dre over the music.

"Everything's good, my nigga," he said before pulling on his blunt.

All of my brothers had a girl or two in their laps as they lay back and enjoyed the night. When Tina strolled in, I reached up from the couch and pulled her down into my lap and kissed her neck. I didn't know what it was, but I had a thing for necks. Kissing them was my way of showing affection without actually having to kiss girls on the mouth. Girls took that kissing shit too far and always tried to fall in love with a nigga. I did almost everything I could to avoid kissing Tina on the mouth. I'd admit that I would give her a peck here and there, because like I said, shawty was needy as fuck, but I'd never really kissed her.

She loved being the center of attention and making other bitches jealous just by being with me. As long as she didn't come talking that shit about us being in a committed relationship or us trying to fuck without a condom, it was all good. We had an agreement that she would be my main girl but that I was free to see whomever else I wanted. I didn't need a girl tying me down, at least not right now. Truthfully, when the time did come, I knew it wouldn't be her. While she was pretty in the face, she wasn't smart or kind enough to really be wifey.

After a few moments passed, the next thing I heard the DJ play was Rich Homie Quan's "The

Most," which I knew was one of Tina's favorite songs. She started slowly grinding and twerking on me like she was giving me a lap dance at Magic City. As I sat back and started to enjoy the dance, I glanced beyond the double doors and saw Raina and her sisters looking right at me.

"Fuck!" I mumbled to myself. I didn't know why I gave a fuck about Raina seeing Tina on my lap, but I did. I immediately grabbed Tina by the waist and pulled her down beside me on the couch.

"What's wrong?" she asked, confused.

"Nothing. I just gotta use the bathroom. I'll be right back," I said.

I got up from the couch and immediately went to go find Raina, but she was nowhere to be found. Truth be told, I didn't even think her nerdy ass would show, but now that I had seen her here, I hoped she hadn't left. I at least wanted to talk to her.

After searching the kitchen and the dance floor inside the house, I decided to look out back. Over in the grassy area beside the pool, I saw more people were dancing to the music outside. That's when I finally spotted her and her sisters dancing.

All of them had crazy bodies. I mean, full breasts, small waists, and nice, round booties.

Although none of them couldn't have been more than a size six, everything they had was in all the right places. Slim thick was what I called it.

I saw Romi twerking with her hands on her knees, while Raina and Raquel ground their hips nicely to the beat of Rihanna's "Work." They looked like they were really enjoying themselves as they laughed and danced. I could tell they were all really close to each other, just like me and my brothers.

Then, suddenly, I saw my nigga Jimmy from the basketball team approaching Raina from behind, trying to dance with her. I didn't know what came over me, but I instantly felt jealous. Before I knew it, I was making my way over to where they were just to make my presence known and shut that shit down. Raina now had her hands up high in the air and was grinding her hips against him with her eyes closed. She didn't notice me coming her way, but Raquel did and quickly tapped her on the arm.

As soon as I approached Jimmy, I spoke low but directly in his ear so that he could hear me over the music. "Nah, this me right here, bruh," I said, pointing toward Raina.

When he didn't immediately back away, I grabbed the back of his neck to drive my point home. "Don't let me catch you or any other nigga fucking wit' her. Tell er'body that shit."

He nodded and put his hands up as if to say, "My bad," then instantly backed away from her. When Raina noticed he'd left, she simply shrugged her shoulders. She began dancing again like she didn't see me standing there, which somewhat irritated me. Shawty was playing games with a nigga, but it was all good because I was in a playing kind of mood.

I grabbed her by the arm and whispered in her ear, "Shawty, you don't fucking see me standing here?"

"Kinda like you didn't see me when I walked in, right?" she quipped, snatching her arm away from me. She was right, so I planned to let her have that one.

"Let me introduce you and yo' sisters to my brothers, beautiful," I said, trying to soften my approach.

She smiled and whispered something into Romi's ear. Afterward, she nodded toward me and simply mouthed, "Okay," because the music was too loud for me to hear her. The three of them took a quick selfie together by the pool. Once they were done, I grabbed Raina's hand and led the three of them back into the house.

As I went into the game room where my brothers were, I was already anticipating some fuckery with Tina's ass, but to my surprise, she wasn't in there anymore.

"Yo, Micah, this is my girl Raina and her sisters, Raquel and Romi. You remember Romi?" I asked, leaning down to his ear so that he could hear me.

Before I could even finish my introductions, Romi flopped down on the couch next to Dre and took the blunt out of his hand. She winked at him and smiled before placing it between her lips and taking a pull. In response, he leaned over and kissed her on the neck, and just like that, it was like old times again with those two. I just laughed and shook my head.

Micah stood up and brought Raina in for a hug. "Yo, this you?" he asked, smiling like a proud parent. He looked at her then back to me for confirmation.

I nodded and gave him a smirk so he would know what I meant.

"She's a beautiful girl, Dame. Don't fuck this up," he said, pushing his index finger to my forehead.

I hated when he did that shit. It was crazy because he didn't know Raina from a can of paint, but I assumed it was just the vibe she put off. She was truly beautiful all around, and nobody could deny that.

Raina looked up at me with a confused look on her face. I wasn't sure if she didn't know what we were talking about because of the loud music, or if she wasn't sure about me calling her my girl.

Micah went in for a hug with Raquel, who was a little less accommodating, but she did halfway hug him back. *Shawty mean as fuck.*

"Yo, Melo, this is the girl Raquel I was talking to you about the other night," I shouted so that he could hear me over the music.

Melo had a girl in his lap and was high as a kite. He looked up at us from the couch, wearing the usual scowl on his face before hitting her with a nod. I just shook my head at this crazy-ass nigga. Raquel rolled her hazel eyes at him and instantly walked away toward my mother's piano in an adjacent room. I watched her as she lightly skimmed her fingers across keys. I wondered if she could play.

I sat down on the couch and pulled Raina down onto my lap. It felt like a natural position for the two of us. "You smoke, beautiful?" I asked in her ear.

She only smiled and shook her head. After taking a long pull from the blunt, I grabbed her face and put my mouth directly to hers. As the smoke escaped through my lips, she opened her mouth and deeply inhaled, accepting her first shotgun. With our mouths still connected, we stared intensely into each other's eyes. That was before we burst into a fit of childish laughter. I guessed we both knew we were gonna get fucked up that night.

As she sat on my lap, I looked her body over and had to admit that she was looking good as fuck. She had on a tight white cropped top that exposed her flat stomach with a fitted white skirt to match. All her long, silky hair flowed over one shoulder with loose curls. I leaned forward and kissed her neck.

"You look nice tonight, beautiful."

"Thank you," she mouthed, wearing a shy expression on her face.

I began running my fingers through her hair and softly tugged at her curls. It felt like she had some white people hair or even Hispanic hair. All the sisters did.

"What are you mixed with?" I leaned in and asked.

"My mother is French Creole, and my father is black. Why?"

"'Cause you have some pretty-ass hair, shawty. I'm mixed too," I said with a smirk.

Her eyebrows raised with curiosity. With the naked eye, people assumed we were just black, especially since none of us had accents.

"Yeah, Moms is Haitian, and Pops is what they call Afro-Cuban," I explained.

She nodded and smiled as she surveyed my facial features.

"Come take a walk with me," I said, nodding toward the door.

As we got up to leave the game room, Romi immediately jumped from the couch. "Where is y'all going?"

"I got her," was all I said.

"Look, don't play, and don't be trying to run no game on Baby Girl. That's my heart right there, and she ain't nothing like me," she said, giving me a serious look.

"I got you, shawty. This my heart right here too," I said, pointing to Raina with a devilish smile. I'd only known her a short while, but a nigga was telling the truth.

Taking her hand in mine, I led the way upstairs. I wanted to talk to her some more, and I knew in the east wing of the house we could have more privacy. My parents were gone to Cuba for the week so that Pops could finalize some business dealings with Uncle Raul. We had the crib to ourselves this weekend. I looked over at shawty as she was taking in all the lavishly decorated rooms of the house and the artwork that hung on the walls. Our house was over 13,000 square feet, with eight bedrooms and eight and a half baths. We also had a movie theater, a basketball court, and a bowling alley.

"You good?" I asked before entering my bedroom.

"Yeah, I love your house. I guess I'm not the rich one, huh?" she teased with a little laugh.

I shrugged and smirked at her. She was cute as hell.

Once we walked into my room, I sat on my bed and patted my hand on the bed for her to sit next to me. "Come sit down with me. I couldn't hear you down there, and I wanna talk to you."

She sat beside me, and I could tell she was a little nervous. I decided to put her at ease the best way I knew how, by kissing her on the neck. She smelled almost edible, wearing Love Spell by Victoria's Secret.

"Why do you always do that?" she asked, pulling back from me.

"Do what?" I asked, leaning forward to kiss her neck again.

"I mean, why do you always kiss me on the neck? It's a little intimate for a tutor and tutee relationship, don't you think?" she quipped with light giggles.

"Nah, this is how I am with all my tutors," I replied with a wink.

"I bet," she retorted with a slight eye roll.

Leaning over to her, I lifted her chin to kiss her on the mouth. As I kissed her soft lips, I could taste the sweet spearmint zest of her wet tongue. For some reason, I ached to kiss her young ass on the mouth. It was something that I refused to do with any other female. There was something about her innocence that had me gone. She was so fucking pretty, and she didn't even know it. That shit alone turned me on.

I found myself getting hard as fuck from merely kissing her. Taking it a step further, I stroked her knees while kissing her. Then I proceeded to let my hand slide all the way up the inside of her thigh, underneath her skirt.

She unexpectedly pulled away. "Wait! I can't."

"You can't what?" I asked.

"Look, I can't have sex with you if that's what you want."

"Shawty, I could have sex with any bitch downstairs. If that's the only thing I wanted, I wouldn't have brought your young ass up here," I snapped. I knew I sounded cruel, but shawty straight offended me with that comment.

"I just wanted to let you know before things went any further, that's all," she added softly, feeling a little embarrassed.

I caressed the side of her face with the backs of my fingers, then kissed her neck again. "I'm sorry, beautiful. I'm not going to try you like that, though. I know you a virgin and shit."

"How do you know that?" she inquired with her nose scrunched.

I could only laugh. "'Cause if you weren't, I would have already hit, shawty," I said with a cocky smirk.

"Wow!" she scoffed and rolled her eyes.

"Like I said, I could fuck any bitch downstairs, but I'm up here with you and your virgin ass."

She giggled and slipped off her shoes before sliding back onto my king-size bed. I guessed now that the air was clear on that subject, her nerves were starting to subside.

"Do you want something to drink?" I offered while getting up to go over to the mini-fridge in my room and shake off my nasty thoughts. I grabbed a cold bottle of water and looked over at her for a response.

"No, thank you," she replied while looking like she wanted to ask me something.

"What's on your mind, beautiful?" I asked, returning to sit down next to her.

"Isn't Tina your girlfriend? I mean, I don't want her coming at me because I'm up here with you."

"Trust me, Tina isn't my girl. You don't have to worry about her or anybody else for that matter."

"Does she know that?"

"Yeah, she's knows what's up. I'm focused on you right now anyway. After this summer, I'm going to Clark for school and shit, but I'll be home often to see you. You okay with that, beautiful?" I asked, rubbing her legs.

"Okay," she whispered, breathing softly.

I could tell I was getting her panties wet, so I leaned over and put my face in the crook of her neck. Gently, I guided my hand underneath her skirt again, but this time, I rubbed my thumb across the front of her panties. Softly, I grazed her clit while gliding my tongue all the way up to her ear.

"Look, I'm not going to make you do something that you're not ready for. But while I'm away at college next year, don't give this away to another nigga or we gon' have some mutha-fucking problems. Okay, beautiful?" I asked, whispering in her ear.

She only nodded with her eyes closed, enjoying the soft strokes I was giving her in between her thighs.

While staring at her beautiful face, I took my middle finger and tenderly slipped it inside her panties to feel her. Just like I had thought, her pussy was slippery wet. As I proceeded to slide my middle finger inside of her, only putting it in about an inch and a half deep, a soft moan seeped from her lips. Her eyes were still fully closed, as I watched her face slightly knot up with pleasure. Instantly, I felt myself beginning to get hard at the sound of her, so I pulled my hand from underneath her skirt to avoid further temptations.

Her eyes finally popped open, and she looked at me as if she wanted to question why I'd stopped. I was hard as a rock. If I didn't pull away when I did, I'd have to go and grab Tina or some other chick just to finish the job. After sticking my middle finger inside my mouth to taste her, I couldn't do anything but shake my head.

"Shawty, you taste sweet as fuck. Come on, let's go back downstairs before you have me fucking some shit up in here tonight," I said, slapping her lightly on the thigh.

Chapter 10

Melo

By this time, Raquel was sitting on the other side of Romi with a red cup in her hand. I could tell she'd loosened up a bit from when she first entered the game room. I'd never put a lot of time in when it came to getting with females because I could fuck just about any bitch I wanted to, effortlessly. That was why I initially hit her with the nod when she was introduced to me. My mother was the first and only woman I'd ever loved, and my intentions were to keep it that way. However, I would say that Raquel was probably the prettiest girl I'd ever seen. Flawless brown skin, bright hazel eyes, and long, silky hair were just a few of her attributes.

As I looked her over, I thought that she was probably part Hispanic or something. Even though she wasn't extremely thick, her body was perfect. She had on a teal bodycon dress with the racer back that fit her curves seamlessly. The crazy thing was, shawty hadn't given me a second look since she'd been here. The girl who'd been sitting on my lap damn near all night had finally decided to get up, so I figured I would go and see what was up with shawty. As I got up from my seat, I stretched my arms out wide, cracking the muscles in my back and chest before walking over and sitting directly next to her.

"Sup?"

"Hi," she replied dryly.

I was a quiet nigga and never really had to rap to a girl to get what I wanted, so I was feeling a little out of my element. I looked her over once again to make sure she was worth it before I asked, "You like the piano?"

"Yeah, it's nice."

"You play?"

"Yeah, I can play," she answered nonchalantly. "Romi, you ready to go?" she looked past me and asked. I could tell she was purposely trying to disrupt the flow of the conversation I was trying hard to carry on with her.

Shawty had me fucked up right now with all the attitude and short-ass responses. She wasn't trying to converse with a nigga for shit.

"So you gon' give a nigga yo' number or what?"
I asked.

"I don't think that'd be a good idea."

"The fuck? Why not?" I asked with my eye-brows together and face twisted in confusion.

"'Cause you're not my type," she said, looking up at me and rolling her eyes. Then she looked back at her sister again and asked, "You ready?"

Romi was high and drunk as hell. With her legs thrown over Dre's lap, she looked back at Raquel. "Not yet. Let's go dance some more," she said, pointing her finger over toward the dance floor.

"Nah, dance right here," Dre told her when she started to get up from his lap.

I knew that nigga didn't want anybody looking at Romi's fine ass. I couldn't blame him, though. Romi got up and instantly started dancing right in front of him to Jeezy's "Magic City Monday." She reached down to grab Raquel's hand and pulled her up from the couch to dance with her.

To my surprise, Raquel actually started dancing, throwing her ass in a circle and all. Although she wasn't dancing for me, I still sat back and enjoyed the view. I found myself inadvertently licking my lips every so often and following her hips with my eyes. She knew how to work that little body of hers, and I could feel myself instantly getting hard.

I noticed the girls had several eyes on them when I looked across the room and saw a few fuck niggas staring and pointing at them and shit. However, there wasn't a nigga in attendance who was bold enough to come into our area and approach either one of them. For some reason, seeing other niggas look at Raquel instantly had me feeling heated. I suddenly grabbed her arm and pulled her down into my lap.

"Excuse me. What the fuck do you think you're doing?" she exclaimed.

"You're drawing too much attention," I simply stated.

"I'm not your girl, and whoever's attention I got ain't none of your concern, nigga!" she snapped.

Shawty's mouth was foul as fuck, but for whatever reason, that shit was turning me on. She got up from my lap and rolled those pretty hazel eyes of hers at me again. Then she whispered something into Romi's ear before walking off. *The fuck?*

"Fuck is she going?" I asked, looking over at Romi.

"Leave her alone Melo. She ain't feeling you like that, nigga," Romi said, smiling at me all high and shit while still dancing to the beat.

"Where did she go?" I stood up and asked firmly again. I was on the verge of spazzing the fuck out.

Romi knew I wasn't going to leave her alone until she told me. "Damn, nigga, can't my sister use the bathroom?" she yelled.

I let out a small laugh before walking off to go find her. This girl already had me acting outside of myself. Females always flocked to me. I was a tall, light-skinned, pretty nigga with light eyes who hardly said shit. I never had to put in any effort to get a girl to fuck with me, let alone to have a conversation.

After walking over to the half bath outside of the kitchen, I pounded on the door like I was five-o, causing some nigga to yell out, "Be out in a minute." I decided to go into the kitchen to pour me another cup of Ace before heading out back to go look for her.

A couple of girls I'd never seen before were standing in the kitchen. "Hey, Melo," one girl said, squeezing past me as I stood between the island and the kitchen sink. She made sure to graze her breasts against my back. She was tall and light skinned with a short Halle Berry haircut. Shorty could certainly get it, but she was nowhere near as fine as Raquel's mean ass.

"What are you getting into tonight?" another girl in the kitchen asked me. She was short and dark skinned with a small, naturally curly afro. I looked down at her frame to notice that she was thick in all the right places. She also had some pretty dark eyes like Naturi Naughton, but she was not my usual type. I liked long, silky hair that I could pull on when I was fucking.

"Just chillin' right now, shawty," I simply stated.

"Can we chill with you after the party?" the light-skinned girl asked. Her smile exposed the gap between her front teeth.

"Come find a nigga after this shit is over," I told her, leaving the kitchen. I knew that by the morning hours I'd have them both in my bed.

When I looked out the back patio door, I saw that Raquel, Raina, and Dame were all sitting around the hot tub with their feet in. I watched as Raquel flicked the water up with her toes, allowing her head to fall back to let out a big laugh. When I approached them, she quickly looked up at me and rolled her eyes. The beautiful smile and laughter she had just displayed moments before were suddenly replaced by an unfriendly scowl.

"Shawty, you mean as fuck," I said, pulling up a chair next to the hot tub and placing my red cup of Ace down on the ground.

She ignored me, so I intentionally stayed there to talk to Dame just to annoy the shit out of her. "This wifey?" I asked him, pointing to Raina.

"In time. In time, my nigga," he replied with a smirk while stroking her hair.

I had to admit that she was beautiful too. All of them were.

"Whatever," Raina cooed.

"Tell him how old you are," he told Raina.

"I'm sixteen," she said as she looked over to Raquel, waiting for her to respond. Instead, Raquel just sighed like she wanted to question why I was even talking to her.

"And she's eighteen. She graduates next month with Damien," Raina continued.

"You see why I ain't wifing her up right now? She young as fuck, bruh," he stated with a chuckle.

"Yes, but my birthday is in a few months. On the Fourth of July, actually," she explained.

"Yo, you were born on the Fourth of July? That's crazy," Dame said.

"Yeah, we usually celebrate my birthday real big each year."

"Well, I hope to be a part of the celebration this time, beautiful," he said before kissing her cheek.

"Of course," she responded as she stared deeply into his eyes. I could tell shawty was already gone over my li'l bro.

"Are you a virgin too?" I asked Raquel, already knowing that Raina was. I stared at her with my arms across my chest, waiting for her response. I could tell that I was irritating her, but I didn't give a fuck.

"You would ask some ignorant-ass shit like that," Raquel retorted.

"It's just conversation, shawty. You ain't gotta answer the muthafucking question if it's like that though," I barked.

"Yes, we're both virgins," Raina quickly responded, noticing the tension that had begun to build between the two of us.

Raquel looked over at Raina with wide eyes that wondered why she was spilling her business.

"What? You waiting for marriage or some shit?" I asked. Although I wasn't big on talking, I knew this conversation was making Raquel uncomfortable as hell, which was all the motivation I needed to keep it going.

"I'm waiting for the right person," Raina corrected me.

"Nah, you're waiting for me. Don't play with me, shawty," Dame said, giving her a serious look.

She just laughed and shook her head. I sure hoped she took li'l bro seriously, because I could already tell that he wasn't playing any games when it came to her.

"And what about you? The fuck you waiting for?" I asked Raquel.

"I've never been in love," she admitted softly. Her eyes remained on the water as she circled her feet.

"In love?" I questioned with a smirk. What the fuck did love have to do with fucking?

"I want to be in love with someone who is just as in love with me before I spread my legs for them. I know you could never comprehend a concept like that," she expressed, rolling her pretty-ass eyes at me again.

Shawty had me ready to snap her little-ass neck with all that eye rolling and neck popping. However, as soon as I was about to speak, I could feel someone behind me rubbing a hand across the top of my back. I turned my head to look back and saw the tall, light-skinned girl from the kitchen.

"We still hanging out after the party, right?" she asked with her hand resting on my shoulder. I didn't answer, I only nodded.

"Well, you never did ask our names. I'm Kela, and my girl is Shante," she said.

I nodded again without saying a word while my eyes remained focused on Raquel.

"Well, I'll let you finish your conversation, daddy. Can't wait to see you later," she spoke seductively before walking away.

"Ugh! Lame," Raquel said, shaking her head.

"Why she gotta be lame? 'Cause she wanna fuck wit' a nigga?" I asked.

"No, she's lame because she 'made plans to fuck wit' a nigga' when he doesn't even know her name," she said, using air quotes for emphasis.

I just laughed because it was obvious she was jealous. Jealousy was cute on her though. "Sometimes it doesn't have to be about love. Sometimes you just need a good nut."

"Ughh! I can't with you," she complained, pulling her feet out of the water to dry them off.

As she was getting up to leave, there was a short, dark-skinned nigga with dreads approaching her. "Ay, li'l mama, let me holla atchu for a minute?" he asked.

That he approached her with me being in her presence was a sign of disrespect. I didn't even give her a chance to respond before I got up from my chair, walked over to dude, and punched him dead in the nose.

Crack!

He instantly fell to the ground with his hands covering his nose, which was rapidly leaking blood. I could hear Raina and Raquel scream out as the crowd around us gasped and gathered at the scene. However, my eyes remained on the fuck nigga lying out on the ground before me.

"The fuck, bruh?" he questioned, looking at his hands covered in blood.

Out of my peripheral vision, I could see two other guys who must have been with him walking toward us. Dame must have seen it too, because he immediately hopped up from the hot tub and stood like he was ready for war. That was why I fucked with my little brother. He always had my back, even in times I didn't need him to.

"Didn't you see me over here talking to her?" I asked, raising my shirt to display the 9 mm tucked in my waist. I was the only one out of the four of us to take my gun wherever I went.

The other two instantly stopped in their tracks and held their hands up to surrender.

"Now get the fuck up outta here, and take these lame-ass niggas with you," I spat before making my way back to my seat.

Once I sat down in my chair, I watched all three of them leave. I pick up my cup from the ground and put it up to my lips to take another sip of Ace. Raquel shook her head and rolled her eyes at me. I responded by blowing her mean ass a kiss just to fuck with her before she got up and stomped inside the house with Raina following her. Dame and I looked at one another for a second before we fell out laughing.

"Yo, you wild, bruh. Why you messing with Raquel like that?" he asked.

"'Cause she's so easy to fuck with, bruh."

Looking down, I realized she left her iPhone on the ground next to where she'd been sitting by the hot tub. I quickly picked it up, and after realizing that she didn't have a lock on her phone, I added my number to her contact list under the name Bae. Then I sent myself a text from her phone so I could have her number. Raquel was a challenge, which was all new for me, but something about her little smart-mouthed ass made me want to be that one nigga she fell for. I was going to leave her alone for now, but it wouldn't be for too long.

Chapter 11

Dre

I hadn't seen or heard from Romi for two months, yet here her pretty ass was, sitting in my lap. She and I kicked it heavy for about a month and a half before she officially tried to lock a nigga down. I was in college an hour away from home, so that was an absolute no-go for me. I mean, not only was I a Borrego, but I was also a fraternity nigga, so bitches practically threw themselves at me all day, every day. The last thing I needed was a girlfriend. Plus I had to dedicate myself to school and the family business, which was hella time-consuming.

However, I would say that if there were to ever be a girl to lock me down, she would be the one. Romi was cool as hell. We could always chill on a friend-type vibe, watching football games, smoking blunts, and talking shit. Then she could switch that shit up and really know how to treat a nigga. She knew when to be affectionate and how to be a good listener, and she could take the dick better than any girl I'd ever been with. Her pussy was perfect: tight, warm, and wet, like it was created just for me. Being here with her tonight had brought back all those feelings I'd been working hard to push away for the past couple of months.

I wanted to call her, but I didn't want to come off like some soft-ass nigga. I also didn't want her to think that I was going back on what I told her, which was that I didn't want to be in a committed relationship right now. After I told her that, she instantly stopped calling and texting a nigga. It was like she just fell off the face of the earth, but now here she was, acting cool. Most girls would have given me attitude or just ignored the fuck out of me all night if they were in her shoes, especially with the way I'd dismissed her, but like I said, Romi was cool as shit. All my brothers loved her. In fact, my whole family did because she fit right in. In just the short period we'd been kicking it, there were times that she'd join in on poker nights with me and my brothers, or I'd call home from school to learn she'd been out shopping with my moms. Even Pops still asked about her every now and then. She was unforgettable, just like the first day we'd met.

I had been back in Atlanta for only about two weeks, and I was over at Lennox with this li'l Puerto Rican baddie named Maria who one of my frat brothers introduced me to. She had a Kim K. booty with a face like Selena. On that particular day, she called herself reacquainting me with Atlanta, and we ended up doing a little shopping. Maria asked if she could stop in Bebe, saying it was one of her favorite stores. I didn't mind, because we had been shopping for me all day. I took a seat on one of the pink suede sofas they had in the front of the store and placed my bags beside me. While Maria made her way through the store, I checked a few texts on my phone.

As the instrumental pop music played within the store, I noticed two girls walking in. One was short with brown skin and shoulder-length hair, and the other was a light-skinned beauty. Shawty's curves and long, silky hair instantly had my attention, but when I caught a glimpse of those green eyes peeking from underneath the fitted cap she wore, I was gone. She had on a red off-the-shoulder cropped top, black leggings with a red stripe down each side, and some red and black Jordans on her feet. She rocked her red and black fitted Braves cap pulled down low like a nigga. In fact, she was wearing the same one I was wearing. By far, she was the baddest, and I mean the baddest, woman I had ever laid my eyes on, whether on TV or otherwise. I closely watched her and her friend as they made their way through the store. They were fingering through items on the racks and holding them up against themselves every so often. When they were finally through shopping and were in line at the register, I heard Maria call out to me from the dressing room.

"Dre."

"Yeah, shawty. What's up?" I hollered, making my way to the outside of her dressing room.

"I wanted you to see this on me and tell me what you think, papi," she said, opening the door and turning around to model a white one-shoulder dress for me.

The dress was cool, but I was no longer thinking about Maria. My mind was on shawty with the red and black Jays on.

"That's cool. You should get it," I stated nonchalantly after giving her a quick look and diverting my attention back to my phone.

After she shut the dressing room door, I made my way back to the sofa in the front of the store and looked down to check IG on my phone. When I looked up, shawty and the short, brown-skinned girl were heading my way out the door.

"Hey, shawty, you forgot something," I told her.

She looked back at me with those beautiful green eyes, then down to the floor and behind her with a confused expression on her face. I guessed she was questioning what I was referring to. Finally, she asked, "What did I forget?"

I passed her my phone and said, "You forgot to give me your number, shawty."

Yeah, I knew that was corny as fuck, but a nigga was out of practice. I couldn't remember the last time I had to spit game or even ask a girl for her number, because women always threw themselves at me. She only looked at me and let out a small laugh. She gnawed on the corner of her bottom lip like she had to think about it. Her eyes roamed me from head to toe as she continued to appear deep in thought.

I shook my head and let out a minor laugh to counter. What the fuck was she contemplating? "If it's going to take all day for you to make up ya mind, just forget it, yo."

"A'ight, I'll just forget it then," she said with a smirk before walking out the door.

Shawty had me fucked up. I'd never had a girl play me out like that, so I was completely thrown. Just as she walked out the door, I got up to follow her. I gently grabbed her arm, turning her around to face me.

"You really not gon' give me ya number, shawty?" I asked with my eyes squinted in confusion.

"I mean, I was, but since you were snapping on me, I changed my mind," she responded with her arms folded across her chest.

"Why'd you hesitate? I mean, what the fuck was you contemplating?"

"Well, I saw you with the Hispanic girl in the dressing room, and I don't like a bunch of drama," she explained as she adjusted her fitted cap.

I smiled because shawty had me feeling insecure and shit at first. I was relieved that it wasn't solely me who caused her to hesitate. "Look, I've only known that girl for all of one week. It ain't even that deep."

As soon as I said that, Maria walked out with her bag in her hand, and she looped her arm through mine. I just bit my bottom lip and shook my head, because now Maria had me looking like a fuck nigga in front of shawty.

"A week, huh?" Romi repeated with a smile.

Her eyes were darting from Maria back to me. She let out a small laugh before she and her *friend turned to walk away. I was an arrogant nigga, and I wasn't ashamed to admit that, so I just let her walk away. Something told me I'd see her again.*

Two days later, I saw a red Camry pull up to the pump behind me at the gas station in Greensboro. Shawty must have seen me pumping my gas when she pulled in, because she was looking at me and smiling when she got out of her car. I just hit her with a nod and a smirk. This time I was acting like I wasn't interested, but it was a straight facade. Just seeing her from behind, walking into the convenience store, ass jiggling in her Pink sweat suit, instantly caused me to brick up. I sighed to myself and shook my head because I knew that shawty was going to make me work for it. Something I never did.

I didn't remember hearing her car lock, so I walked over and opened the driver-side door so that I could pop the gas tank. I walked around and swiped my debit card to fill her up. I knew that $28 and a full tank of gas wasn't going to be enough for me to get at her, but it might be a start. When she came out of the convenience store, she had a little brown paper bag in her hand and a frown on her face.

"Excuse me, did you just go into my car?" she asked with one of her eyebrows raised.

"You should learn how to lock yo' car door, shawty," I said, continuing to fill up my tank.

She rolled her eyes at me and leaned in the car to pop the gas tank.

"I already filled you up," I told her, but she didn't respond. She walked around her car to close her tank, then made her way back around to the driver seat. When I saw that she was about to get in the car, I got a little heated.

"You ain't gon' open up yo' mouth to say thank you?" I questioned with my head cocked to the side.

She smiled at me and leaned back in her car without saying another word. Shawty had officially pissed me off now. I was prepared to say fuck it and turn back to get on my bike, but before I could start it up, I heard her yell for me to, "Wait!"

"Wassup?" I inquired, hopping off my bike with a pissed look plastered on my face.

"I was only reaching into my car to grab my phone. You wanted to exchange numbers, right?" she asked with her pretty-ass smile.

I brushed my hand down my chin because shawty had me all confused at this point. When I looked at her, I couldn't help but smile back, *because she still had the prettiest face I had ever seen. We exchanged numbers, and before I could even get out of the gas station, she'd already sent me a text.*

Ro: Thx for the gas, love.

Me: Anytime, shawty.

Ro: Glad I ran into you again.

Me: I knew we would meet again.

Ro: How?

Me: Destiny.

Ro: Ha-ha, whatever! What are you doing tonight?

Me: You, if you lemme.

Ro: Never mind.

Me: Just chillin' tonight. You wanna roll thru?

Ro: Maybe.

Me: Still playin' games, I see.

Ro: I wanna see you later, but I'm not sure what my plans are yet.

Me: Cancel them shits. You fuckin wit' a real nigga tonight.

Ro: Okay.

That night, we rode out on my motorcycle and hung out in downtown Atlanta with Melo and a few of my frat brothers. They all immediately fell in love with her and said how cool she was for a pretty chick. I even had to check a few of my boys because they were doing too much with eye raping her and shit. Other than that, we all had the best time clowning and bar hopping. I quickly learned that Romi was the homie-lover-friend type of girl and someone I definitely wanted on my team for the long haul. We even shared our first kiss that night, which was beyond describable. Of course, a nigga wanted to take it further, but she shut that shit down with the quickness. In just the short time we'd spent together that night, I had already gained so much love and respect for her that I didn't push the issue. A nigga like me always smashed on the first night, so she had me acting out of character from the jump. Plus, I also knew it would only be a matter of time before I'd be dicking her down anyway, so I played my position that night.

As I collected my thoughts reminiscing, she stood in front of me and began to dance again, now on the fifth song, which was Meek Mill's "All Eyes on You." She seductively swayed her body in front of me, mouthing Chris Brown's words: *Are you here lookin' for love? Got the club goin' crazy. All these bitches, but my eyes on you.*

And I'd be damned if she wasn't mouthing exactly what was going through my mind. I stood in front of her and wrapped my hands around her waist. She reciprocated by putting her arms up around my neck before looking up at me to smile. I was six foot four inches, so I towered over her small frame. After pushing her hair out of her face, I leaned into her ear and whispered, "I missed yo' crazy ass."

"I know you do," was all she said before laying her head against my chest.

"You gon' chill with a nigga tonight?"

"I can't. I got my sisters with me. Plus if I remember correctly, the last time I saw you, you weren't feeling me like that," she said.

"I'm always feeling you, shawty. You already know that shit," I said, looking into her sparkly green eyes.

"Prove it!" she quipped cockily with her hands on her hips and her head cocked to the side.

I laughed before grabbing her sexy ass up and throwing her over my shoulder. As I made my way through the house and up the stairs to my bedroom, she giggled until I threw her ass back onto my king-size bed.

"What are you doing, Dre?" she asked between her fits of giggles.

I didn't respond. I figured since she had to leave to take her sisters home soon, there was no time for talking. I'd be better off showing her how I felt about her. After pulling my shirt off over my head, kicking off my Balenciagas, and taking off my pants, I looked at her and noticed she was eying my mans. I was never one to brag on my dick, but I also knew that I was working with almost ten inches and a stroke game that was out of this world. That look on her face told me she hadn't forgotten.

Slowly, I pushed her dress up to her waist and began pulling down her red lace panties. In that moment, I knew for sure that she hadn't forgotten a nigga, because she knew red was my favorite color. It was also my fraternity color. In the short time that we were together, I had bought her several red bra and panty sets from Victoria's Secret so that she could always wear red whenever she was with me. That she remembered that shit made me happy as fuck.

"What are you smiling at?" she asked knowingly.

"You wore these for me?" I asked slowly, holding up her panties with my index finger.

She blushed and turned her eyes away, which I took as my answer of yes. I kneeled and began to softly kiss her on her thighs.

"Dre, what are you doing? I'm not fucking with you like that no more," she whined while allowing me to kiss on her.

I ignored all that shit she was talking and pulled her legs down closer toward me right before putting my mouth directly on her clit. As I began to taste her, I first let my tongue gently stroke her clit up and down then around in a circular motion until she let out a soft moan.

"Oooh, Dre. Baby, wait!"

Just hearing her moan my name had a nigga bricked up and ready to bust one. Firmly, I palmed her cheeks and continued to suck on her clit with even more hunger, causing her to go wild.

Looking up at her sexy face, I saw that she was biting her lower lip and that her eyes were tightly closed. I could feel her legs tensing up, too, so I knew she was on the verge of cumming. At that moment, I began to fuck her with my stiff tongue. I made sure to thrust it in and out of her until she just couldn't take it anymore. She grabbed the back of my head and pushed my face and tongue deeper inside of her.

"Oooh, Dre, fuuuckk!" she moaned, creaming all over my tongue in the process.

I lapped up all her sweetness before getting on my knees and looking over her relaxed body. Romi was beautiful from head to toe. I pulled her dress over her head and removed her matching red bra. After laying her back onto the pillows beneath my headboard, I took her C-cup breast into my mouth. I lightly sucked and teased her caramel-colored nipple while listening to the sound of her breathing amplify.

"Don't do this, Dre," she whispered.

When she said that, I moved to the other breast and took it into my mouth. "Shawty, you know you want this dick." I knew she could feel my hard manhood pressed against her leg, so I ground it against her so she'd know exactly what she'd be missing out on if she kept trying to play hard to get with a nigga.

"You already know I want you, Dre. I love you. But you're not ready, and I don't want my heart to get broken again."

I stared at her face and noticed she actually had a tear streaming down the corner of her eye and running down into her hair. Now instead of feeling like I wanted to fuck, shawty had me feeling bad. I slid up and lay directly on top of her, wedging my body in between her thighs with my weight resting on my forearms.

Staring directly into her green eyes, I wiped away the wetness from her face before softly pecking her full lips. In response, she turned her head, refusing to look at me, like she was ashamed for me to see her cry. I had never seen Romi cry, not even the day I told her that I didn't want to be in a relationship. She wasn't even the crying type, and that she'd confessed to loving me had me feeling some type of way.

"Don't cry, shawty. I'll be back home next month when school ends, and I'll make shit right with you. I promise," I said.

"You promise, Dre?" she asked, looking me dead in the eyes for reassurance.

I nodded, knowing I had made a commitment that would be damn near impossible for me to keep. In that moment, though, all I could think of was never seeing my girl cry like that again. She was a keeper and I knew it, so from that point on I planned to make a serious effort to get my shit together.

She lifted her head from the pillow and grabbed my face to passionately kiss me. I wasn't about to say that I loved her back. However, being with her like this made me realize how much I truly did miss shawty and how I probably did love her crazy ass.

She reached her soft hand down between us, grabbing my dick and lifting her hips to guide me inside of her. A slight moan slipped from her lips as I filled her body up one inch at a time. I grabbed one of her thighs with one hand and used my other to palm her cheek, allowing me to penetrate her deeper. I bit my bottom lip in pleasure as I felt her tightness wrap around me. Once I was all the way in, I started to slowly grind my hips because I remembered that she liked it when my pelvis would graze against her clit. She told me that it was the best feeling to have that sensation on her clit while feeling me inside of her at the same time.

"Daamn, daddy," she cooed in my ear.

I slowly ground a few minutes more, watching the pleasure unfold on her face. Then in one swift motion, I switched my rhythm and began hitting her with slow, deep strokes in and out. She tried putting her hands up on my chest to prevent me from going in too deep, but I just knocked them shits away and told her to, "Take it!"

"Aah, Dre! Aaah! I'm about to cum," she moaned.

"Nah, fuck that. Hold that shit," I commanded.

I quickly pulled out because I desperately wanted her from behind. She looked at me like I was crazy for taking my dick out right before she was about to reach her peak.

"Turn over," I instructed, smacking her on the thigh.

She did what she was told and turned over on all fours. I grabbed her hips and entered her from behind, which sent me over the top. Shortly after, I began hitting her with my best moves, and she began throwing it back, matching me stroke for stroke.

Romi's pussy was the best I'd ever had. I wasn't ashamed to admit that in my 21 years I'd experienced a lot of pussy. Seeing her big, bright, jiggly ass bouncing on my dick had a nigga wanting to propose and put a baby inside of her to lock her shit down. I got so excited that I began to increase my speed, causing her to cry out in ecstasy.

"Tell me what the fuck I want to hear," I leaned down and said directly in her ear. I tightened my grip on her hair so that her back could arch some more. "Tell me."

"Ooh, fuuck," she moaned in pleasurable pain.

"Tell me what the fuck I want to hear," I commanded again, hitting her with harder strokes and gripping her hair a little tighter.

"I'm cummingg, daddy!" she moaned, causing me to fill her up with my seeds. I knew that I should have used a condom, but she felt too good. Plus I remembered that the last time we were together a few months ago, she told me that she was on the pill.

After our lovemaking session was over, we lay in my bed, holding each other in silence for a while before we got up to wash off and put our clothes back on.

"You all right?" I asked her as we made our way back downstairs hand in hand.

"As long as I got you, I'm all right," she said with a gentle squeeze to my hand.

It was now a little after two in the morning, and people were starting to clear out. When we finally found Raina, Raquel, and Damien, they were all standing out in front of the house. The April night's air had become cool, so Damien held Raina from behind to keep her warm while Raquel wore one of his jackets.

"You ladies need to get home. You want me to drive you, or are you straight?" I asked Romi.

"I'm good," she replied.

"Text me when you get in the house," I instructed before grabbing her chin and planting a long, wet kiss on her lips.

"Will do, daddy," she replied with giggles.

"Don't start that daddy shit again or else yo' ass ain't going nowhere tonight," I threatened, eyeing her up and down while licking my lips.

"Sounds like I need to drag your ass to this car so we can get home and take this ass whipping for being out so late," Raquel said.

When the girls all fell out laughing, I assumed their parents had given them a curfew that they had broken. After Damien and I walked them to their car, I kissed Romi one more time. Damien kissed Raina goodbye and told her to text him when she made it in.

I didn't know how Romi and I were going to make out moving forward, but right now, I was just happy to have my girl back in my life.

Chapter 12

Risa

Finally I had taken all my exams, and I had even made it all week without one word from Zo. While he usually gave me a few hours or even a day to cool off after one of his blowups, he had never gone an entire week. Although I felt a sense of relief, I also felt like there was something off about the situation. In all the years I had dealt with Zo, he always made sure to keep close tabs on me. He would text or call me several times throughout the day, and if I didn't answer, he'd beat my ass.

After we graduated high school, we'd spent most nights together, which of course put some distance between me and my family. My father disapproved but didn't speak on it much because he knew I was headed to Spelman. Still, no matter how much Zo tried to distance me from my sisters, we always remained close. Whether it was through phone calls, texts, or weekend trips to my campus, we always stayed connected. To say the least, we had an unbreakable bond.

It was late Sunday morning when I pulled into Zo's parking garage. I noticed his black Escalade was parked in its usual spot. After hitting the alarm to my white Audi, I tried to mentally prepare myself for the bullshit as I made my way to his apartment. I had already packed up my dorm room for the summer. Now all I needed was to get the rest of my things from Zo's place before I headed home to Greensboro.

Truthfully, I didn't know what had come over me this past week, but I had already made up my mind that if he tried to attack me, I was fucking his ass up, no questions asked. I was tired of feeling weak and trapped by Zo, so if he came at me, we were just going to be Ike and Tina in the limo. Over and over, I had replayed this scene in my mind, preparing for the worst-case scenario. If I had to leave this earth at the hands of Zo, I knew I was going down fighting.

When I finally reached the door, I knocked a few times, but there was no answer. Happily, I used my key thinking that he wasn't home, and I silently thanked God for not allowing our paths to cross. After letting myself in, I looked around, noticing that the place was a wreck. He had leftover pizza in a box sitting on the living room coffee table with open bottles of half-drunk beer. There were little clothes piles scattered all throughout the floor, and the putrid stench from the trash reeked as if it hadn't been taken out all week. I shook my head in disgust as I made my way back to his bedroom.

When I got closer to the bedroom door, I noticed that there were bloody handprints on the walls and on the doorknob. My heart began to beat fast within my chest. The door was closed, but against my better judgment, I slowly opened it with trembling hands. Laid out on the floor was Zo's lifeless body in a pool of blood.

"Oh, my God," I whispered to myself.

His cold eyes were still partially opened when I kneeled to check his absent pulse. Zo's skin was still warm to the touch, which told me that he was most likely killed moments before I arrived. Even though I was done with Zo, it still hurt me to see him like that because we had been together for over four years, and we had history. He was the first and only man I'd ever slept with and the only one I had ever given my heart to.

When Zo and I first met, he stalked me for weeks, showing up at my cheerleading practices, following me to class, sitting at nearby tables during lunch just to watch me eat. Shit, if I had

had any sense then, I would have known that the nigga wasn't right in the head, but at the time I thought it was cute. While all the girls in school desired him and fought for his attention, he had specifically chosen me. That made me feel special.

Nevertheless, that special feeling lasted all of eight months before he put his hands on me for the first time. He punched me in the face like I was a man because he saw me talking to another guy after class. He was a new guy in school on his first day, asking for directions to his next class. Even after explaining that to Zo, he still threw blows to my face and to my body while shouting repeatedly that I'd disrespected him.

That was the first and only time Zo had hit me in the face. It took almost three weeks for my face to heal, along with a broken jaw and a fractured rib. We had to lie to my parents and tell them that I had been in a terrible car accident driving Zo's car and that the airbag deployed on my face, causing my wounds. I tried to leave him then, but he and his brother, Timo, had just gotten into the drug game heavily. Word on the street was that Timo was a straight killer. So when Zo threatened my family's life, I didn't second-guess it. I stayed with the hope that I was protecting them. For a few months after that, he went back to being the sweet, caring boyfriend I first fell in love with. That was until the next incident, and then the one after that, and so forth.

Trembling with fear and shock, I quickly gathered most of my things and pushed the thoughts of calling the cops out of my mind. With everything Zo and his brother were into, there was no telling who did this, and I didn't want to be involved. I ran for the door as fast as I could with my duffle bag draped across my shoulder. The clothes that I was wearing, along with my hands, were stained with his blood.

Quickly jumping into my car, I headed home with unsteady hands on the steering wheel and tears streaming down my face. It was the weirdest feeling because I felt remorse for leaving Zo that way, but even more so, I felt a sense of relief. I was on the way to see my family for the first time since Christmas. They didn't know what I had been through the past four years, but I really needed them now more than ever.

Chapter 13

Micah

It was the day after the party at the crib, and I was driving Damien and Dre over to Romi and Raina's house. Apparently, the family was grilling and having a small welcome home party for one of their other sisters who was coming home from college. Raina told me to swing through with my brothers and get a plate, so that was what I planned to do.

In just one night, Raina was already my baby sister. She was sweet, smart, and everything that li'l nigga Dame needed to keep his head on straight, but he was only 18 and had pussy on the brain. I couldn't be too mad at him though because I used to be the same way.

I pulled up to the front of the house in my black Range and checked the all-black G-Shock on my wrist to see what time it was before getting out of the car. I had planned on staying only for about thirty minutes or so because I needed to head back to Atlanta and handle business tonight with Pops. I also needed to meet up with Zo at Club Nixx. Romi said she would take Dre and Damien back home, so that wouldn't be a problem.

As we headed out to the backyard, the smell of charcoal and good barbecue filled the air. I could hear the Isley Brothers' "Groove With You" playing along with happy sounds of family and laughter. The first person to greet us, of course, was Raina. She was smiling brightly, and her long hair swung from side to side as she ran over to us. She wore a blue and green floral-print romper with gold thong sandals. She gave Damien a tight hug, then Dre, followed by me. I reciprocated with a peck on the forehead.

"What's up, sis? You made my plate already?" I asked.

"You're not just gonna eat and run, are you? Let's go say hey to everyone first," she said, slightly pouting.

As we followed her across the backyard, I noticed there were about fifteen picnic tables set up under a huge white tent. There was even a DJ and a dance floor where people of all ages were dancing. I spotted a few tables that had card games going, and others with dominos being played. I could tell they really knew how to have fun, and it was certainly my type of vibe on some family-type shit.

We walked up to a table where Romi and another small, brown-skinned girl sat.

"Why didn't you come over here to get me when you saw me?" Dre asked in a serious tone.

"My bad, baby. I was coming out of the house with the baked beans in my hands when I saw you all walking over here," Romi explained before reaching out to give him a hug. She greeted me and Dame with a hug as well, then informed us, "This is my bestie, Sherry. Sherry, these are Dre's brothers, Damien and Micah."

"Hey," she greeted us shyly.

We all sat down. Romi was sitting in Dre's lap, and Raina was sitting in Dame's. "Where's Raquel?" I asked.

"In the house somewhere. You know she doesn't like people," Raina said, causing us all to start laughing. It was true, Raquel was a harder nut to crack, but she was still good peoples.

"Where's Melo?" Romi asked.

"He's in Atlanta right now," I answered.

"Where's your other sister, the one who's home from college?" Damien asked.

"Oh, Risa's over there with Aunt Marlene and our cousin Leah," Raina explained, pointing her finger in their direction.

We all glanced over to where Raina was pointing, and there she was, the beauty from Club Nixx. She looked even more striking in the natural light of the day than she did that night at the club. And even that night she had been the sexiest woman I had ever laid my eyes on. She sat a few picnic tables away, appearing flawless in a cream-colored romper with her oiled legs crossed and gold sandals adorning her feet. She wore half of her hair in a high bun with the rest of it cascading down her back. Simple gold hoop earrings sparkled in her ears.

Shawty had no idea that she had my full attention as I watched her throw her head back in laughter, exposing all thirty-two of her perfect set of white teeth, pretty neck, and deep dimples. I couldn't take my eyes off her, and I guessed it didn't take Dre and Dame long to notice.

"Damn, nigga, there you go drooling again," Dame said, snickering.

I started laughing because that was exactly what he said to me the night I saw shawty at Club Nixx. I didn't know what it was about her that had me so mesmerized, but it was something that I just couldn't shake no matter how hard I tried.

"Let me go get her so I can introduce y'all," Romi said, getting up from Dre's lap.

Moments later, they were making their way to our table when, suddenly, her beautiful brown eyes locked with mine. It was as if she had also recognized me from the club the other night. Even as Romi introduced her to Damien and Dre, her eyes remained on me. Being the boss nigga I was, I wouldn't break eye contact with her, but I hadn't wanted to either. Then, with the sweetest voice I'd ever heard, she simply said, "Hi."

"And this is Micah," Romi introduced me. Risa smiled at me and tucked a little piece of wispy hair behind her right ear.

"Wait, do you two know each other?" Romi said, noticing the way she looked at me.

"Nah, he was just eye raping her at Club Nixx a few nights ago," Dre informed her with laughter. I quickly cut my eyes at him, letting him know that shit wasn't funny. He became quiet mid-laugh as expected, so I went back to focusing on Risa. I fell back that night at Club Nixx because of everything going on with the business, and also Keesha, but today I felt like I definitely needed to say something to shawty. It was more than obvious to everyone at the table that we had an undeniable connection, so I merely said, "Shawty, come sit next to me," then patted the seat beside me.

She let out a little laugh before submitting.

To get a better assessment, I looked over her body as she made her way around. She'd acquired feminine, toned legs and arms with soft, full breasts and hips. Her ass was plump and juicy, but not too much. She was slim thick, just how I preferred, and naturally curvy while remaining in shape. She was Melyssa Ford-ish. I didn't like the "fake ass and titties" look that was popular these days.

When she finally sat next to me, I noticed that the table had gotten completely silent. All eyes were on us. I let out a small laugh and shook my head, because these li'l niggas were nosy as fuck. I decided to stand and reach for her hand to grant our privacy. "Matter of fact, come take a walk with me, shawty," I told her.

I looked back and saw Raina low-key pouting because she wanted to be able to pry into our conversation. I winked and mouthed to her that we would be right back. As I led Risa to the front of the house, I placed my hand on the small of her back. Touching her gave me a sense of familiarity for some reason. It was like being with someone I had known all my life.

I took a seat on the hood of my Range and had her sit next to me. "Our paths cross once again, I see," I said. She smirked. "Why didn't you come talk to a nigga when I saw you at Club Nixx the other night?" I asked.

"Because I don't approach strangers. I don't talk to men I don't know." She shrugged.

Although I knew she was being serious, I chuckled at her comment. I was used to women throwing themselves at me, which meant I never had to spit game or even try to get pussy. However, I knew that with the right woman, the woman who was created just for me, I'd have to put in some effort.

"Why didn't you say anything to me?" she asked while looking down at her iPhone.

"Honestly, I wanted to, but I had a lot on my mind that night," I admitted.

"Well, I can definitely understand that, because I had a lot on my mind too. That's one of the reasons I let my girl convince me to go out," she said, still scrolling through her phone.

That shit was irritating the hell out of me because I wanted shawty's undivided attention. Being the aggressive nigga I was, I decided to grab her phone out of her hand and put it in the pocket of the fatigue cargo shorts I had on.

She instantly looked up at me with wide eyes. "Hey! What are you doing?"

"Shawty, if you talking to me, then I need your undivided attention. Anything different I take as a sign of disrespect. You feel me?" I explained, giving her a serious look.

She just sighed and folded her arms across her chest like a brat. A cute brat. I could sense she had a little attitude, but ultimately, I meant what I said.

"Now tell me, Ms. Lady, what's been so heavy on your mind that you had to get out to the club to relax?" I asked.

She let out a small, irritated laugh, which let me know she was still pissed that I took her phone. I didn't give a fuck, nor was I giving it back until our conversation was over. I wanted to know what she had going on in her life, and I wanted to get to know her better.

"I recently broke up with someone I had been dating since high school."

"How long were y'all together?" I quizzed.

"Four and a half years."

"Damn, four plus years? That's a long-ass time. Were you two engaged?"

"Ha! Absolutely not," she said, shaking her head vigorously.

"Why you say it like that? Most women don't invest that much time in a nigga if she knows she isn't going to be his wife in the end."

"That's true, but our relationship was over a long time ago. I just stayed because . . ." She hesitated, then softly said, "Because I had to."

Her head dropped, and since she no longer had her phone in her hand, she began playing with her fingernails. I could sense that whatever went on in her past relationship damaged her. I gently grabbed her chin and lifted it so that I could look into her pretty brown eyes. In them, I could sense a sadness that I felt the need to take away.

"Why did you have to?" I asked.

"I really don't want to get into all that right now. Tell me about yourself instead."

"I'll tell you all about me once I know why you felt like you needed to stay with a fuck nigga," I pressed.

She smiled and shook her head. Suddenly, her expression turned serious as she said, "Let's just say he wouldn't let go of me that easily."

Her beautiful smile had now faded, and she turned her face away from me. She looked back toward the house while flicking imaginary lint from her clothes.

It wasn't my first time dealing with a woman in an abusive situation. Plus I'd known plenty of niggas growing up who thought it was okay to hit a woman. So looking at her, I immediately knew that the nigga she'd been dealing with had been putting his hands on her. I instantly grew heated at the thought of someone hurting her, because she was the most beautiful woman I had ever seen. She had the most tender spirit about her.

Not knowing exactly what to say, I grabbed her chin again and forced her to look at me before I placed a gentle peck on her lips, then another to her forehead. To my surprise, she closed her eyes and accepted my displays of affection for her. It was crazy, because I had only known shawty for all of thirty-five minutes, but already she had me prepared to body a nigga over her. I didn't believe in that "love at first sight" bullshit, but if I did, shawty right here would have been it for me.

Glancing down at my G-Shock, I realized that I had stayed longer than I had anticipated. I reached into my pocket and grabbed her phone. After storing my number in her contact list, I handed it back.

"Call me if you need me. Day or night, no matter the time," I said while gently smoothing back the fine curls that were blowing in her face.

"Thanks, Micah."

"I gotta get outta here, but I'll be back in a few days. Can I take you out?" I asked.

"I think that may be possible, but I'll need to check my schedule first and get back to you," she quipped with a smirk.

"Yeah, a'ight! Check yo' schedule and let me know. You got my number, so I'll be waiting for a text or a call from you," I said, giving her a wink.

I pulled her in for a tight hug, then kissed her cheek before walking her to the backyard. After saying my goodbyes, I grabbed my plate that Raina made for me, and I headed back to Atlanta. The entire ride there, Risa stayed on my mind.

Later that night, I walked into Club Nixx and headed upstairs to the VIP lounge where I'd told Zo to meet me. I hadn't seen this li'l nigga in about five years, so I wasn't sure what he looked like now. I figured he was the same light-skinned, rat-face nigga, just with longer dreads. Shaking my head, I laughed to myself thinking about how Timo and I used to beat him up when we were younger. It was crazy, because as tight as we were, I kept my little brothers far away from Zo.

As I made my way up, I could feel there were eyes on me, mostly females, but I wasn't there to party. I'd only gone out looking like a boss because I had an image to uphold, but as soon as I discussed a few things with Zo, I would be leaving. I sported black Tom Ford jeans, a red Tom Ford button-up, with black and red Jays on my feet. In addition, the finest diamonds gleamed in my ears and on my wrist.

After taking my seat, I looked over at the cocktail waitress, Mimi, whom I had already smashed a few times since being back in Atlanta. "Shawty, you already know what I want to drink," I told her.

"Yes, one Coke and Hennessy coming up," she said.

That was one of the things I liked about Mimi. She always stayed professional on the job and never got caught up in her feelings, even if she'd peeped me with another woman. I couldn't help but look Mimi over as she stood next to me. Her thick body oozing from the tight red dress she was wearing exposed at least ten inches of her full thighs. She had the body of a stripper, and I couldn't take my eyes off her.

As I waited for Zo, I got up from my seat and leaned over the rail to take in the crowd below. The smoke-filled club was packed to capacity. Women were twerking and grinding their asses on niggas from wall to wall to the sounds of "Both" by Gucci Mane. I kept looking at the club entrance, but there were still no signs of Zo.

Mimi approached and set my drink down on the table in front of me before walking away with a hard switch of her hips. After fifteen additional minutes of waiting, and several unanswered calls and texts to Zo, I tossed my drink down my throat and got up to leave.

As I began to make my way downstairs, I could see Mimi behind the bar staring at me. I hadn't fucked with her in over a month, and she was probably looking for some dick. My mind was set on having Risa, but I couldn't control how Mimi had me bricked up just from looking at her. She possessed long, bone-straight bundles that flowed down her back. She harbored big brown eyes and big, full, juicy lips that I wanted nothing more than for her to wrap around my dick.

Making my way over to her through the crowd, I saw a few ladies staring and calling out to me. "Hey, Mr. Borrego," I heard along with, "Damn, that nigga fine."

"What's up, shawty? What's good with you?" I asked Mimi.

"Nothing much, just wanting to see you again," she flirted.

"Oh, you want to see daddy again?" I asked, licking my lower lip seductively.

She nodded bashfully because she knew that when I called myself daddy, I was referring to my dick. I pulled her closer to me, placing my hands on her fat ass, and whispered in her ear, "I'm heading out, but if you want to see me off, I won't mind."

She smiled and walked behind me as I headed out of the club toward my car.

Behind black illegally tinted windows, she quickly began unbuckling my jeans. Her mouth watered greedily from anticipation. Closing my eyes, I allowed my head to fall back onto the leather headrest at the feel of her moist lips sucking my dick. With my hand on her head, I guided her up and down as she continued to slurp.

"Fuuuck!" I groaned.

Gripping me tighter in her hand, she sucked on the tip like it was a lollipop. She began gagging on my dick, only to come back up and tease the tip again. She rotated that motion repeatedly, each time getting sloppier. Her mouth skills had me going crazy inside. Not being able to take any more, I gripped her head tight and released down her throat. After she wiped the corners of her mouth, I dismissed her from my car and was on my way.

After making my way home and taking a much-needed shower, I lay in my bed, naked and deep in thought. I had a lot on my mind, and

I was thinking of how I could hold Timo down
and not fuck up what Pops and I were building.
As I cut the television on to ESPN, I heard a text
message chime through my phone. I looked to
see that it was an unfamiliar number and a text
that read, Now you have my number too.

I smiled because I instantly knew that it was
Risa. I also knew that if she was texting me
already, she must have been feeling me as much
as I was feeling her. After saving her number in
my contacts, I replied.

Me: Yes, I do, beautiful. Have you given any
thought to where you want our first date to be?

Wife: No. You're the man. I want you to take
the lead.

Me: I most certainly am the man, so that I will
do.

Wife: Ha-ha! Well, have a good night.

Me: You too. I'll hit you tomorrow, beautiful.

Wife: K.

That's right, I was already claiming shawty as
my wife. I knew that it wouldn't be long before
she'd be mine. I just had to figure out how I was
going to deal with Keesha's crazy ass.

After Keesha's persistence and me missing
Zaria like crazy, I went ahead and made moves
to get them here. I signed a one-year lease for a
nice two-bedroom apartment close to my place

and paid the rent up for a year. Keesha was
prepared for them to be here by next weekend.
I only prayed she would fall back so we could
successfully parent Zaria. I wished she would
allow me to move forward with my life, which
would hopefully be a life with Risa.

Chapter 14

Risa

After my welcome home party, Micah and I immediately took to one another. We were calling and texting each other several times throughout the day. Although texting was convenient, I preferred to talk to him on the phone because he had a deep, raspy baritone that I found very sexy. Throughout the course of the week, Micah and I made plans to go out the following Friday, which had me super excited. I was anxious to see his handsome face again.

I could admit that I felt a little guilty for moving on so quickly after what happened to Zo, but as soon as those thoughts would enter my mind, I would remind myself of everything I had been through with him. For some reason, I kept looking for the cops to turn up at my door or give me a call, but so far there was nothing, and I was perfectly content with that.

I was on my summer break, so when he told me that he wanted to spend the whole day with me starting with breakfast, I didn't protest. He instructed me to dress down and wear sneakers because we were going to be active. I was a little disappointed because I really liked to dress up, but I was looking forward to spending time with him nonetheless. Zo never took me anywhere, so I had a bunch of nice clothes with the tags still on them. When Micah told me to bring a change of clothes for that evening, I instantly got excited knowing exactly which dress I was going to wear.

To begin our day, I decided on a pink, blue, and black workout outfit from Fabletics, which I paired with black-on-black Nike Air Max and no-show socks. I wore my hair in a high ponytail with small one-karat diamond studs in my ears and no makeup, just gloss. My skin was flawless, and I didn't need to wear makeup. These dimples, long lashes, and dark brown eyes were all I needed. As I finished packing my bag, I got a text from Micah.

Micah: Be there in five min.

Me: Okay.

It was 8:15 when I made it downstairs and saw Mama in the kitchen making breakfast for everyone. She was standing at the stove when I approached and gave her a tight embrace from behind, startling her. When she discovered it was me, she allowed me to continue hugging her as I rested my head on her back. Without saying anything to me, she tightened her grip around my hand that rested on her stomach. It was as though she could sense my need for love and affection. After a few moments, she turned to face me and saw that I had a duffle bag over my shoulder.

"Where are you headed off to this early in the morning, ladybug? The gym?"

"Micah is taking me on a date, and I don't know where. He just said it was going to be active and to dress down, but I think we may be getting dinner later because he said to also bring a change of clothes," I explained.

Me and Mama were cool. I could talk to her openly about love and relationships, even sex. I just couldn't bear to tell her about Zo though. When she asked me why we broke up, I just told her that we were in different places in our lives. I completely left out the part of him beating my ass over the years, and how I'd found him lying on the floor dead.

After kissing my mother on the cheek, I heard the doorbell ring. On my way to open the door, I gave myself a once-over in the mirror that hung in our foyer, and I smiled at my reflection.

When I went to open the door, a cheesy smile was plastered on my face as I stared at Micah's fine chocolate ass standing before me. He had on some army fatigue cargo shorts, a black V-neck tee, black-on-black Jordans, and an all-black fitted cap. Like me, he also had diamond studs in each ear, but while mine were only a karat, his were more like five karats.

When he stepped in the house, he immediately pulled me in for a tight hug. Being in his strong arms felt like I had known him all my life. What surprised me even more was when, without hesitation, he went in for a kiss. Even more surprising, I reciprocated like he was my man, and like my mama wasn't in the next room. It wasn't a deep, passionate kiss or anything, but he definitely slipped me a little tongue.

I looked over to find my mother had come into the room and was smiling at me. "Hey, Ma, you remember Micah?"

"Of course," she said, approaching us to pull him in for a hug. "Where are you taking her today?" she asked.

"Ma'am, it's a surprise, but if you give me your cell number, I'll text you all the information," he said. That made my mother smile as she called out her cell phone number to him.

"Should I even ask what time you'll be back?" she wondered.

I looked at Micah for him to respond, but he merely let out a small chuckle and scratched his head before saying, "Probably not, ma'am."

I looked at him with wide eyes before covering my face in embarrassment, because he had basically just told my mother that I was staying out all night with him. I mean, yes, I was 21 years old and would be 22 in three more months, but I still didn't feel that damn grown.

To my surprise, my mother replied, "Well, hey, there's nothing wrong with that. Take care of my baby, that's all I ask."

"I wouldn't have it any other way," he said while stroking my ponytail.

After saying our goodbyes, he took my bag from me and carried it to the car. Before I got in, he scanned my body slowly with his dark, alluring eyes. "I can already see you gon' have a nigga fighting out here today."

"What do you mean?" I wondered.

"You and them tight-ass workout pants, shawty, is what I mean. I ain't gon' lie though, you sexy as fuck right now, so it's all good," he said, shaking his head.

"Thank you," was all I could manage as I felt myself blushing.

After opening the door to his Range Rover for me and making sure I was buckled in, he got in the car, and we headed to IHOP for breakfast. For the duration of breakfast, we talked about his daughter and how she was moving to Atlanta in a couple of days with her mom to be closer to him. I thought it was sweet how he talked about her. I could tell that she was his world, which only made me like him more.

He spoke about wanting to open a dinner lounge in Atlanta that would have live music. I thought his idea was dope, and I loved seeing the excitement in his eyes when he talked about it. He was ambitious, which was a perfect match for me. It led me into explaining the degree I was pursuing and the career I ultimately hoped to have.

Talking to him was easy. It felt more like catching up with an old friend rather than a first date. Surprisingly he didn't ask me about Zo, and I was grateful, because being with him had me wanting to focus on my future and forget about my past.

After breakfast was over, we got in the car and drove for about an hour before I finally asked Micah where we were going.

"I wanted it to be a surprise, but I do need to know if you are afraid of heights."

"Yes, I am," I lied. A surprised expression spread across his face, which made me laugh. "I'm kidding, Micah. I'm not afraid of heights. Now where are we going?"

"Oh, you think that shit was funny?" He circled his finger inside my ear, which irritated me.

After swatting his hand away, I quipped, "Your face was priceless though. So I guess we are doing something that involves us being high up. Let me guess: we're going rock climbing."

"Wrong!" he shouted cockily.

"Are we going on a plane ride, maybe?"

"Wrong again!" he stated with a smirk.

"Um, what about—"

"Shawty, just let a nigga surprise you. Please!" He shook his head.

I rolled my eyes and gave in. "Fine," I pouted.

He didn't know now, but he'd soon find out that I hated surprises. After another thirty minutes in the car, we pulled up to Historic Banning Mills. I immediately knew that we were there to go zip-lining, something that I had been wanting to do for years.

"What the fuck you cheesing for?" Micah asked, referring to the huge grin on my face.

"We're going zip-lining?" I asked excitedly as if the mystery were officially solved.

"Is that what you want to do?" he asked.

"Hell yeah!" I exclaimed with excitement.

"A'ight, then leggo," he said, putting his finger in my dimple.

After getting out the car, he grabbed me by the waist to pull me into him to kiss my forehead. The touch of his lips against my skin felt amazing. We continued to walk hand in hand as if we had been in a relationship for years.

I was so nervous for the first line that I was holding my breath the entire time the instructor explained what we needed to do. Micah must have sensed my apprehension, so he approached me from behind and began giving me a little shoulder massage before kissing my temple. He was very affectionate, something I wasn't used to from being with Zo, at least not in the past three years. Micah handled me with care, and I loved that he wouldn't allow too much time to pass before the next time he touched me. It was like there was a silent alarm on me that would go off, signaling him that I needed to feel his warmth again. I silently wondered how long that would last, or if Micah would change the way he was with me.

My thoughts were interrupted when it was my turn to go. I looked back at Micah with worried eyes, and he just shook his head and laughed. "You'll be all right. You want me to go first?"

I shook my head and preceded to step up on the platform for our guide to hook the line to me. After I heard, "One, two, three, go," I felt a slight push. I held my legs up high as instructed, and let the wind take me across the line that was 115 feet up in the air. I squeezed my eyes tight and let the cool breeze whisk across my face. Slowly, I opened one eye at a time to look down in awe of the beautiful tree lines below me. For the first time in a long time, I felt free, so much so that tears began rolling down my face. I felt like this moment was a confirmation from God that I would no longer have to endure the pain of my past, and that I was truly being set free.

When I finally reached the platform on the other side, my tears were streaming uncontrollably, but I didn't even care who saw them. After the line was unhooked from me, I went over to a small grassy area where no one was, and I kneeled down to pray. I couldn't let another moment pass before giving thanks to the Man Upstairs. He had brought me out of one of the darkest places in my life and led me straight to Micah, a man who made me feel safe and cared for. And for that, He deserved my honor and praise.

Kneeling on the ground with my eyes closed shut, I suddenly felt someone touch my shoulder. I looked back. It was Micah, reaching for my hand to help me up. I instantly hugged him and buried my face into his muscular chest, allowing him to hold me. He never asked if I was okay or if I was scared from zip-lining. Instead, he tightened his embrace, almost as if he knew what was going through my mind.

After a full day of zip-lining and eating lunch on site, we headed back to the car. "Where are we going now?" I asked.

"I got us a room in Buckhead," he said.

"A hotel room?" I asked with a concerned tone.

"I'm not going to try anything, shawty. We just need to shower and rest up before dinner, that's all."

"One bed or two?" I asked with a smirk.

"I reserved a suite, so there is one bedroom with a king-size bed and a living room with a pullout sofa."

"Wow, you went all out. You definitely took the lead when you planned all of this."

"I have no problem leading when the woman doesn't mind following," he stated with his deep, raspy baritone before grabbing my hand to kiss it.

When we finally made our way back to Buckhead around 3:30, we pulled right into the

Ritz-Carlton. I was pleasantly surprised at how much thought and detail he put into our first date. After we checked in and headed up to the presidential suite, I took in the beautiful city view from the floor-to-ceiling windows that bordered the living room area.

"Wow, this is beautiful, Micah," I said in awe, my nose pressed against the window.

"Yeah, I think it will really be nice when we come back up here tonight and the whole city is lit up," he responded.

I nodded to agree before walking around to admire the rest of the suite. In the kitchen, there were chocolate-covered strawberries and champagne. I quietly giggled to myself because he thought he was getting some tonight. I glanced over my shoulder to see the muscles in his back exposed through his T-shirt as he remained standing in front of the window, taking in the view. *Damn, he's sexy.*

"Our dinner reservations are for eight o'clock, so I figured we could shower now and maybe take a little nap if you're tired," he said.

"Sure, you wanna hop in first?"

"Nah, ladies first."

After I got out of the shower, I wrapped the towel around me before heading into the bedroom. When I opened the bathroom door, he was standing beside the bed naked as the day

he was born and staring directly into my eyes
with a sly grin on his face.

"Oh, my gosh!" I screamed, covering my eyes
like a child.

I had covered my eyes, but not before I took in
his perfect dark chocolate pecks and sculptured
abs that led down to a perfectly shaped V. *Lawd,
have mercy!*

"My bad, shawty," was all he said, straight-
faced, without a laugh or smile.

Afterward, he took his sweet time to wrap the
towel around his waist as he looked me directly
in the eyes. He was definitely playing games,
and I could tell that he wanted me to see that
anaconda between his legs. Zo was the only man
I'd ever been with sexually, and although he
had worked with a good eight inches, he was no
match for what I had just seen.

Still covering my eyes, yet peeking through
the crevices between my fingers, I asked, "Are
you covered up yet?"

"Yeah, you can look now," he responded.

Wedging past me to make his way into the
bathroom, he ever so lightly grazed my breasts.
The smallest touch of his body connecting with
mine instantly made my clit pulse, matching
the thump of my fast-beating heart. I let out a
deep exhale before crossing my legs and tightly

pressing them together, trying to dissipate my yearning.

Moments later, I was dressed in an oversized white T-shirt with powder blue cotton panties. I was tightly tucked underneath the thick white down comforter that lay on the bed. My hair was out, and again I had no makeup on, just some Carmex on my lips. I heard the bathroom door open, and standing there in only black Versace boxer briefs with the rest of his beautiful body exposed, he looked at me and chuckled.

"So, I guess I got the pullout, huh?"

I smiled and hesitated before responding. With an innocent shrug, I said, "We're only napping, right?"

Without responding, he came over and pulled back the covers and quickly got in the bed with me. My thumping clit had now progressed into a powerful pounding between my thighs. He instantly reached for my face and began planting soft kisses all over it before passionately kissing my lips. Although my mind was telling me that we were moving way too fast, my body submitted to his touch. I got wetter by the second as his big, masculine hands rubbed up and down my hips and thighs. Suddenly, embarrassed that I let out a couple of unfamiliar moans, I immediately pulled away. I was no match for him, because he brought my body right back close to his and continued kissing me. Our tongues aggressively intertwined as his fingers raked through my hair. We moaned and panted together in unison until he pulled his lips away and groaned, "Damn!" as he shook his head.

I giggled. After one of the most intense make-out sessions I'd ever experienced, we could only lay there with our bodies entangled like two perfectly fitted puzzle pieces drifting off to sleep.

It was right at 6:30 when I heard the alarm on Micah's cell phone go off. I quickly shot up and reached over him to grab his phone off the nightstand.

"Here, turn this is off," I groggily said while shaking him to hand him his cell phone.

While I went into the adjoining bathroom to wash my face and brush my teeth before getting dressed, Micah went into the half bath. I wore a cream-colored Michael Kors cold-shoulder dress that fit my body like a glove, paired with pewter-colored heels and jewelry to match. And since I felt like dressing up a bit more than usual, I even wore a little BB cream on my face, pink cheek highlighter, pink MAC gloss, and black mascara to complete my look. My long hair hung down my back and was brushed to its perfect natural sheen.

When I came out of the bedroom and stepped into the living room area, I found him sitting on the sofa, talking on his cell phone while smoking a blunt. He immediately jumped up, scanning my body from head to toe with a sexy smirk on his face.

"Keesh, I'm gonna have to call you later," he said into the phone before ending his call.

"You like?" I asked, spinning around for him to get a better assessment.

"You look sexy as fuck, shawty," he complimented me while eyeing my body lustfully.

I blushed and scanned his body, confirming that I could certainly return the compliment. He had on an all-black Armani suit that had to have been tailored the way it fit his body to perfection. Those signature diamonds beamed in each ear and on his wrist, while he wore black Louboutins on his feet. The deep, thick black waves of his hair were brushed to precision.

When we made it to the extravagant restaurant, the hostess asked for our reservation name.

"It's under Mr. and Mrs. Borrego," Micah said before grabbing my hand and bringing it up to his mouth to kiss it.

He was over the top with his romantic gestures, but I wasn't complaining because I loved all of the attention he was giving me. In fact, it was something I could get used to.

Later that night, as we lay together in bed, Micah had the eleven o'clock news on. I was tucked in tight, resting my head on his chest, close to letting sleep overcome me when I heard, "This morning, police found twenty-one-year-old Zo'mire Johnson shot and killed, alone in his Twin Oaks apartment. Forensics say that his body had been there for at least five days. No suspects have been named at this time."

Both Micah and I sat up in the bed immediately.

He sighed. "Damn," he mumbled in disbelief.

I didn't know what expression my face was wearing, but it must have been one of guilt, fear, or nervousness, because Micah looked over at me and asked, "Did you know him or something?"

"No," I lied quickly. "Did you?"

"Yeah, that's my man's little brother. Fuck! I gotta get in touch with Timo ASAP. I already know this nigga gon' spaz the fuck out."

I lay back in the bed with my thoughts racing a mile a minute. *How did Micah know Timo and Zo? And what in the world have I gotten myself into?*

Chapter 15

Raina

Six Weeks Later

It was graduation day for both Raquel and Damien. Waking up with Damien on my mind, I rolled over in my bed and grabbed my cell before deciding to send him a text.

Me: Congrats on your big day, Dame. I'm so proud of you. U got a B in Ms. Waters's class! Can't wait 2CU in your cap and gown.

Dame: Thanks, beautiful! I can't wait to see you too. Moms and Pops are doing something at the house afterward. I want you to cum.

Me: U so nasty! I will see what Mama and Daddy have planned for Raquel and let you know.

Dame: Nah, I don't need you to try to see. I want you with me. Invite the whole fam. Me and Raquel can celebrate together.

Me: You sure you ready for your parents to meet mine?

Dame: Fo' sho.

Me: What are we?

Dame: We'll talk later, beautiful. Gotta finish getting ready.

I hated when he did that. Anytime I asked him what the status of our relationship was, he would change subjects or avoid it altogether. I didn't know what being in love felt like to compare it to anything I'd experienced, but I swore I had all the symptoms. I never wanted to imagine a time when Damien was not in my life.

Pushing all those feelings aside, I focused on getting dressed. I put on a peach form-fitting BeBe dress and nude Louboutins. After lightly oiling my legs and looking myself over in the mirror, I chose to put my hair up in a high, messy bun. I'd kept my makeup light with a hint of highlighter on my cheeks, black mascara, and to finish, a simple coat of pink MAC lip gloss.

I smoothed my dress down and walked across the hall to Raquel's room. I could hear her singing one of Mama's favorite songs by Tamia called "Stranger in My House." I had to give it to my sister, her voice was beautiful.

"Hey, Raquel. You ready for your big day?" I interrupted.

Raquel looked beautiful. She had her hair bone straight with a part down the middle. She wore a white off-the-shoulder bodycon dress with nude red bottoms. Simple gold stud earrings and gold bangles on her wrist complemented her flawless makeup. Today was truly her day.

"Ready to get it over with," she said, lightly spraying on her perfume.

I swore Raquel could be such a downer sometimes. She hardly ever got excited about anything unless it was music. Maybe Damien was right when he said she probably just needed some dick. I laughed aloud a little as I remembered his comment.

"What's so funny?" Raquel asked, rolling her hazel eyes.

"Ah, nothing. Damien wants everyone to celebrate you all's graduation together. He said his parents were doing something afterward at their house and invited the whole family."

"Melo's annoying ass isn't going to be there, is he?"

"I'm sure he is, Raquel, he's family. Just don't talk to him."

"Uhh! Fine, it's whatever. Let's just get this day over with," she huffed.

"Let me go check with Mama and Daddy first," I said excitedly before running out of the room.

As I was walking down the hall toward the steps to do go downstairs, I heard Romi in the hall bathroom, and it sounded like she was throwing up. I knocked on the door and asked if she was okay.

"Yeah," she managed to reply.

"You sure? Are you throwing up?"

"Yeah, something I ate probably," she explained weakly.

I continued downstairs to the kitchen where I saw Mama next to the refrigerator, drinking a glass of ice water. She was already dressed for the graduation in a fancy tan pantsuit from Loft with nude Michael Kors sandals. She had her silky hair down, which fell to the top of her butt. We all had long hair, but hers was the longest.

"You look nice, Mama," I complimented her.

"Thanks, baby, you do too." As she smiled, she gave me a once-over and nodded.

"Um, Damien asked if we could all celebrate together today after the graduation. He said that his parents were having a little something and invited us. Raquel wants to go, too," I lied.

"I think we were just going out to eat at Ruth's Chris, but we can cancel our reservations. Shouldn't be a problem. We just gotta let your father know," she said, giving me a funny look. I knew getting Daddy to go over there wasn't going to be as easy, but I'd let Mama handle him.

Suddenly, Risa entered the kitchen behind me. "It feels so good to be home, Mama. You have no idea," she said, closing her eyes and inhaling to take a deep breath.

"And it's good to have you home, ladybug," my mother replied.

Risa had been home from Spelman for several weeks now, but she kept saying how grateful she was to back home with family. She was beautiful, just like the rest of my sisters, and I admired her as she stood there in a fitted green cold-shoulder dress with nude Louboutins. Although she probably wouldn't have been considered dark skinned, she had the darkest complexion of all of us sisters. Her deep complexion was flawless, and her hair was long, black, and silky, which she modestly wore parted down the middle. With long, curly eyelashes that sat over her dark eyes, and deep dimples displayed on her face just like Mama, she beamed.

"Oh, we're going to Damien's house after the graduation to celebrate. His family invited us," I said.

"I know. Micah told me last night," she sang with a smile.

She had only been home for a little over a month, yet I could already tell she was madly in love with Micah. Not once when she was with Zo had I seen her that happy.

"Oh, this was a whole setup I see," I mentioned with laughter.

"You know those boys want to be around us every chance they get."

I shook my head and laughed, knowing she was right. "Have you heard from Zo's family since you've been home? That's so awful what happened to him," I quizzed.

My sister had simply told us that she and Zo broke up before he got shot and killed. However, when she said it, it was like she was unbothered by their breakup, and she didn't provide any additional details. We had all known Zo for a long time, and he was crazy about my sister, so I found it hard to believe that he would have let her go without a fight. There had to be more to the story at least.

"I talked to Timo briefly, but they're all holding up," she replied nonchalantly, shrugging her shoulders. I raised my eyebrows, confused as to how to respond to her.

A few moments later, Romi made her way into the kitchen. She was wearing a simple navy blue romper pantsuit with lace sleeves and the back out, with gold accessories. She had her hair curled and pinned to one side so that it could cascade down one shoulder. She looked gorgeous as always.

"You have a glow about you today. Gorgeous!" Risa said, complimenting Romi.

"Thanks, sis," Romi responded weakly as she took a seat.

"We're hanging out with the guys after the graduation. Did Raquel tell you?" I asked.

"Yeah, she told me," Romi responded with her head down on the kitchen table. I could tell she didn't feel well.

Thirty minutes later, we packed in the cars to head to graduation. Mama and Daddy rode together in Daddy's Yukon while the four of us all piled in Risa's Audi. When we got out of the car, Raquel immediately ran inside the Coliseum to meet up with her classmates because she was a couple minutes late for lineup. We spotted Damien's brothers and parents outside, preparing to head in from the parking lot. Romi, Risa, and I immediately ran over to speak to them.

"Hey, Mr. and Mrs. Borrego," I said, giving Damien's mom a hug.

She hugged the three of us right before Romi found her way into Dre's arms. "Are you guys coming over after graduation?" Mrs. Borrego asked me. Her neat shoulder-length dreads hung down, framing her dark chocolate-colored face. She was extremely beautiful and had a beauty mark under one of her eyes, just like Micah.

"Yes, ma'am. You said my parents could come also, right?" I double-checked.

"Of course. This is a celebration for both Damien and Raquel. We even got her name added to the cake."

"Aw, thank you," I said, just as my parents were walking up behind me.

"Hi, I am Damien's mother, Calisa, and this is his father, Anton," she said, extending her hand to my mother. Instead, my mother pulled her in for a hug. I guessed with Damien being at the house all the time, and sometimes Dre and Micah too, she felt like they were family.

"I am Ernestine, but everyone calls me Ernie, and this is my husband, Brad," she said as Daddy reached his hand out to shake Mrs. and Mr. Borrego's hands.

I was so happy with everyone meeting that I decided to send Damien a quick text.

Me: Our parents have officially met. Went perfectly.

Dame: I knew it would. Your fam is cool just like mine, beautiful.

Me: I'm gonna be screaming 4U.

Dame: I already know.

Me: CU afterward.

Dame: Okay, beautiful.

***

The graduation went great, and my throat was so sore from cheering for them. Both Raquel and Damien graduated with highest honors, Damien with a 3.8 GPA and Raquel with a 4.0. Unfortunately, Raquel got beat out for valedictorian and salutatorian by the twins, Chip and Chris Robinson. I didn't think she cared though, because she wasn't really into giving speeches or the attention that it would attract.

After the graduation was over, we scooted through the crowd to make our way down to meet up with Damien and Raquel outside. I couldn't wait to hug and kiss them. I was so excited that I led the pack to where they told us to meet them. Most of the graduates were already outside taking pictures with each other and family members. While the girls wore all white, the boys wore red caps and gowns, which was Damien's favorite color.

As we waited outside, I looked up to finally see Damien walking out the door. A smile quickly spread across my face as I took off running toward him. Suddenly, I was stopped in my tracks. Tina was coming out of the door behind him, and I noticed they were holding hands. My smile instantly faded, and I looked back toward Mama and Daddy and the rest of our family to see if they'd witnessed what I had. The looks on their faces told me everything, and embarrassment quickly flooded my spirit.

Here I was, thinking that he was my boyfriend and I'd even gotten our families together, yet he was playing me the whole time. Tears were beginning to form, but I refused to let them fall because I knew that he'd never made us official. I would be the same as every other girl he'd complained about. So I turned around and went back to stand beside Romi, who instantly put her arm around me, allowing me to lay my head on her shoulder. Everyone could see the sadness in my eyes, which was really hard for me to disguise though I tried my best to. I hated that Daddy had to see me that way, because although I was mad at Damien, I didn't want Daddy to dislike him.

Once Damien saw all of us standing there, he quickly dropped Tina's hand, and I could read his lips telling her that he'd check her out later. First, he walked up to his mother to give her a hug, then embraced his father. His brothers went up to hug and congratulate him next while I stood back. He looked over to me as I stood there with my parents, Romi, and Risa.

"Congratulations, Damien," my mother chimed, giving him a hug and trying to break the ice.

"Thanks, Mrs. B," he said.

My father also shook his hand and congratu-
lated him, but Romi and Risa weren't budging.
The three of us only stood there together because
with us it was all for one and one for all. Damien
walked toward us, staring at me before he spoke.
"Hey, beautiful."

"Congratulations, Damien," I said subtly.

He already knew he'd fucked up, but I wasn't
going to get into all that with him being that my
parents and his were standing there.

Moments later, Raquel walked out of the
building. Romi, Risa, and I all ran to her and
gave her a big group hug. "Congratulations!"
we all sang in unison. Once we were together,
both Damien's family and mine began taking
pictures with the two graduates. I tried to just
push Damien and Tina to the back of my mind
because it was their day and I didn't want to be
the Debbie Downer of the group.

As we were all getting ready to leave, Damien
said, "Shawty, ride with me."

I looked back at my sisters and my parents for
their consent, then nodded because, again, I did
not want to cause a scene. Once we got into his
Charger and began heading to his house, he tried
to make small talk with me, but I wasn't having
it. I simply hit him with one-word answers or
ignored the shit out of him altogether.

"Look, before we get back to my house, is there something you need to get the fuck off yo' chest?" he snapped.

My eyes grew wide as I turned to look at him. I couldn't believe he was coming at me like that when he was the one in the wrong.

"What were you doing with Tina? And why were you holding her hand?" I asked, already near tears.

"Shit, we just graduated together, and I grabbed her hand so we could fight the crowd together to get out of the building."

"Well, it looked like more than that to me," I snapped.

"Look, shawty, you need to calm the fuck down. I ain't never said yo' young ass was my girl. I ain't made no commitments to nobody, so don't be questioning me about shit," he spat.

When he said that, it felt like someone had just punched me in the gut. Here I was thinking we were building something, thinking our families were becoming one. His words were like a slap in the face. Again, I held back the tears that were forming and managed to let out a low, "Okay," through the tightness building in my throat.

Chapter 16

Damien

I knew as soon as I walked out the door holding Tina's hand and saw Raina's face that I had fucked up. Everything I said about grabbing her hand to fight the crowd was true, but what I didn't say was that Tina and I never really stopped fucking around. After the night of the house party, I told Tina that I wanted to start rocking with Raina and that she needed to fall back, but even with that being said, I would still see her for extracurricular activities. I mean, Raina wasn't fucking, and although I respected that, a nigga still had needs. Point blank, period. Because I was still fucking with Tina, she and I still had a connection, and I knew that was the shit Raina saw between us.

I hated that I had her over here sad and shit on what was supposed to be one of the best nights of my life, hell, of our lives, because I knew in my gut I would end up settling with Raina one day. Our families coming together was only the beginning, but I managed to fuck that shit up. The look on her daddy's face was crazy. I knew that nigga was ready to try to lay hands on me, but Mrs. Ernie had that nigga in check and on his best behavior. I was appreciative of that, because I would've hated to have to fuck that old nigga up, especially with him being my future father-in-law and all.

After pulling up in my driveway, I put the car in park and reached over to grab Raina's hand. She tried snatching it away, but I held on to it tight enough that she couldn't.

"Look, before we go in here, are we good? I don't want you mad at me, beautiful," I said.

"We're not together, so I don't have a reason to be mad at you," she replied dryly while looking away from me out the window.

I just shook my head because I knew it wasn't going to be easy to get back in her good graces. With most girls, I could just give them the dick or some nice gifts to make them calm down, but Raina was different.

As we got out of the car and headed to the house, I saw Micah and Risa waiting there for us. He instantly walked over to Raina and gave her a hug. He didn't give a shit that I was his blood or that today was my graduation, all he wanted was his little sister to be okay.

"Are you two lovebirds back on track now?" he asked, looking at Raina then back at me.

"No lovebirds here, only friends. But yeah, we're cool," she answered with a shrug.

I knew she was still pissed, but I'd make it up to her in time. "We straight, nigga. Now stop instigating shit," I snapped.

He mushed me in the back of my head, making me trip forward. "Fix it, bruh!" he scolded me. I sighed as I shook my head.

When we all got in the house, we learned that my mom had outdone herself. She had a chef come and prepare grilled filet mignon topped with crabmeat, grilled asparagus, and garlic red potatoes. We also had shrimp cocktail and bacon-wrapped scallops as appetizers. Moms was crazy about some seafood, and luckily, Raina's family was too. She had ordered several dozens of tulips with red and white balloons to decorate the house, and I even saw a red and white three-tiered cake with both my name and Raquel's on it. Everyone was impressed.

"Wow, you have such a beautiful home, Calisa. You have truly outdone yourself. And thank you so much for putting Raquel's name on the cake," Mrs. Ernie said.

"It was my pleasure. I have grown very fond of your girls these past few weeks. They are like the daughters I never had."

"Well, I feel the same about your boys. Can I help you with anything?"

"No, but do you drink wine?"

"Of course I do." Mrs. Ernie smiled.

"Then let's go down to the cellar and pick us out something nice."

I went into the kitchen to steal some food before dinner was served while Raina sat with everyone in the game room. Pops and Mr. B were outside on the back patio, talking and smoking Cuban cigars, while Raquel, of course, was at the piano by herself. I looked at Melo and noticed him staring at her. I shook my head because that nigga was wide open and shawty wasn't even given his ass no play.

"How long you gon' make a nigga wait?" Micah said to Risa, rubbing his hand down his beard.

Everybody fell out laughing because we all assumed he was talking about sex. She could only cover her face and shake her head in embarrassment as he tried to peel her hands back.

"That's not what I was asking her. Y'all some nasty li'l niggas. And you?" he said, pointing at Raina, who was laughing. "I thought you were better than that, Baby Girl."

She held her hands up to surrender.

"So you done already hit? What she making you wait for?" I asked.

"Nah, I ain't hit yet," he replied with a sly grin while looking over at her. Her hands were still covering her face. "She won't be my wife until she graduates from school."

"Wife!" everyone shouted.

"Look, you are moving way too fast for me, Micah," Mrs. Ernie yelled unexpectedly.

We all fell over laughing because even though she was joking, she was still dead-ass serious. You could tell Mrs. Ernie didn't play any games when it came to the girls.

"Mrs. Ernie, no disrespect, but some things you just know. This is my wife right here," he simply stated, looking over at Risa while stroking her long hair. No laugh or hint of a smile was on his face.

"Uh, hmm. Well, she's right. At least let her graduate from school, and then we'll talk," she spoke candidly. My mother laughed at their exchange.

"Well, Risa, when the time comes, I myself would be happy to have you as my daughter-in-law," my mother said.

Risa smiled and silently mouthed, "Thank you," to my mother before Micah kissed her on the lips. It was crazy how Micah had just met shawty a little over a month ago, and he was already talking about getting married. I ain't never seen him this way over any female, and he'd been with quite a few bad ones. Shit was crazy. Plus I knew that he was still fucking around with other bitches, but I figured she might've just been on that same bullshit as her sisters—celibacy.

Out of nowhere, Raquel stood from the piano bench with her hands on her hips and said, "Well, today is all about celebrating me and Damien. We have a whole year and some change to plan this damn wedding."

Everybody burst out into laughter. It was shocking to actually see Raquel lightening the mood in the room, because she was one of the grumpiest chicks I had ever met.

Dinner was fairly quiet, but the food was on point. I was glad that Raina decided to sit next to me even though she hadn't said two words to me since we'd entered the house. After the cake was cut, my father stood up and told everyone how proud of me he was. He and my mother presented me with keys to a black-on-black Lamborghini Aventador SV, which was sitting outside in the driveway. I was happy as fuck and couldn't wait to drive it, but before I could make my way outside, Mr. and Mrs. Brimmage handed me a card with $500 cash in it, which was nice of them. They didn't know we were rich as fuck and that $500 was less than pocket change to me. Still, it was all good.

Mrs. Ernie looked over at Raina and asked, "Baby Girl, are you going to give Damien the gift you got him?"

Raina looked uncomfortable as shit, but she managed to give a half smile. "Oh, here," she said, passing me a small gift box wrapped in red paper before looking back down at her lap. I could already see that she was going to make a nigga feel like shit for the rest of the night.

I tore the red wrapping paper off before opening the little black box. Inside there was a simple platinum Bulgari watch with small diamonds framing the face. I smiled because I knew that even though this wasn't the expensive, flashy shit I was used to wearing, it was a classic, something that I could wear until the end of time. I also knew that she had probably spent her last dollar on it, which made me care for her even more. Leaning down to where she was sitting, I hugged her from behind and simply whispered my gratitude in her ear.

"You're welcome," she politely replied, but her eyes never focused on me.

As I took the watch out of the box and began to place it on my wrist, I noticed that the back of it was engraved. It read, "You have my heart."

That shit right there instantly had a nigga's stomach hurting. Quietly, I sat back down in my chair next to her and leaned over to show her the words on the watch as though she hadn't already seen it. She gave me another sad half smile, making me feel even guiltier for still messing around with Tina and talking to her the way I had earlier on. I really didn't know how to respond to the message she gave me on the back of the watch, so I just kissed her cheek and humbly said, "Thank you, beautiful."

Romi must have known what was going on, because she instantly wrapped her arm around her and whispered something in her ear. Raina laid her head on her shoulder while Romi gave me the stare of death.

A few moments later, Mrs. Ernie stood up and said, "Well, we also have a surprise for Raquel. As most you might already know, she has received a full scholarship to attend Clark Atlanta in the fall for her music. We also know that she is going to need transportation back and forth from school, so this is for you."

She handed Raquel a set of BMW keys and pointed outside. Raquel ran over to the window to look out at her brand-new white BMW X6. "Oh, my God, Mama," she exclaimed with tears running down her face. "Thank you, Mama. Thank you, Daddy," she cried while hugging her parents.

"No need to thank us. You deserve it. All the money we saved for your college education, we didn't even need to use a dime of it because of all your hard work and talent. I couldn't ask for anything more, baby," Mr. Brimmage said before kissing her on the forehead.

Afterward, Melo quietly stood and walked over to Raquel to hand her a gift wrapped in red with a white bow on top.

"What's this?" she asked.

He shrugged his shoulders as he kept his cold hazel eyes on hers. When she opened it, she saw a platinum and diamond tennis bracelet worth at least twenty stacks gleaming back at her.

"Oh, my Gawd!" she shouted. "Melo, I . . . I can't accept this. It's too much," she said, covering her mouth in shock.

"I bought it for you, so if you don't take it, it'll just sit here," he stated with a nonchalant shrug.

She paused for a minute, admiring the bracelet. Then she looked over to her parents for their approval. Mrs. Ernie smiled, but I thought everyone in the room was practically speechless.

Finally, she broke the silence. "Thank you, Melo." Still with wide eyes and in slight shock, she gave him a tight hug as he nodded, somewhat expressionless and not really reciprocating her gesture.

Just like Raina, she had to stand on her tippy toes to hug his neck, with Melo being six foot three and her being about five foot four. It was the most affection I had ever seen Raquel show to anyone other than her sisters, so I knew she was happy as fuck.

While she continued hugging on Melo, he looked over at me and winked on the sly. I could only shake my head because that slick-ass nigga knew exactly what he was doing. He was working his way inside her panties, but if he knew like I knew, he'd be working on much more than that because her mean ass looked like she didn't play.

After he placed the bracelet on her wrist, we all ran outside to check out our new whips. Raquel jumped in the driver seat of her new BMW and asked Melo, Romi, and Dre to ride with her. I jumped in mine, asking Raina, Micah, and Risa to ride with me. Raina immediately jumped in the back with Risa, forcing Micah to sit up front with me. Micah smirked and shook his head as we all got in the car to ride off, leaving our parents behind.

Chapter 17

Raquel

No one knew, not even my sisters, that Melo had been texting me and playing on my phone for the past two weeks. One day I had been downstairs in the parlor playing the piano when I felt a vibration besides me on the piano bench. I flipped over my iPhone, and there was a text message from Bae. Of course at first, I was like, *who is playing games on my phone?* Nonetheless, I had opened the text.

Bae: I miss your beautiful face.

Me: Who is this?

Bae: What does the contact name say?

Me: Bae?

Bae: Exactly!

Me: I don't have time for this shit.

Bae: Mean ass. What are you doing?

Me: Again, who is this?

Bae: Secret admirer.

Me: Okay.

Bae: I think we got off on the wrong foot. Can we start over?

Me: Who is this?

Bae: The nigga who loves that you are still a virgin. Can't wait to punish that pussy for all that shit talking and eye rolling you be doin'.

Ugh! At that moment, I had known exactly who had been playing on my phone. I was going to kill Raina if she gave out my number to that psycho.

Me: I wouldn't let you touch me with a ten-foot pole.

Bae: A'ight, we will see about that. I'll let you get back to your piano.

Me: How do you know I'm playing the piano?

I had gotten up to look out the window to see if I had a stalker on my hands, but I didn't see anyone, nor did he respond to my text.

Today, Graduation Day, was my first time seeing him since the night of the party. To my surprise, he looked even better than he did that first night. He wore an all-white True Religion shirt and blue jeans with all-white Balenciagas. His Caesar fade had the edges lined to perfection from being freshly cut. Each of his ears shined brightly with a three-carat diamond stud, while the sexy scent of the Creed cologne filled my car.

"I'm in love!" I shouted. The soft leather, new-car smell, and smooth ride of my new BMW had me all geeked up. I couldn't wait to go to Clark to stunt on bitches.

As soon as that thought crossed my mind, Melo looked over and commented in a low tone, "Don't be thinking you the shit up at Clark, shawty. I can already see that I'm going have to keep a close eye on you."

It was as if that nigga was over there reading my mind. "Nigga, you ain't my daddy," I said, rolling my eyes. That was why I couldn't stand him, tennis bracelet or not.

"There you go with that slick mouth. I told you I got something for that," he spoke low so only I could hear.

Romi suddenly said, "Raquel, pull over."

"What you mean pull over? What's wrong?"

"Yo, she car sick or something. Pull over before she messes up your new whip," Dre said.

I pulled over on the side of the road, and Romi quickly jumped out from the back seat and began throwing up while Dre held her hair for her. Damien had to have noticed me stop the car, because in the rearview mirror I saw him bust a U-turn and pull behind us.

"You still throwing up?" Raina said as she was getting out of the car.

"Still? You sick?" Dre questioned her with concern.

"Pregnant more like it, bruh," Micah said, wiping his hand down over the waves in his hair.

"Shut up," Romi struggled to say while still throwing up.

"You pregnant?" Dre asked in a more aggressive tone with a scowl on his face.

Romi shrugged, indicating she didn't know if she was. After making sure she was okay, we all got back in the cars and headed back to the house. The car was completely silent, and I was sure everyone was in deep thought, wondering if Romi was pregnant.

When we arrived back at the house, Mama and Daddy were already gone. Raina looked like she was ready to go just like I was, but Romi and Risa were already headed back in the house with Dre and Micah following them. So, unfortunately, Raina and I would have to suck it up for a little while longer. I knew she was still hurting from seeing Damien's dumb ass holding Tina's hand, and I could tell she was trying her best not to ruin my day. That was one of the reasons I loved her most. She was selfless.

As Melo and I made it back in the house, we saw Raina, Micah, and Damien all sitting in the game room. I was on my way in there to join them when Melo gently grabbed my arm. "Nah, come with me, shawty," he said, nodding down the hall.

"Get off me. Grabbing me like I'm your child," I hissed, yanking my arm away from his grasp.

"Yo, if you don't bring your li'l mean ass on . . ." he threatened through gritted teeth.

His demeanor somewhat scared me, so I followed him down the hall that led to a music studio downstairs. This house had everything—a wine cellar, music studio, bowling alley. It was crazy.

"Wow, you guys have a music studio?"

He nodded and stared at me with an expressionless face. I just stood there waiting, gnawing at the corner of my mouth. I couldn't read Melo, but I knew his cold, vacant hazel eyes staring back at me did not belong to someone I wanted to associate myself with.

"What are we doing in here?" I asked, looking around at the impressive equipment.

"Sing for me," he said, slowly pointing toward the booth.

"I never told you I could sing. Raina . . . Fuck!"

"You too pretty to be doing all that cussing. Now get your li'l mean ass in there," he repeated, still wearing the usual scowl on his face.

"Look, I don't know who you think you are or what you're used to, but you don't tell me what to do," I snapped with my hand on my hip.

Slowly, he entered my space with barely an inch between us. He looked down at me with a furious expression on his face. As much as I tried to front, he was surely intimidating. I couldn't even look him in the eyes. Instead, I just looked down to the floor.

"What's that shit you talking now?" he asked.

"I . . . I said . . ." I stuttered.

"That's what the fuck I thought. Now take your ass in the booth and sing something fo' yo' nigga."

For my nigga, I thought, scrunching my face up in the process before childishly stomping into the sound booth. "What do you want me to sing?" I asked dryly, rolling my eyes again.

"Whatever," he simply replied, waving me off.

"Whatever?" I quizzed, consistently rolling my eyes.

Melo was working my last nerve thinking that I was his puppet and that he could tell me what to do, or talk to me any kind of way just because he bought me a damn tennis bracelet. Shit, he had another think coming if he thought I'd be that easy. Nevertheless, I got as comfortable as

I could inside the booth and positioned the microphone in front of me before taking in a deep breath and closing my eyes. I started singing the lyrics to an older song that my mother would sometimes play called "Put That on Everything," by Brandy.

Before I could even really get started, I noticed him in the studio, smiling and motioning for me to come there. It was the first time I'd ever seen that nigga smile, and I couldn't even lie and say it wasn't sexy on him.

When I walked out, he said, "Yo, your voice is dope as fuck."

He let out a light laugh, and it was obvious he was in disbelief. He was such a quiet person, so for him to be complimenting me, it made me feel happy inside for some reason.

"You think so?" I asked, smiling ear to ear.

"Fo' sho," he said in all seriousness while nodding.

I was pretty confident when it came to my singing abilities, but hearing him say how good I was actually gave me more confirmation that this was what I was meant to do with my life.

"That's your song?" he inquired.

Giggling, I shook my head. "That's Brandy's song. Ol' school."

"Oh, with the way you was in there singing to a nigga, I thought that shit was your song," he said.

After a small pause, we looked at one another and fell out laughing.

"You should laugh more often, Melo," I told him, attempting to lighten the tension that was always between us.

"Don't shit be funny half the time," he said, getting serious all over again as he prepped a blunt on the soundboard. "Is that how you would treat a nigga, shawty?" he asked quietly with his eyes still trained on the blunt he was rolling.

"What are you talking about?" I quizzed.

"'Pull a star out of the sky, go to the edge of the earth,' all that shit in the song," he replied.

"If I loved him," I said low.

Unexpectedly, my heart began to race, and there was now an unfamiliar throbbing between my legs. His conversation was making me uncomfortable, and I'd never felt that way before.

Melo must have sensed my discomfort, because he commented, "Shawty, you not ready for all that." He smirked before placing the blunt between his dark pink lips.

"What is that supposed to mean?" I asked, rolling my eyes. I hated that he could always read my damn mind and call me out on my shit.

"Keep on and those pretty-ass eyes gonna roll right up outta your fucking head one of these days. Shit is unattractive, shawty," he said before walking out of the studio.

I just stood there by myself, speechless, feeling quite stupid and even more confused.

Chapter 18

Romi

As soon as Dre and I got back to the house, he literally snatched me by the arm and told me that I needed to go upstairs to his room. When we entered his bedroom, he rushed into his bathroom and instructed me to come to him. I walked into his bathroom to find him holding an EPT pregnancy test for me to take.

"Go ahead and make it happen, shawty," he snapped, motioning for me to get on the toilet.

After peeing on the stick, I told him that we had to wait about three minutes to get the results. Neither one of us said a word to each other during those three minutes. I just lay down on his bed while he sat in a chair across the room in the corner. As he sat in the chair, I noticed he had his head hung low with his hands covering his face. Just seeing his reaction alone told me that he wouldn't be happy if I was pregnant.

When the stopwatch on his phone went off, we both jumped up and headed to the bathroom. I grabbed the test first, and sure enough, it read, "Pregnant."

"Shawty, what the fuck?" he hollered in disbelief with his hands on top of his head.

"Do you want me to get rid of it?" I immediately asked. I didn't know if I was ready to be a mother yet, so I wasn't exactly opposed to getting an abortion.

He never answered my question. Instead, he just yelled, "Why the fuck wasn't you on birth control?"

"I don't know, Dre. Let's not play the blame game right now. If you want me to get an abortion, I will," I assured him.

He suddenly slammed me against the wall, pushing his forearm up to my neck, slightly cutting off my air supply. I was scared shitless. I had never seen Dre this mad, nor did I ever think he would put his hands on me.

"How the fuck you gon' say some dumb shit like that to me, shawty? You not killing my seed, and that's the end of that fucking conversation," he spat before releasing his arm from my throat.

I tried to regain my breath, but now the tears were coming down my face hard. His face softened a little as he tried to grab for me, but I ran away from him and out of his room.

When Raina saw me, she immediately ran over to me. "What's wrong? What happened?" she questioned.

"I'm pregnant, and he's pissed at me," I cried.

"Pissed at you for what? Both of you did it. And why is your neck all red like that?" she asked, examining me with her eyes.

My sisters and I were extremely close. So close that most times we didn't even need to speak words to know what the other was going through.

"Dre, get the fuck down here. Now, mutha-fucka!" she yelled, storming up the stairs. I knew she was pissed because Baby Girl didn't cuss.

Damien flew by me, rushing to follow Raina up the stairs to try to intervene. "What's wrong?" he asked, looking from Raina to Dre and then to me.

"I'm pregnant, Dame, that's all," I cried, shaking my head in disbelief.

"This nigga put his hands on my sister, and now we've got a problem," Raina yelled.

"Dre, what the fuck?" Damien asked, looking at Dre for an explanation.

Now everybody was in the bedroom with us, including Micah, Risa, Raquel, and Melo.

"I fucked up," Dre said with his hands on his head, pacing the floor.

"Yeah, you fucked up, nigga, that's for sure," Raina said, refusing to back down. At this point, she was in his face while Raquel and Melo were still trying to figure out what had happened.

"Will somebody please tell me what is going on?" Raquel shouted.

"Romi is pregnant, and he was so pissed with her about it, he put his hands on her," Raina spat as she tried to explain.

"You did what, li'l nigga?" Micah said as he gave Dre a look like he was getting ready to beat his ass.

"I fucked up, yo. I fucked up. I'm sorry, Romi, but please don't kill my seed, shawty. Please!" Dre said.

"Nah, we don't believe in abortions, so there won't be killing of anybody's seeds around this muthafucka. Y'all hear me?" Micah said, looking from Raina to Raquel to Risa then back to me as if he were talking to his children.

"We'll figure this shit out, sis. Don't you worry your pretty li'l head, shawty. We'll figure it out," Micah told me, giving me a tight hug and a kiss on the forehead as Risa came over to rub my back.

Raquel grabbed my hand before leading me downstairs and out the door. The four of us left and headed home without saying another word to the guys. I was so shaken up that Risa drove my car while Raquel drove home in her new BMW.

"What are you going to do?" Raina asked.

"I guess make me a doctor appointment and go from there," I cried. I couldn't stop the tears from streaming. I was so scared of becoming a mother and even more scared of once again losing the only man I'd ever loved.

Two Weeks Later

I was sitting in the doctor's office waiting for Dr. Mahoney to come back with the results of my blood test. Raquel, Raina, and Risa all went with me to the doctor's office. They promised to let me be the one to tell Mama and Daddy if the blood test indeed proved I was pregnant.

"Well, Ms. Brimmage, congratulations. Looks like you were correct. You are indeed pregnant."

"I see," was all I could manage. Raquel, Raina, and Risa all hugged me as I began to sob.

"It will be okay, Romi. I promise it will," Raina assured me.

"Well, let's see how far along you are. Let's do an ultrasound," Dr. Mahoney suggested.

After she turned on the machine and started the ultrasound, I could instantly hear my baby's heartbeat. A huge smile quickly appeared on my face as I wished Dre were with me. We hadn't talked since the night of the graduation, and I really didn't know what to make of that.

"Okay, so it's too early to determine the sex, but it does look like you are about eight weeks pregnant. And the heartbeat sounds strong," she said.

"Wait, you said eight weeks?" I asked the doctor, then looked at Raina. She was the only one who knew about my affair with Mr. Charles. I slept with Charles four days before reuniting with Dre. *Fuck my life.* When I began to cry, Raina came to my side and grabbed my hand.

"What's wrong, Romi?" Risa asked, but I was speechless. I couldn't talk. "Talk to us, Romi. Are you scared? 'Cause if you are, there's no need to be," she continued.

She looked over at Raina, who was now rubbing my hair and sweetly shushing me. "Raina, what's wrong with her?" Risa asked.

Raina just shook her head, feeling torn between not wanting to betray me yet not wanting to betray the sisterhood we all shared.

"Raina, what the fuck is wrong with Romi?" Raquel yelled.

I couldn't take it anymore, and I didn't want to keep Raina in the middle, so I sat up and shouted, "I don't know if the baby is Dre's or if it's Mr. Charles's!"

When I looked up and saw Dre standing at the door behind Risa with a bouquet of red tulips in his hands and a scowl on his face, all of the breath instantly left my body. I could no longer breathe.

"Fuck you mean?" he asked, his eyes already red and filled with anger.

"I'm sorry, Romi. I texted him because I thought you would want him to be here," Raina said, looking at me with apologetic eyes.

"Dre, the doctor just told me that I was eight weeks pregnant, which was the week me and you first got back together. The night of the party."

"And?" he asked.

"I slept with someone just days before that, and I just don't know," I cried, trying my best to explain.

"Fuck you, Romi! Don't call me until you get a DNA test," he yelled before throwing the flowers in my face and storming out of the room.

I realized he was hurting, but so was I. I had only wanted to be with him from the jump, but he'd told me he didn't want me to be his girl, so now I was being punished for trying to move on. My sisters all gathered around me for a tight group hug while Raquel quietly sang "Over the Rainbow" in our ears. It was the song Mama used to sing to us growing up to make us feel better.

"'Somewhere over the rainbow, skies are blue, and the dreams that you dare to dream, really do come true.'"

By the time Raquel had finished singing, all our faces were soaked with tears, including Dr. Mahoney's. I loved Dre with all my heart, and I could only pray that the baby was his, but for now, I knew that everything would be okay as long as I had my sisters beside me.

The whole way home, I explained everything to them, from Dre breaking my heart to me sleeping with a few random guys, and even my embarrassing affair with Mr. Charles. Telling them was like a huge weight being lifted off my shoulders. The only thing left to do was to tell Mama and Daddy, but how was I supposed to tell Daddy about his friend of twenty years?

Chapter 19

Damien

It had been three weeks since I'd last seen or heard from Raina. What was supposed to be one of the best days of my life ended up being one of the worst. I'd lost my girl that night, and my brothers had even thrown blows after the girls left because Micah was still pissed about Dre putting his hands on Romi. I tried sending Raina a few texts after that, but she never responded. Now today was the Fourth of July, her birthday, and I was sick like some soft-ass nigga because I wanted to see her and wish her a happy birthday. After taking a deep sigh and running my hand down my face, I decided to call Mrs. Ernie.

"Hey, Mrs. Ernie, how are you?"

"I am fine, Damien. How are you?" she replied.

"Well, you already know how I am. Raina hasn't talked to me since the graduation."

"I see," was all she said in response. I guessed Raina had turned the whole family against me.

"Mrs. Ernie, I know today is her birthday, and I wanted to see her. I have something that I'd like to give her."

After a long pause, Mrs. Ernie finally said, "Well, she'll probably kill me, but we're having a barbecue for her here at the house around four today if you'd like to stop by. I believe Melo is coming by."

"Oh, he is? All right, thank you, ma'am. I'll see you then," I said. Cocking my head to the side, I was thinking that sneaky-ass Melo hadn't said shit about going over there.

It was thirty minutes after four when I pulled up to Raina's house. There were several cars parked outside, and I even saw Micah's Bugatti parked close by, so I knew he had to be here with Melo. I knew Micah wasn't going to be loyal to me if the choice was between me and Raina, because that was his Baby Girl. Plus any free time he had nowadays was spent in Greensboro with Risa.

The backyard was booming and in full effect the same way it was the day of Risa's welcome home party. I could hear "Knuck if You Buck" blaring, with people around my age dancing and shit. Some I knew from school while others I didn't know at all. I noticed girls across the yard eying me from afar, but I was there for one girl and one girl only.

After whiffing the same good smell of barbecue that filled the air, I decided to walk in the house first to find Mrs. Ernie rather than going out back to look for Raina. As I made my way through the house, I finally spotted her in the kitchen, pulling potato salad out of the fridge.

"What up, Mrs. Ernie?" I called out.

She turned around with a smile and gave me a half hug. "Better question is what's up with you?" she replied while grinning.

"On a scale of one to ten, how mad is she?" I asked, pulling up a barstool to sit at the kitchen counter.

Mrs. Ernie laughed. "Well, the day of your graduation I'd say she was about a ten. And today, today she's a nine."

"A nine! Damn, she ain't cutting a nigga no slack, is she?" I said, forgetting who I was talking to.

"What's the problem, Dame? Raina was at your graduation, and that was the first time I had ever seen my baby in love."

My eyes grew wide at her words.

"Yes, I said in love, Damien! Here she is thinking that you're her boyfriend, and you were holding hands with someone else. And then you tell her that y'all never had a commitment so she shouldn't even be mad."

I was feeling like shit as Mrs. Ernie recounted the events that went down after my graduation. I put my head down in my hands and shook my head, not knowing what I was thinking, coming in here to talk to her first.

"What's the problem, Damien? My daughter was good enough to help tutor you, good enough for you to take to prom, good enough to meet your family, but she's not good enough to be your girlfriend? You already know I love you boys. All of you! But you tell me how that shit sounds," she said in her hood voice.

"I'm going to college in a few months, Mrs. Ernie. I don't want to hurt her," I admitted.

"Boy, you are going less than an hour away for school. If you care for her how I think you do, then you'll fix it."

"I know, Mrs. Ernie, I know," I said before grabbing one of the trays of potato salad from her and heading out to the backyard.

After setting the food down on a table on the deck, I spotted her. She was pretty as ever and playing spades with Melo, Raquel, and some nigga I didn't know. There were a few of my peoples out there from school who I stopped to speak to before I nervously made my way over to her. Walking closer, I spotted Micah with Risa in his lap and Romi sitting across from them. Romi saw me first and rolled her eyes before saying something to Risa. It was some smart-ass comment, I was sure. Walking up directly behind Raina, I covered her eyes with my hands.

"Hey, Damien," she greeted me with sarcasm.

"How'd you know it was me?" I asked, removing my hands from her face.

"Your cologne," she answered quickly. "I got four," she said, continuing to play her game of spades.

I just shook my head, realizing how much she really was still mad at me. I looked over at Melo, and he cut his eyes at me and hit me with a nod. *This nigga.*

After that, I saw Micah, and he was kissing and caressing Risa without a care in the world. I doubted either one of them even saw me walk up. Romi was shooting her usual daggers at me with her eyes. I figured she was probably taking some of her anger with Dre out on me, but I didn't give a fuck. I blew her a kiss just to fuck with her, and she kindly gave me the finger in return. I laughed before turning my attention to Raina's card partner.

"Yo, who the fuck is this?" I asked, pointing at that nigga.

"Arnell, this is Damien. Damien, this is Arnell," Raina flatly introduced us while continuing to play cards.

"Arnell, huh?" I said, letting out a small laugh and feeling myself getting heated as I rubbed my chin. "I need to talk to you, shawty. Now!" I spat.

Raina let out a heavy sigh before getting up and walking off. I was quick on her heels as we entered the house and walked into the living room.

"What do you need to talk to me about, Damien?" she asked with her arms folded over her chest. Her weight was shifted to one hip, and her body language was full of attitude.

"Who is that nigga outside?" I spat.

"Why does it even matter, Damien? He's a guest. Is that all you wanted to talk about?"

"No, I wanted to wish you a happy birthday."

"Thanks. Now are we done here?" she asked, rolling her eyes. She definitely wasn't letting up.

"I bought you a birthday present," I said, pulling out the small gift wrapped in red paper from my cargo shorts pocket.

She sighed again before unwrapping it with a scowl on her face. As she opened the box, I thought I might have seen the corners of her mouth slightly turn up. She pulled out the platinum Bulgari diamond-faced watch that matched the one she gave me.

"Thanks, Dame," was all she said.

"Can I put it on you?" I asked.

She nodded and gave me a half smile. I was winning her back slowly but surely, I could feel it. As I took the watch out of the box, I flipped it over so that she could see that it was engraved.

"Wait, what does it say?" she asked. I held it up so that she could read it: "Dame & Beautiful."

After seeing the huge smile spread across her face, I knew I had her. She tried pulling me in for a hug, but I killed all that hugging shit. Instead, I put my face directly in front of hers to let our lips collide. To my surprise, her body submitted to my touch. She wrapped her arms around my neck and returned my kiss with her eyes closed. As I tightly held her body close to mine, I continued to kiss her deeply. I genuinely missed the way her young ass felt and the way she smelled.

"Wait, what does this mean?" she asked, breaking our kiss.

"It means I'm all yours if you still want me, shawty."

She smiled and came back up to kiss me. After she put the watch on her wrist, we made our way back outside with everyone else. With my arm draped around her shoulders, I leaned over and lightly licked her on the ear. She giggled while listening to me tell her how much I missed her.

"You know you're mine, right?" I whispered. She merely laughed and nodded. "And who the fuck is that nigga?" I asked again, pointing to the guy at the table.

"That's just our cousin Arnell, babe." She laughed.

"Why the fuck ain't you just say that the first time I asked?"

She giggled and shrugged, knowing she was playing games with a nigga. I shook my head and playfully smacked her on the ass. "Go fix a nigga a plate, shawty," I said as I made my way over to the table where Micah, Risa, and Romi were.

"Where's Raina?" Romi asked.

"She went to go fix me a plate," I boasted.

Micah started smiling and slapped hands with me. If Baby Girl was happy, shit, he was happy too.

"So, are you guys okay now?" Risa sweetly asked.

"Yeah, we straight."

"Are you two together? As in you're not going to break my sister's fucking heart again?" Romi spat. She hated me right now. Shit, I thought it was safe to say that she hated all niggas right now.

"Yeah, we straight," was all I said.

"Uuhhmmm." Romi rolled her eyes.

I turned around to see Raina putting my plate in front of me. The sticky sauce glistened on my barbecue ribs and grilled chicken. She also had nice portions of potato salad, green beans, and macaroni and cheese piled up high on my plate.

"Here ya go," she said.

"Thanks, beautiful," I said, puckering my lips so she could kiss me before taking a seat next to me.

"Babe, my feet hurt," Risa whined.

"Lemme rub them for you, babe," Micah said, sliding her down from his lap and taking her feet into his hands.

"Really, nigga! You really finna rub her crusty-ass feet right here at the table where I'm eating?" I spat. Everybody at the table burst out laughing, including Romi, but I was serious as fuck.

"Nigga, she got pretty feet," he said, holding one of her feet in the air. She covered her face and shook her head from embarrassment. Although she did have some pretty-ass feet, I still didn't want them around my food.

"Let's just go to my room, and you can finish rubbing my feet up there," she said with a smile.

"Nah, I don't wanna have to fuck yo' pops up for being up in yo' room. Let's go sit on the couch," Micah said.

Risa just laughed and nodded. After picking her up bridal style, he carried her into the house. I shook my head and looked over at Raina, who was observing the two of them interact.

"Is that what you want from me, beautiful?" I asked knowingly while stroking her silky hair. She gave a small smile and nodded.

"I got you," I simply responded before kissing her neck. Damn, I'd missed that neck.

After finishing my plate, I sat with Melo and Romi as we watched Raquel and Raina in the yard dancing the Wobble. They were smiling and laughing and simply having the best time. The shit made me smile just looking at the two of them. When the song finished, she glanced over, and I waved for her to come back and sit with me. Their faces glistened from being covered in the summer night's humidity as they swatted the bugs from their path. I pulled her down into my lap, and Raquel took her seat just before the fireworks started to go off. Loud, bright bursts of red, blue, and white lights sparkled in the dark night sky. Raina placed her head in the crook of my neck while I softly stroked her hair and continued to watch the show.

"Happy birthday, beautiful," I said before kissing her softly on the lips. She was happier than I'd ever seen her before, and I was solely thankful to be in her presence again.

There were blankets scattered all throughout the backyard, with couples and families watching the fireworks in the distance. They were pointing and clapping, their faces filled with amusement. Even Micah and Risa had finally made their way back out of the house and were sitting out on a blanket in the yard. As I continued to scan the backyard, I spotted Mrs. Ernie and Mr. B cuddled up together, watching the sky. When Mrs. Ernie saw me looking at her, I gave her the thumbs-up, letting her know that Raina and I were good again. She smiled contently and placed her head against Mr. B's chest, allowing him to wrap his arms around her.

In the middle of the fireworks show, I saw an older man walking over to sit with Romi. At first glance, he looked like he was probably a family member or something, but then I saw him place his hand on her knee. She quickly swatted his hand away and scrunched up her face. I could read her lips saying, "Nigga, get off me." Being that Dre wasn't here because he was still in his feelings about her possibly being pregnant by somebody else, I instantly jumped up in his place. Raina sat up and looked at me like I was crazy when I walked over to where they were sitting and looked the old-ass nigga dead in the eye.

"Is there a problem here?" I spat. I guessed from my tone, Melo instantly stood ready for whatever.

"No, young blood, there's no problem," he coolly replied.

"You all right, Romi?" I asked. She looked at me with sad eyes but never responded. I took that shit as a no.

"Yo, she doesn't want you here. You need to get up and move the fuck on," I snapped.

"Li'l nigga, who the fuck do you think you are talking to?" the older man spat back as he took a stand.

"You, nigga! Now get the fuck on," I scolded, making my way closer to him. Micah and Risa were now behind me as well.

"Mr. Charles, can you please leave this area? I don't think Romi wants to talk with you," Risa said, attempting to quickly mediate the situation.

"Charles?" Micah inquired, cocking his head to the side like he recognized the nigga's name. "Are you the same Charles who might have gotten my brother's girl pregnant?" Micah asked. Now all three of us—Micah, Melo, and I—were up in this nigga's face.

"Pregnant? What the fuck is he talking about?" he asked, looking down at Romi, who was still seated with her face in her palms.

"Charles, what is going on?" Mr. B approached me from behind me and asked.

That nigga Charles was dumbstruck. His mouth hung open, and he wasn't saying shit. He was speechless.

"Romi?" Mrs. Ernie spoke.

Lifting her wet face from her hands, Romi looked at her parents then back at Charles.

"Mama. Daddy," she cried softly as Raina and Risa went over to embrace her from behind. "Me and Mr. Charles had an affair," she cried and paused to swallow hard before finishing. "I'm eleven weeks pregnant, and I don't know if the baby is Charles's or Dre's," she shamefully confessed, crying aloud in Risa's arms.

Before Charles could even react, Mr. B jumped over the table, taking Charles to the ground with his bare hands, wrapping them tightly around his neck.

"Muthafucka, you took advantage of my daughter. You were like my brother, nigga," he spat.

With spit flying from his mouth, he continued trying to choke the life out of Charles. Mr. B reached back, making a closed fist that landed hard on Charles's face. He continued raining one blow after the other until his fist was covered in blood.

"That's enough, Brad! That's enough!" Mrs. Ernie yelled with her face wet with tears.

Mr. B jumped up and off of Charles before storming into the house with his hands on top of his head in disbelief. Mrs. Ernie followed him, sobbing. While Romi continued to cry, Micah and Risa escorted her into the house. The rest of us followed, leaving Charles lying on the ground, breathing heavily with his face covered in blood.

Chapter 20

Micah

A month had passed since Mr. B whooped that nigga's ass on Baby Girl's birthday, but Dre still wasn't fucking with Romi. Even Risa and I disagreed on the matter, which was completely unlike us. We always stayed on some lovey-dovey, kumbaya-type shit. I mean, I honestly couldn't blame my brother for how he was acting. The last thing he wanted to do was to get back involved with Romi and get excited about a baby that may not even be his. Plus he would be heading back to school in a couple of weeks anyway, and that was where his focus needed to be until Romi told him otherwise.

So here I was, on a Friday night in my apartment with Keesha and Zaria. Keesha was dropping Zaria off for the weekend, but I asked her to hang out for a bit. I knowingly omitted the fact that I wanted her to meet Risa. Risa was going to stay the night with me and Zaria, so I thought the mature thing to do would be to introduce her to my baby mama. I only hoped that Keesha was on her grown-woman shit tonight. I knew I probably should have forewarned Keesha about Risa coming over, but I was doing everything possible to prevent any drama. I knew Keesha still had feelings for me, but I honestly just wanted to be happy with Risa.

I looked at my daughter while the three of us sat on the floor building castles and battleships with the pink and purple Legos that I'd bought for her. My baby was a pretty, brown-skinned 3-year-old girl with long, curly hair that Keesha always kept in a high ponytail with a ribbon accent. Seeing how happy Zaria was to be in our presence at the same time made me smile. I just hoped that she would take a liking to Risa the way I had, because if she didn't, we would have a serious problem. Zaria was my world, and anybody who couldn't fit in it just wasn't for me.

As I showed off my battleship to Zaria, there was a sudden knock on the door.

"Who is that?" Keesha asked.

"I don't know," I lied. I quickly got up from the floor and opened the door to see Risa standing there with her Spelman T-shirt, skinny jeans, and burgundy Chucks on, looking like a for-real college student. Her long hair was pulled up in a high ponytail, exposing her flawless naked brown face and neck with diamond studs shining in each ear. Even wearing the most basic shit, Risa was always killing the next bitch. Here Keesha was, sitting in the house with little cutoff jean shorts that exposed her ass cheeks and a pink cropped top. She wore a long, wavy weave that draped down her back, wedge heels, and all this gaudy gold jewelry up and down her arms. I could only shake my head at the comparison.

"Hey, baby," I greeted her with a hug and a kiss before letting her into the house. I turned around to see Keesha's scowling expression glaring at the two of us.

"Keesha, this is my girlfriend, Risa. Risa, this is Keesha and our daughter, Zaria."

Risa politely held out her hand to Keesha, but Keesha merely scrunched her nose at her hand and rolled her eyes. Risa played it cool though, putting her hand back to her side before sitting down on the floor with Zaria.

"Hi, Zaria, my name is Risa. Nice to meet you," she said, extending her hand to my daughter.

Zaria smiled and politely shook her hand. "Wanna play wit' my blocks?" she asked Risa.

"Sure," Risa said, smiling before beginning to build with Zari.

"Keesh, let me holla at you for a minute," I said before leading Keesha to my bedroom. "What the fuck is the problem?' I snapped.

"Nigga, why the fuck you ain't tell me you had a girlfriend? And how the fuck you gon' have some bitch around my child."

I shook my head and took a deep breath. I was trying to keep my cool because she already had me heated over calling Risa outside of her name.

"She and I have been kicking it for a few months, and things are getting serious with us now. I wanted you to meet her 'cause she's gonna be around Zari."

"But I thought you moved us up here so that we could work on being a family again," she whined with tears brimming her eyes. I sighed deeply, searching for the words to convey my emotions without breaking her in the process.

"I love you, Keesha, I do. But I'm falling in love with Risa."

"Well, what was all that bullshit last month when you came down to see us? Nigga, you had me sucking yo' dick, and you slept in my bed that weekend. Does that bitch know that?" She pointed toward the door for emphasis. "Since y'all been so-called 'kicking it for few months,'" she continued, using air quotes for emphasis. Tears were beginning to fall.

"No, she doesn't know, and I'm sorry about that. It will never happen again. I don't want to hurt you, shawty. I just need you to understand what's up," I said, reaching out to hug her, but she quickly pushed me away and stormed out of the room. When I trailed behind, I saw Keesha snatch Zaria up out of Risa's lap from where they sat on the floor together.

"What are you doing?" I spat, growing more agitated.

"I'm taking my baby home, Micah. Call me when you decide what you want," she snapped.

I looked at Keesha with my head cocked to the side. Then I looked over at Risa's confused face and took another deep breath.

"I've decided what I want, Keesha. I'm very clear on that. Risa is my girlfriend. You and I are no longer together. I'm introducing the two of you because she is going to be around Zari when she's with me."

"Well, nigga, I couldn't tell when you were in my bed last month," she shouted, looking at me with her nose turned up.

Risa just let out a small, irritated laugh and stood up. "Look, you two obviously have a lot to talk about. Micah, I'll come back and hang out with you and Zari another day, okay?" she said, offering a half smile.

"No, sit down, Risa! You not going nowhere tonight," I snapped.

Now Keesha was really pissing me off. I was trying to play nice and do the right thing for Zaria, but at this point, all bets were off. I told Keesha that Risa didn't know anything about me staying with her last month, yet she still tried to put me on blast to be spiteful. The last thing I wanted was for Risa's feelings to be hurt.

"Keesha, it's time for you to go. Now! I'll call you Sunday and let you know what time I'm dropping Zari off."

She rolled her eyes and hesitated, but she must have noticed that I wasn't playing with her ass. She placed Zaria back on the floor and kissed her on the forehead before storming out the door.

"Have you eaten yet?" Risa asked. Zaria shook her head. "You like pizza?" Risa asked. Zaria just nodded, which caused Risa to pull out her phone to order a pizza for us.

To my surprise, not once the whole night did Risa mention Keesha to me. Instead, she just catered to Zaria's every need and bonded with her. She gave her a bath, combed and brushed her hair, and even played dolls with her. Zaria took right to her, too, following her around everywhere she went. My baby must have tired Risa out though, because when it was time for Zaria to go to bed, Risa looked over at me from the couch with her head laid back and sternly said, "You're tucking her in."

I held my hands up in submission and laughed.

After putting Zaria in the bed, I joined Risa on the couch, pulling her cold feet into my lap. I began roughly rubbing her feet the way I knew she liked it as I watched her beautiful face staring back at me in silence. Only sounds of the TV and the dishwasher could be heard.

"You slept with Zari's mom last month?" she asked softly. She was expressionless while she took her hair down from the ponytail she wore. I knew it was coming, but I was prepared to tell her the truth, so I didn't care either way.

"No. I let her suck my dick, but either way, I was wrong for leading her on and for disrespecting you," I explained shamefully. I faced down as I rubbed her feet.

"I mean, I didn't think I had to ask, but apparently I do. Are we in a committed relationship?" she inquired, letting out a small laugh.

"Yeah, we are. I fucked up. It's just . . ." I paused with a deep sigh.

"It's just what, Micah?" she wondered, sitting upright as she waited for me to continue.

"Shawty, I'm a twenty-five-year-old man, and I've been fucking since I was thirteen. I'm not used to not having sex, and a nigga is being patient as fuck right now."

"I know, Micah. That's the only reason I'm not spazzing out on you right now. Whether you know it or not, you already have my heart, but once I give you my body, you only have one time with me," she said, pointing to her chest for emphasis.

"I can respect that, shawty."

She grabbed my chin, making me look her directly in the eyes. "Can you be a faithful man, Micah?" she asked softly.

"I don't see nobody but you, Risa. You got a nigga's heart, that's my word."

Looking deeply into her eyes, I saw the half-moon of her luminous white teeth peering wide as she smiled. Her deep dimples were full on display. I leaned up, and we sealed our commitment with a closed-lip kiss. When she moved up to straddle my lap, she allowed her arms to snake around my neck. As our kiss deepened, my hands gently moved to squeeze her soft ass. A slight moan escaped her lips as the passion between our mouths continued to grow more forceful. As she permitted my hands to roam up the back of her T-shirt, I unsnapped her bra with anticipation. I could feel my dick rise as she tightly wrapped her legs around my waist, allowing me to carry her to my bedroom.

I laid her on my California king-size bed and pulled her shirt up over her head, exposing her smooth, cocoa-colored breasts. As I took one into my mouth and lightly flicked her morsel with my tongue, the sound of another moan lightly skated through her lips. After sliding her pants down, I gently placed a kiss between her breasts before gliding the tip of my wet tongue down to her belly button. The sound of her breathing coming to a complete stop as she anticipated the feeling of my mouth on her most sensitive place made my dick jump. After kissing and sucking on her flat stomach a little more, I continued making a trail with the tip of my tongue down to the front of her clit.

"Mmmm," she moaned.

After sliding down her red cotton VS panties, I draped each of her legs over my shoulders and softly licked her center, making slow circular motions. Gently sucking on her sensitive bud, I could hear her moans getting louder and louder. Repeatedly thrusting my stiff tongue in and out of her, I made her call out my name.

"Micah, oh, my Gawd! Aaaah, Micahhh!" she moaned, coming hard into my mouth.

Although I wanted our first time to be romantic for her, at this particular moment, all a nigga wanted to see was how she could ride the dick. Selfishly, I lay on my back and flipped her body on top of mine. Watching her face, I saw her eyes tightly close while her mouth hung open slightly from pleasure. She eased her way down onto me and felt good as fuck.

"Damn, you tight as shit," I muttered.

Instinctively, I grabbed her waist and began pumping in and out of her, but she pushed my hands away and began slowly grinding her hips onto me. Up and down her body went as she squeezed her muscles tighter and tighter around my dick like a pro. I reached my hand up to fondle her breast when she slipped two of my fingers into her mouth. While deep throating my fingers, she took complete and total control.

"Shhit," I hissed.

She had a nigga ready to nut, but I needed her to cum for me first. I flipped her over onto her back and began giving it to her deep. She rocked her hips up, matching me stroke for stroke as I watched her beautiful face twist from pleasurable pain.

"Ooh, Micah, I'm about to . . . ahhhh."

I quickly pulled out of her, causing her eyes to open wide, Quickly, I turned her over, softly pushing her head into the pillow. She eagerly lifted her ass toward me, permitting me access to her from behind. Holding on to her waist, I stroked her slow and deep, wanting her to feel every inch of me. Hearing her murmured sounds hidden within the pillow turned me on even more.

"I'm cumming, baby!" she yelled, throwing her ass back onto me before trembling and creaming all over my dick. I grabbed a hold of her long hair and began stroking her faster and faster until I pulled out, spreading my seeds all over her ass.

After cleaning ourselves and getting back in bed, I held Risa tightly in my arms, thinking about how much she truly meant to me. I knew I always joked around about her marrying a nigga one day, but after the way she just put it down, I truly felt like she was the one. I doubted that in this lifetime I would find a girl who was more genuine, smart, and ambitious. Plus I had just discovered that she had something special between her legs.

The next morning, I rolled over to Risa's side of the bed to feel for her, but she wasn't there. As I wiped the crust out of my eyes, the mouth-

watering smell of bacon and maple syrup hit my
nose. I sat up and stretched wide to crack the
muscles in my chest and back before throwing
on my basketball shorts. After taking my morning piss and brushing my teeth, I made my way
into the kitchen, where I saw Risa and Zaria stir-
ring a bowl of pancake batter together. Flour
lightly dusted Zaria's little face and her wild,
curly hair, which was all over her head. I glanced
at Risa, who stood there in burgundy cheerleader shorts and a gray camisole. Her feet were
bare and pretty on the cold tile floor.

"Good morning, Zari." I greeted my daughter with a kiss before picking her up from the
counter.

With Zaria still in my arms, I approached Risa
from behind and kissed the side of her neck.
"Morning, bae."

"Good morning," she said, leaning back to give
me a peck on the lips. She looked sexy to me
with her long hair flipped to one side.

"How long before breakfast is ready?" I asked.

"Ten minutes tops." She smiled, showing her
deep dimples.

"I need to head over to the office for a little
while today. Do you mind watching Zari for a
few hours for me?"

"Of course I don't, and you don't need to ask me that," she commented with her back to me as she focused on cooking.

That right there was why she was a keeper. In less than twenty-four hours, she had already taken to my daughter like she was her own and fell right into the role of my future wife. I put Zaria down and turned Risa around to face me before planting a kiss on her lips to show my gratitude.

After breakfast, I got dressed and headed to my office in my all-white 745. I had some paperwork to complete for the new hotel that we would be opening soon. Plus I needed to get up with Timo and see how he was holding up. Growing up, Timo always had a nigga's back, so there was no way I could let him down now that he needed me.

Sitting at my desk, I heard a knock on the door. "Come in," I said.

"Mr. Borrego, I have that paperwork you asked for," Melody explained. Melody had been my assistant for the past two years. She was a beautiful woman with a golden skin tone and long legs. She gave off a Keri Hilson vibe with her short haircut and light-colored eyes. For the most part, she and I kept it professional, but there were times I'd let her top me off. Still, Melody never acted crazy or obsessive over me.

She gave a familiar flirty smile as she walked over to me in her charcoal gray dress that hugged her ass perfectly and sexy pewter pumps that showed off her legs. After setting the documents down on my desk in front of me, she moved behind me and began giving me a shoulder massage. It was something she did for me several times throughout the week. I was a little hesitant because of what I was trying to build with Risa, but then I figured it was what assistants were for. A little shoulder massage never hurt anybody, right?

"You feel tense, Mr. Borrego," she whined seductively while massaging my shoulders.

At this point, my head was lying back and my eyes were closed, because her hands felt so good on me. I felt her hands slide from my shoulders and down to my chest before she whispered in my ear, "Can I take care of that for you too, sir?"

Shit!

When I looked down at my lap, there was a tent in my pants. I was coming to realize that I couldn't be a faithful man. I'd never really had to try up to this point in my life, so I didn't realize how hard it would be for me. Before I could even respond, Melody was spinning my chair around and getting down on her knees.

"Ohh, shit!" I hissed as I felt her warm, wet mouth wrap around my dick. My head fell all the way back, and my hands instantly went to the top of her head, allowing her to do what she did best.

"Damn," I groaned as she teased the tip with her tongue, then sloppily deep throated my shaft. Suddenly, there was a knock on the door, followed by my office door opening.

"Oh, shit! My bad, Micah," Timo apologized after seeing Melody giving me head.

He quickly closed the door, and because I was on the verge of finishing, I allowed Melody to continue to do her thing until I released my load down her throat. After taking a tissue to wipe the corners of her mouth, she straightened herself up and left so I could get myself together to speak with Timo.

Timo had finally been released on bail a few weeks ago, but unfortunately, it wasn't before Zo's funeral.

"My bad, bruh. I didn't see nobody out front, so I walked on back to your office," he explained with a little laugh before slapping hands and reeling me in for a hug.

"No problem, man. I don't think she was expecting you to be here for another thirty minutes or so."

"That's you?" he asked, referring to Melody.

"Nah, nigga, that's just my assistant."

"Damn, I gotta get me an assistant. For real, for real!"

I let out a light chuckle and shook my head. "What's good wit'cha? How does it feel to be a free man?" I asked, trying to quickly change subjects because I felt guilty for cheating on Risa. It was like I just couldn't control my wayward dick.

"Everything is everything. The whole family is still fucked up behind Zo's death and shit, but I've already got my people on it. Whoever did it is gonna wish they hadn't fucked with my family, ya feel me?" he said.

I could tell my nigga was stressed, so I offered him a blunt and a glass of cognac that I always kept in my office for celebratory times or stressful ones like this.

"Thanks, man. I 'preciate it," he said.

"I do need a favor from you, though, bro."

"Just say the word," I responded while fixing my own glass of cognac.

"Because of all that shit that went down with Zo, my connect's not fucking with me right now. Says shit is too hot, but you already know the streets drying up. I need to link up with Raul."

"You want me to put you on with Uncle Raul?" I questioned before placing the blunt between my lips and taking a pull.

"Yeah, I need that hookup, bruh."

"Lemme see what I can do. Oh, my wife just texted me and said she wants to go to lunch," I said, looking down at my phone.

"Oh, shit, you married now?" he asked in shock, giving me a disapproving look. I knew that was because he'd literally just caught me with my dick down Melody's throat.

"Nah, not yet, but I do plan on marrying this one. Shit, you already know I wouldn't have a wedding without my right-hand man being present anyway."

"Oh, a'ight, I'm just making sure, shit." He laughed before getting up. "Well, I'll definitely have to meet her. Just holla at me once you talk with Raul though," he said before dapping me up and heading out the door.

Chapter 21

Risa

After Zaria and I got dressed for the day, we headed to Micah's office so we could grab some lunch together. I wore simple jean shorts with a white off-the-shoulder bodysuit that I paired with modest gold hoop earrings and flat gold sandals to match. Memories of the night I shared with Micah engulfed my thoughts, causing a slight quiver, accompanied by moisture between my thighs. Images of his dark, chiseled body overpowering mine as we made love for the first time turned me on. All of the colorful artwork tattooed across the top of his big, strong back and muscular arms fascinated me like abstract paintings hung in a museum. And that deep, raspy baritone of his alone made me weak. I was falling hard for Micah. I just hoped he would protect my heart in the process.

For some reason, I really trusted him. Maybe it was because he introduced me to Keesha or he was completely honest when he told me about their dealings last month. Perhaps it was because he continuously told me that he wanted me to be his wife without a smile or hint of a joke in his voice. I really didn't know what it was, but this man had me wide open like a 15-year-old girl experiencing love for the very first time.

I wasn't sure how much longer he was going to be at the office today, but I wanted to head back home to Greensboro after we had lunch. I was even planning to take Zaria with me, as long as he didn't mind. My mother and sisters would go crazy over how cute she was, plus I was sure Micah's parents wanted to spend time with her. I already had a full schedule planned solely for the two of us.

As I walked hand in hand into the downtown office building with Zaria, she looked up at me and said, "You're so pretty, Risa."

"Aw, thank you, Zari. You're so pretty too, sweet girl!" I cooed, smiling back at her.

"You my daddy's girlfriend?" she asked.

"Yes, baby. I'm Daddy's girlfriend."

This was Zaria's tenth time asking me that question today, but I didn't mind repeating myself. I wanted her to get it clear in her cute little head just in case her mama had any questions when she went back home. As we continued to walk hand in hand, my eyes were still down on her sweet little face when I accidentally bumped into someone.

"Oh, excuse me," I said, looking up from Zaria.

"Risa!" he said.

When my eyes landed on Timo, Zo's brother, I let out a loud gasp and instantly grew nervous. "Ex . . . excuse me, Timo," I stuttered, squeezing Zaria's hand a little tighter, attempting to move out of his way and continue to Micah's office.

With a firm grip on my arm, he softly yanked me back, causing me to let out a gasp. The last thing I wanted was to scare Zaria or put her in harm's way. I instantly calmed myself down and held back the fearful tears that were threatening to fall. Timo had always been nice to me, but my own guilt of leaving Zo's lifeless body on the floor took over my nerves, and I felt certain that he could read me.

"I'm surprised you didn't attend Zo's funeral. My mother was looking for you," he said.

"Zo and I broke up before he died, Timo," I responded, still trembling in fear.

"So what? That means you don't show up to the funeral of your childhood sweetheart? A nigga you been dealing with for years? Shit don't sound right to me, Risa," he questioned with his eyebrows scrunched.

"And you also know that nigga beat on me for years, so let's not even go there, Timo," I snapped, covering Zaria's ears. I realized that Zo was dead and Timo was probably still hurting over it, but I wasn't going to act like Zo was a saint just because he had suddenly gotten shot and killed. Truth be told, he probably got exactly what he deserved.

"You right. My bad, shawty. Do you know anybody he had beef with lately? While I was away? Anybody who could have done this?" he questioned sincerely.

"I have no idea, bro. You already know he was into a lot of shit, but I was still surprised to see . . . hear that he was killed," I said, almost letting out that I'd seen Zo's lifeless body probably moments after he was murdered.

"Hmmm," Timo said, looking me over suspiciously as if he was contemplating something. "Well, let me know if you need anything. Anything at all. You've always been like a little sister to me, so if there's anything you need, I got you," he told me before giving me a tight hug and walking away.

After taking a sigh of relief, I took Zaria by the hand and quickly scurried to the elevator to head to Micah's office. I could no longer hold back the tears due to the wave of guilt I felt, but I kept them silent and quickly thumbed them away before they could even fall. When we reached the office, there was an attractive lady sitting out front in the reception area.

"May I help you?" she asked me before her eyes immediately traveled down to look at Zaria. "Oh, hey, Zari. How are you?" she asked, kneeling to pinch her chubby cheeks.

"Hi, I'm Micah's girlfriend, Risa. Is he in?" I asked, already knowing the answer.

"Let me call him up," she said. She stood and walked behind her desk to dial his line. "Mr. Borrego, you have someone here to see you. She's here with Zaria," she said as if I just hadn't told her who I was. She was giving me a weird vibe, but I let her make it because I didn't like drama.

"He'll be right up."

Moments later, Micah walked to the front of the office suite and greeted me with a peck on my lips before picking Zaria up into his arms. "How's Daddy's baby?" he asked, kissing her cheek.

"A man grabbed Risa downstairs," she said, snitching on me.

"What man?" he asked with his brows scrunched together, looking at me with his head cocked to the side.

"Just someone I bumped into by accident," I lied.

Before making our way back to his office, I notice his assistant giving me a nasty look. When I turned to face her, letting it be known that I saw how she was eyeing me, she quickly displayed a phony smile. Something about her just wasn't sitting right with me, so I made a mental note to mention it to Micah later.

After going into his office, I sat on the leather sofa with Zaria in my lap while he closed out something on his computer and gathered up some of his paperwork. I couldn't help but admire this fine dark chocolate man who was officially all mine. He was business casual in simple tan Ralph Lauren slacks and a white Ralph Lauren button-up dress shirt with brown leather Pradas on his feet. He had his sleeves rolled halfway up, showing hints of his tattoos and looking as if he'd been working hard all morning long. Even at the office, he still wore his diamond-encrusted watch, just without earrings, which was sexy as hell.

"Hey, bae, I want to head back to Greensboro after lunch," I said, looking around his office and making a mental note to get a picture of us to put on his desk.

"You leaving me already, woman?" he asked in his sexy, deep, raspy baritone voice.

"Well, I wanted to take Zaria to my house so my mom and sisters can meet her. Then I wanted to take her to your parents' house."

"You got it all planned out I see. Where does that leave me?"

"Um, driving back to Greensboro this evening." I smiled with a shrug.

He let out a deep laugh and shook his head. "Anything for you, sweetheart."

During lunch at the Olive Garden, I mentioned to Micah how his assistant was low-key mean mugging me. He brushed it off and told me not to pay her ass no mind and that he would mention something to her about it later. I ordered the shrimp primavera, and Zaria had a grilled cheese and fries while Micah went for his favorite, classic meat lasagna. After about an hour and a half of good conversation and playing with Zaria, we went on our way to Greensboro, leaving Micah behind.

"Hey, Ma," I yelled excitedly as I entered my house with Zaria.

"Hey, ladybug. And who do we have here? What is your name, pretty girl?" my mama asked, walking out from the kitchen and smiling down at Zaria.

"Zaria," she softly replied.

"Oh, yes, Micah's daughter. She is beautiful, Risa," my mother said with a smile.

After grabbing us a few of my mother's home-made cookies out of the kitchen, I took Zaria upstairs to check out my sisters. When I got to Raquel's room, I saw Raina laid across the foot of the bed while Raquel sat propped up against a pillow by the headboard. With a tan towel laid underneath her feet, she painted her toenails a soft shade of pink while slightly bopping her head to the music coming from her earbuds.

"Hey, y'all. Look at this little visitor we have," I sang, making our entrance.

They both turned to look our way, and immediately Raina rushed over to see her while Raquel wobbled on the heels of her feet, trying not to let her toes hit the floor.

"Awww," they cooed.

"Oh, my gosh, Risa, she looks just like Micah. She even has a teeny beauty mark under her eye," Raquel said.

"She's so pretty. And look at all this pretty, curly hair," Raina chimed in softly, pulling at Zaria's curls.

"I know," I cooed, swiping the side of my finger gently across Zaria's chubby cheek.

Raina and Raquel made their way back onto the bed as I grabbed the remote to cut *Doc McStuffins* on for my baby.

"Tell us what happened with the baby mama last night," Raquel said. Like always, she wanted the tea because she didn't have a life of her own.

"I don't think he told her I was coming, so I could tell she was caught off guard. She pretty much went ham on him."

"Why?" Raina asked.

"'Cause she still has feelings for him, I guess. I mean, to be honest, I don't blame her," I said, smiling to myself about the way Micah put it on me last night.

"Let me find out . . ." Raquel said, catching on to my thoughts.

"How did he introduce you?" Raina questioned.

"As his girlfriend. But apparently he went to Florida last month sometime and let her give him head. She thought that meant something, so of course she was pissed."

"He told you that?" Raquel asked.

"No, her salty ass did, but I put my foot down and let him know that if we are going to be official, he needs to be faithful. But enough about me and my man," I gloated with a big smile. "Where is Romi?"

"In her room like always these days," Raina said with a sigh.

"Let me go check on her," I said.

I walked down the hall and knocked on Romi's door. When she didn't answer, I turned the knob to find that her door was locked. I knocked again but this time harder.

"Romi, open up the door!"

After a few seconds of silence, I could hear her feet shuffling toward the door. Once the door opened, she stood before me with her black wiry hair all over her head. Her face was bare and sad, as hints of green glared back at me through her red, puffy eyes. Wearing nothing but a short, dingy T-shirt with "Greene County High" faded on the front and powder blue period panties, I watched as she turned back around, trudging, and climbed back into bed. The girl before my eyes was no longer the confident, damn near conceited beauty I had grown up with. My sister was hurting bad, and I hated to see her like this.

As I walked over to her bedside, I noticed the blinds were tightly shut and there were small piles of clothes scattered across the floor. I sat down on the edge of her bed, her back facing me, and gently began to rub her frizzy, unkempt hair. The only sound in the room was the ticking of the large, round clock that hung on her wall.

"What's going on, sis? How are you feeling, mama?" I asked.

There was no response, so I rubbed her some more, allowing my fingers to gently massage her scalp in hopes that it would soothe her.

"I've got Micah's little girl, Zaria, here with me. She's so pretty, Romi. I want you to meet her," I said, hoping for any kind of response, but there was nothing. I sighed and kissed the only part of her forehead that was exposed from the comforter being pulled high over her face.

"Look, Ro, I know you're in a sad place right now, and I get it, I do. But you gotta pull yourself out it. For the baby's sake, at least. Do you want me to call Dre?" I asked.

"No!" she shouted quickly, sitting upright in her bed.

"What's going on, Ro? Talk to me," I said, staring into her sad eyes.

"The only reason I didn't get an abortion is because I'm praying it's Dre's baby. It's my only hope for us," she cried in desperation.

"So you don't want the baby? You just want Dre?" I asked, trying to clarify and also allow her to hear how crazy she sounded.

"I don't know, Risa. I just love him, and I don't know why. I've tried everything to get him out of my system and I just . . . I can't," she choked with tears welling her eyes.

"I get it, but you have to put this baby first," I said, putting my hand up to her growing belly. She was only four months, but her belly had already begun to protrude.

"I know I need to do better, but every time I think of him being so disgusted with me, I start to cry and get depressed all over again. I hate my fucking life right now."

"Well, what's done is done. If he can't get over it, then that's on him, and if he wants to miss out on this pregnancy with you, then that's on him too," I said as she nodded.

I thumbed away the tears threatening to fall down her face, and then I gave her a tight hug. "Come on and get dressed. We're going over to Mr. and Mrs. Borrego's house. I gotta take Zari."

"What if he's there?" she asked, pulling her knees up to her chest.

"So what! That's his problem, not yours," I told her, pointing my finger to her chest for emphasis. "Now get yourself cleaned up, and we'll be waiting for you downstairs."

Chapter 22

Romi

After taking a much-needed shower, leaving my hair wet and face bare, I slipped on a light pink sundress that slightly revealed my new baby bump. After adding some Carmex to my naturally pink lips, I put a diamond stud in each ear before making my way downstairs. Immediately recognizing the sweet smell of vanilla and brown sugar from mama's homemade cookies, I entered the kitchen. Mama had Zaria sitting on the kitchen counter, drinking a cup of milk. They turned back to look at me when I entered.

"Aw, she's beautiful," I cooed as I admired Zaria.

"I'm glad to see you're up and about," Mama said to me, still watching Zaria to make sure she didn't spill her milk.

"Just riding over with Risa to take Zaria to Mr. and Mrs. Borrego's house."

"Do they know?" she asked low.

"I don't know. I'm sure they do, but I haven't said anything to them."

"Are you sure that you're ready to go over there?" she inquired, finally facing me with concerned eyes.

Although I knew she was pissed with Charles, my mother was even more disappointed in me. First it was with me not going to college, and now this. My sisters always thought our mother favored me the most, but with that came a lot of expectations and a lot of pressure. I was her twin physically with the same green eyes, long black hair, and pale complexion. My natural video-vixen body matched hers exactly at the age of 21. But the truth was, she always wanted to live vicariously through me because she was just a stay-at-home mom with a bachelor's degree in hospitality. She had big dreams of running her own restaurant one day, but it never happened for her. Now that I was here, in her physical form, she wanted me to be all that she couldn't.

"You ready, Ro?" Risa called out to me with Raina and Raquel trailing in the kitchen behind her.

Mama kissed Zaria on the cheek before passing her on to Risa as we all headed out the front door. I could hear light sounds of thunder in the distance as the sky began to gray. The faint smell of rain approaching swirled in the warm summer air as we piled into Risa's car. I could tell that there was a storm brewing.

Sitting in the front passenger's seat, I stared out of the window while hearing the faint sounds of chatter and laughter. The soft music on the radio faded into the background of my thoughts. The whole ride there, I kept wondering, what would happen if his mama decided to kick me out of the house? What if he was there?

As we entered through the large iron gate and drove up the circular driveway to their home, I released the breath that I had been holding in for the past ten minutes. On and off, of course. My eyes freely roamed to search for Dre's car. Emotions of both relief and disappointment washed over me when the realization hit that he wasn't there. While my sisters and Zaria had already made their way outside of the car, I remained seated, taking a few last-minute deep breaths in hopes of getting my nerves under control.

"Beautiful!" Damien called out, grinning wide as he opened the door for us. His facial features looked exactly like Micha's other than his complexion being a shade lighter and no beauty mark under his eye. He greeted only Raina at first before his eyes quickly fell on Zaria.

"Ay, com'ere, Unc's li'l baby," he said, reaching out for her and kissing her on the forehead.

Raina stood on her tippy toes to give him a simple peck on the lips, which he accepted before kissing her again on the neck. I only mushed him in the head and rolled my eyes before we all walked past him, making our way through their enormous house and into the kitchen.

"Mama! Ay, Mama!" he hollered out.

"Boy, stop yelling in my house!" she said before her eyes lit up at the sight of Zaria in his arms. "There goes GiGi's sweet pea," she cooed, taking her in her arms for a hug.

Mrs. Calisa was beautiful as always with her flawless dark skin glowing and her dreads pulled up in a high bun. She had a small beauty mark under her eye that added to her good looks.

"Hey, Ma," Risa greeted her before giving her a hug and a kiss on the cheek, then Raina, then Raquel, and lastly me.

"Finally showing your face over here, huh?" she asked knowingly with a smirk.

"Yes, ma'am," I replied with my head hung low.

She gently lifted my chin, forcing my eyes to look at her. "It's okay. You're only human, Romi. My son will be all right, and so will you. We've got us a little one on the way. I don't know about y'all, but I'm exciittedd!" she sang as she looked around the room for everyone else's reaction.

"I . . . I'm not sure if it's his, Ms. Calisa. I'm so embarrassed," I whispered, immediately feeling myself tear up.

"Well, it may not be his, but it'll still be my little grandbaby, so it's okay. Now stop all that damn crying," she fussed.

I nodded and wiped my wet face with my hands. I still felt ashamed that I didn't know who the father of my unborn child was. *Dre or Mr. Charles?*

"Where is Dre at anyway?" Risa asked, making my eyes grow wide, followed by a hard roll.

"I don't know. He and Melo are out and about somewhere. Where's my eldest son? I thought he was coming too," she said.

"He'll be here later, Ma. What are you cooking?" Risa asked, peeking in Ms. Calisa's pots on the stove and allowing the Italian aromas to escape.

"Get out! Get outta my damn pots, Risa," she fussed, smacking at Risa's hands. We all just laughed because that was Risa. She did that same shit to Mama.

"You gonna do us like that, Ma? You not gon' feed us?" Risa asked, pouting with her bottom lip poked out.

"I gotta put the lasagna together and put it in the oven. Salad, corn, and garlic breadsticks. Y'all already know you can eat here," she said.

I glanced over to Raina and Dame, who were off in the corner by themselves. She was seated in his lap while he playfully twirled her hair with his fingers, pecking her lips every so often.

"Ugh!" I quietly sighed to myself. I was so jealous of their young, budding love, but I was happy to see Baby Girl experience it for the first time. If any of us deserved a perfect love and a happily ever after, it was her.

Suddenly, the sound of the front door chiming followed by recognizable voices could be heard throughout the house. It was definitely Dre and Melo. Locking eyes with Risa, I braced myself to see the man I loved for the first time in months. Quickly, I was trying to remember all the things I needed to say to him in hopes that he'd give us another try. When I looked at his mother, who was staring off and awaiting their entrance, I noticed her eyes grow wide, which caused me to turn around in my seat.

There he stood with his deep brown skin, thick black shiny eyebrows, and full lips that were turned up into a scowl as soon as his eyes landed on me. It was the ugliest face I'd ever seen him wear as he draped his arm over a pretty, petite brown-skinned girl. Wild, naturally spiraled hair the color of cinnamon fell just above her shoulders. She had a small, perfect mouth and a nose she had pierced with a small silver stud. She was undeniably pretty. She had tattoos displayed on each arm, which I could see thanks to the black tank top she wore. Several earrings stacked all the way up to the top of her cartilage. She gave off a biker chick vibe with her black destroyed jeans and combat boots in the summer, but still, she was very much a pretty girl.

"What up, y'all?" Melo asked in a low, unemotional voice, breaking the awkward silence that had fallen upon the room. He immediately walked over to Raquel and gave her a lustful stare while she rolled her eyes in response.

"Who do we have here, Dre?" Mrs. Calisa asked with confusion on her face.

"Ma, this is my girlfriend, Brandi. Brandi, this is my mother, Calisa," he said with his cold eyes remaining on me.

"Girlfriend?" she quizzed, bringing her eyebrows together as she reached her hand out to greet this Brandi girl.

"This is Beautiful, I mean, my baby, Raina," Dame interrupted, pointing at Baby Girl, who just waved with a half smile. "That's my oldest brother's girl, Risa, right there. And this Melo's girl, Raquel," he finished with a laugh.

Raquel looked at him with her nose scrunched up, and she rolled her hazel eyes. "Nigga wishes I were his girl," she mumbled under her breath before flipping her long hair over her shoulders, not even bothering to acknowledge Dre's girl.

I had to admit that my little sister was a bit of a meanie as I chuckled inwardly to myself.

"And who are you?" Brandi politely asked, looking at me.

I stood up and smoothed down the front of my dress to expose my little pregnancy bump, and I walked directly over to her. Dre's cold eyes grew wider with every step I took toward them.

"Hi, I'm Romi, and these are all my sisters," I said, extending my hand for her to shake.

She shook my hand and smiled at me. "Wow, sisters. I wish I had a sibling," she said, oblivious to the situation. "How far along are you?" she asked.

"Four months," I answered as I walked back to my seat.

"When do you find out if it's a boy or a girl?"

"On my next visit. That's when I'll be seventeen weeks," I explained.

"Do you want a boy or a girl?" she asked, making her way into the kitchen to sit right next to me and still having no clue who I really was.

"It doesn't matter to me. I just want a healthy baby."

"Well, I know you want your baby to have those pretty green eyes of yours. Personally, I want one boy and one girl," she said, grinning back at Dre. I just looked back at him with my lips twisted to the side. *Really, nigga?*

"How long have you and Dre been dating?" I pried, noticing from my peripheral vision that Mrs. Calisa gave me a scolding look.

"About a month or so," she started to say when Dre came over and roughly grabbed me by the arm.

"Let me holla at you for a minute," he said, still bearing that mean and hard expression on his face. His eyes were shooting not daggers but bullets directly into me as he pulled me into the hallway.

"Fuck is you doing over here, shawty? Didn't I tell you I don't wanna see yo' ass 'til we get them DNA results?" he spat.

"Look, I just rode over with Risa to bring Zaria over. I didn't think you were even going to be here, Dre," I said, somewhat lying. I felt my attitude surfacing as my arms began to fold over my chest.

"Don't come over here no more, shawty. I got a girl now, and things are going good," he stated before I interrupted, not letting him finish.

"Does she know about us? About this baby?" I asked, pointing to my belly for emphasis.

"No, and she won't know until I know. So keep all that drama to yo'self," he spat, running his hand over the waves in his hair and down onto his face out of frustration.

"What if this baby is yours? You don't want me anymore because of something that happened while weren't even together?" I quizzed.

He sighed while shaking his head. He was unable to respond, let alone look at me. Moments of silence fell between us until I could no longer hold in what was on my heart.

"Dre, I love you," I whispered, looking at him for a response or anything that said he felt the same about me, yet there was nothing.

"I can't do this with you, Ro. Just let me know if it's mine," he said, slowly backing away from me.

I could feel the tears starting to burn, but I refused to let them fall in front of him again, so I quickly walked away. When I entered the kitchen, I could tell that everyone noticed the sadness on my face, even Brandi. Risa walked over to me and gave me a tight embrace.

"I'm okay, y'all," I said, trying to sound strong as I looked around the room to provide clarity. "Mrs. Calisa, I'm going to go, but I'll be sure to call you later. Definitely next week when I find out what I'm having," I said before giving her a tight hug.

"And it was nice meeting you, Brandi," I said, giving her a small smile before exiting the kitchen.

My sisters walked me out of the house before I got in Risa's car and began driving home alone. By this time, it was pouring rain outside with streaks of lightning sporadically scattering across the sky. My sisters had all tried to convince me to stay until the weather subsided, but all I wanted to do was be alone in my own thoughts and feelings. I could hear sounds of Carrie Underwood's "Jesus Take the Wheel" playing on the radio between the loud periodic claps of thunder. Risa low-key stayed listening to the country music radio station, but right now this song was exactly what I needed to hear. I sang along as tears fell abundantly down my face.

I turned the radio up and began to sing even louder, hoping that all my heartache and pain would just go away. It was crazy how one relationship had taken all of my confidence from me.

Here I was, thinking I was God's gift to all men, when this one man came and shut all that shit down, causing me to feel like I wasn't worthy of anyone anymore.

Suddenly, I could see that there was a red light coming up ahead. When I began to slowly break, the tires hydroplaned. Before I knew it, the car started gliding into the intersection out of my control. By then it was too late, because to my left I could see a big blue truck coming at me full speed. Might have even been a sixteen-wheeler. It was almost as if everything appeared in slow motion or even a dream. I could only close my eyes and wait, bracing myself for what was next to come.

Chapter 23

Dre

I was so pissed that Romi would even show her face over here after I told her I didn't want shit to do with her until we get those DNA results. She just had to come over here, looking beautiful with those damn green eyes and that small protruding belly. If only she knew that I wanted nothing more than to be rubbing and kissing on her, loving on her through this whole pregnancy process, but I just refused to set myself up for heartbreak in the end. She was the only woman who could even do that shit to me: break a nigga's fucking heart.

I moved on and started dating Brandi six weeks prior. I met her at the race track one Saturday, racing motorcycles for money, she wasn't half bad on the bike either. Shit, she almost beat me. I didn't know who I was racing until we crossed that finish line and I was like,

"Yeah, nigga, run me my money!" Shawty took off that helmet. I saw all those pretty curls falling around that sweet baby face of hers, and a nigga was gone. I was still in my feelings over Romi up until I saw Brandi's sweet face. It was like a breath of fresh air or some shit like that. That was six weeks ago, and we'd been inseparable ever since. I was even trying to convince her to transfer to Clark next semester. I'd barely even thought about Romi up until now. That's how much I really liked Brandi.

"Why did you make that girl leave, Dre?" my mama yelled.

"I ain't make her leave," I said dryly, trying to brush it off. I knew I was going to have to tell Brandi what was up sooner or later, but I didn't want to have to do that shit today. Not like this, at least.

"Yes, you did, nigga. She told me what the fuck you said to her," Raquel jumped in.

"Watch the way you talk to my son, chile," my mother snapped, rolling her eyes at Raquel. Mama didn't play that disrespectful shit in her house, especially not when it came to her sons.

"I'm sorry, Ma, but that's my sister, and he's wrong," she responded apologetically to my mother.

"I know he is. That girl loves you and is carrying your child, Dre. Do you know what that is like for a woman? To do that by herself?"

I just shrugged nonchalantly, not wanting to feel any emotion or remorse for Romi in the moment.

"To see the man she loves in here with another woman while carrying your child?" my mother continued, pointing at me for emphasis.

"That baby ain't mine, Ma," I defended myself as Brandi rose from her seat.

"I'm sorry, y'all. I didn't mean to cause any kinda confusion. I didn't know Dre was expecting a child or even in a relationship for that matter," she said low while cutting her dark brown eyes at me.

"We know you didn't," Risa said, going over to her and placing her hand on her shoulder in a comforting manner. That was Risa, always the peacemaker and mature one of the sisters, being the oldest.

"Look, Bran, I'm sorry I ain't tell you. I just didn't want you to worry about something that may not even be a factor. That ho was fucking me and some other nigga at the same time," I tried to explain.

My mother, Risa, Raquel, and Raina all jumped up toward me, fussing over my harsh choice of words.

"Don't be disrespectful, Dre," Ma fussed.

"Really, nigga! You gon' call my sister a ho?" Raquel spat with Melo standing behind her with his hands firmly gripping her arms in an attempt to keep her calm. "Nah, nah, lemme go. You know it wasn't even like that. She was with someone before you came back in her life. The same week, yes, but that doesn't make her a ho. She loves you and hasn't been with anyone since you and she started up again," Raquel said.

"Pshh! Yeah, a'ight!" I countered in disbelief. I just couldn't get the images of Romi having sex with another man out of my head, and for that, she was always going to be ho in my eyes.

I knew it was an immature way to think, but that's how I felt. With any other girl, I might have felt differently about the situation, but not Romi. Romi was my heart, and to know that she was giving away what I felt was mine and possibly having a baby by another nigga hurt me to the core.

"Look, you have a lot of things going on in your life that I didn't know about," Brandi said with her hand held up to my chest for a soft pat. "Just call me when you find out. Okay?" she spoke softly.

I just sighed and put my hand up to my forehead out of frustration before I realized she was walking away. "Brandi, wait!" I yelled, following her as she began to walk toward the front door.

She turned around, pushing her wild spirals out of her hurt face. "What do you want, Dre?" she asked with her arms crossed over her chest.

"Hear me out. I'm falling hard for you, and I don't want to lose you," I pleaded, pulling her chin up to look her in the eyes. "Is it that you can't deal with me having a child by someone else?" I asked.

"No, that's not it at all. I can deal with a child who was before me, but I can't deal with my man being in love with someone else," she retorted before pushing the curls out of her face.

"I'm not in love with Romi. I'm falling for you, and that's my word, shawty," I said, trying to convince both her and myself.

"I don't know, Dre. It feels like . . . almost like you hate her."

"Okay, so maybe I do. So what?" I asked with a shrug.

"You don't get it. Love and hate. That's the same emotion, Dre. You're in love with her."

"Huh?" I retorted, squinting my eyes and snapping my head back in complete and utter confusion.

"Call me when you figure it out, Dre," she said.

As soon as shawty turned to walk out the door, we immediately heard yelling and screaming from in the kitchen. I ran back in with Brandi trailing closely behind me, trying to figure out what all the commotion was about. My mother and the girls all had tears running down their frantic faces. Their expressions were nothing short of sadness, panic, and pure shock rolled into one.

"Ma, what's wrong?" I asked, feeling that queasy feeling in the pit of my stomach. You know, the feeling you get when you know you're about to receive the worst news that could ever be delivered.

"Ernie just called," she said, sniffing back the water from her nose. "Romi's been in a terrible accident, Dre. She's at St. Josephine's, and they said it's bad. Had to pry her body out of a flipped-over car kinda bad," she said with another sniff.

I just stood there frozen and in disbelief of it all. She was just here less than thirty minutes ago, and now they were telling me that she was in the hospital, so badly fucked up to the point that I may never see her again? May never even know my unborn child?

"Come on, y'all, we gotta go!" Mama panicked.

Brandi softly rubbed my back while I stood there frozen in time, taking it all in. She quietly said, "Let's go, bae."

On our way outside to the cars, I could hear Risa on the phone with Micah, telling him what happened and to meet us at the hospital, while Damien was consoling Raina. He was stroking her long, pretty hair and assuring her that everything would be all right.

The whole ride to the hospital I couldn't say shit. The tight knot in my throat wouldn't subside, and my hands were mildly trembling with fear and uncertainty. All I kept thinking was, *it's all my fault*. Brandi held my hand on the middle console of the car, occasionally rubbing her thumb across the top in a small attempt to somewhat comfort me. As she told me that everything would be all right, I couldn't help but feel guilty. Knowing it was me who made her leave in the bad storm with her pregnant emotions all over the place was haunting me. If she didn't make it or if the baby didn't make it, I already knew it was on me.

My mother had been on the phone with Ms. Ernie the entire way to the hospital, so when we got there, we all went straight to the waiting room. As we entered, I could see lavender vinyl chairs with square wooden arms neatly lining all four walls, off-white tile floors, and a large flat-screen TV that hung in the crook of the room. There was only one other family with us in the waiting room.

Mr. Brimmage was holding Ms. Ernie in his arms as she sobbed, slowly rocking her back and forth in one of the corner seats of the room. My mother immediately went over to hold her too, as they had gotten very close over the past few months, talking on the phone a few nights a week, shopping at the mall together, and having lunch dates here and there. For some reason, they both wanted us all to be one big, happy family.

"What are they saying, Daddy?" Risa asked, kneeling in front of her parents.

"We don't know anything yet. We just have to wait. And we have to pray," he said in a deep, solemn voice, trying to sound strong for his family.

Just as we all stood and began holding hands in prayer, Micah rushed in and immediately went over to comfort Risa, who was holding Zaria in her arms. He gave Risa a tight hug before running his hand down her ponytail and kissing her on the forehead. Moments later, Romi's best friend, Sherry, walked in and quickly held hands with Raquel after realizing that we were about to pray.

"Dear Heavenly Father, we come to you in the name of Jesus to watch over my li'l girl, Romi Renee Brimmage, and her unborn child. Let them know that they are loved and wanted by many, dear Lord. We ask that you heal her in her time of need. Bless the hands of the men and women in there working on her as we speak so that we can keep her here with us, if it is in your will, dear Lord. In Jesus' name. Amen!" Mr. Brimmage finished.

"Amen!" everyone said in unison with closed eyes and bowed heads. Not a dry face was in the room, other than Melo's, whose face wore a somber expression.

Another forty-five minutes or so had passed when the doctor finally came out to speak to us. "Family of Romi Brimmage?" he called out, looking around the room.

"We're her family," Mr. Brimmage said, standing to adjust his pants around his waist.

"Well, Ms. Brimmage sustained several injuries to her head during the collision, both contusions and a severe concussion. She also has a broken collarbone in addition to her left arm being broken in two places."

"Is she alive, Doc?" I asked impatiently.

"Romi is in a coma from what we believe to be caused by the traumatic brain injuries she suffered. We don't know when or if she will come out of it."

"And the baby?" I asked weakly, hearing the crackling sound of my own voice being on the verge of tears.

"Well, that's the good news I have for you all. The baby boy is just fine."

"Boy?" Raina asked as my eyes instantly lit up.

"Yes, Ms. Brimmage is carrying a boy. Looks as though she's right around sixteen to seventeen weeks, and he is doing perfectly fine. The longer Romi is in her coma resting with strong vitals, the longer the baby will have a chance to continue growing and the better his chance of survival. That is, unless she wakes up and makes a full recovery, in which case both she and baby will most likely be fine."

"Do you know what the effects of her brain injuries will be if she does wake up?" Mrs. Ernie asked.

"We won't know until she wakes up, ma'am. I'm sorry," he said.

"Can we go back and see our daughter?" Mr. Brimmage asked.

"Yes, we will allow two at a time, but visiting hours are over in an hour. And just a warning to

you, she won't be responsive. Just make sure
to keep calm in the room, for her and the baby's
sakes," he offered.

After Mr. and Mrs. Brimmage came out of
Romi's room, it was my and my mother's turn
to go in. I couldn't even take two steps inside
of the room without breaking down crying like
a bitch. I shook my head in disbelief as I looked
her over. Seeing all the tubes and wires running
throughout her helpless body and hearing that
constant beeping sound in the background did
something to me. While her head was completely wrapped in bandages, her swollen purple
eyes were fully shut, and her face was cut up
from what I assumed was the shattering of the
windshield. Those were the images that made
me feel weak all over as I walked over to the side
of her bed. I softly grabbed her hand while my
mother remained on the other side.

"You gon' pull through this, baby. You hear
me?" my mother softly spoke to her. "Are you
going to say something to her, Dre?" she asked.

I just stood there, still speechless, not knowing
what to say or do at the moment. I felt nothing
but vulnerability and guilt because I knew that I
was the one who put her there.

"I'm so sorry, Romi," I whispered before taking
a deep breath. "I never meant for anything like

this to happen to you, shawty. Or the baby. Just wanted you to hurt the way I've been hurting. That's all. Last words you said to me was that"—I paused, swallowing with a deep breath—"you loved me, and . . . and shit, you already know I love you too. I do. Ever since the first day I saw your pretty ass at the mall, I loved you. If I could trade places with you right now, I swear I would, Ro. Just hold on, baby, and I promise you I'll make shit right," I cried as my mother made her way around the bed just to hold me.

The next morning, around 4:00 a.m., when we finally made it back home from the hospital, Brandi started to leave on her bike, but I needed her now more than ever.

"Hold up! Brandi, hold up," I yelled, running over to her and grabbing the motorcycle helmet from her hands. "Can you stay with me? Just for tonight?" I asked with pleading eyes.

She closed her eyes briefly, deep in thought, before letting out what seemed to be a bottomless breath. "If you need me, I'll stay, Dre," she said softly with that sweet, innocent face of hers. Her soft brown curls were wildly strewn about from the awful night we'd had.

When Brandi and I made our way upstairs, I could see Risa walking into Micah's room before closing the door. She just shook her head in what I took to be her disgust and disapproval of me. I completely understood, especially with her seeing Brandi following me. Raina and Raquel went back home with Mr. and Mrs. Brimmage, but Risa had decided to stay over with Micah. Those two were inseparable and already married in my eyes.

After stripping down to just my boxers, I quickly got in the bed. I let my head fall against the headboard and stared up at the ceiling while wondering to myself how I'd let all this happen. Brandi slowly crawled up next to me. She kneeled beside me in just her black bra and panties before gently stroking my face.

"How can I help, Dre?" she asked softly.

"Nothing you can do, baby. Just stay here with me. I don't want to be alone tonight."

Brandi gently kissed my lips and threw her thin brown leg across to straddle me. I didn't have any intentions of having sex this morning. In fact, I didn't even think my mind was in the right space for it. But when I felt her soft lips against my neck and her soft, tiny hands on my chest, I closed my eyes. I allowed my hands to caress her soft body, and I just lost myself, my guilt, and everything in her.

That was one thing I really liked about Brandi. She always knew what I needed and how to comfort me. It was crazy, because when she slid her body down onto mine, intensively staring into my eyes, the feeling was nothing short of soothing. There was nothing overly sexual about that moment in the least. It was her way of consoling me when she glided herself up and down me with ease. Our eyes stayed connected until I reached my peak and released every emotion I had inside of her. I knew that I still loved Romi, but I couldn't deny that I was falling for Brandi too.

Chapter 24

Raina

It had been six long weeks after Romi's car accident, and she was still in the hospital in a coma. However, she was still alive with progressive brain activity, and the baby was still growing and healthy at twenty-three weeks. The doctors were talking about possibly delivering the baby early in another month if Romi wasn't awake by then. We all regularly went by to visit her, and each time, they would allow us to hear the baby's heartbeat. It was the most beautiful sound I'd ever heard, the fast, drumming sound of new life. Even Dre had gotten a sonogram picture that he'd taken back to school with him.

Speaking of school, I rode up to Clark with Raquel and Dame a month prior. It was their freshman year of college, and they were both living on campus. They lived in dorms right across the street from one another, where I'd helped them unpack and set up their rooms. While I talked to Raquel several times a day between calls and text messages, I actually hadn't heard from Damien at all since the day we dropped him off. The first week he was there, I called him nonstop, but he wouldn't answer for me or even return my calls. I'd tried texting, but he'd never respond. Finally, I asked Raquel what he was up to because I hadn't heard from him. She informed me of what I already knew: that he was out and about with other girls between football practice, class, and partying. And to think I actually thought he was serious about me this time around. I had allowed Dame to break my heart for the second time.

Walking to class by myself these days made me miss Damien even more. I had gotten so used to the feel of his strong arm around my shoulders while he carried my books to class. I missed the sound of him calling me beautiful echoing throughout the hallways of our school, and I missed those soft, frequent kisses that he'd plant on my neck throughout the day. However, I would say that ever since we'd been dating, my whole high school life had changed. Every girl wanted to be my friend, and every guy wanted to date me, it seemed. But I hadn't changed. My only focuses remained school and dance . . . and healing this broken heart of mine.

It was early Friday morning before class, and I was in the gym, getting our dance line uniforms together for the big game tonight. Our red and white sequined uniforms were strewn about the bleachers where I carefully tagged each with a girl's name and hung them up neatly one at a time. As I sorted through the clothes rack, I saw Big Rob and Codi coming in and clowning around with a few guys from the football team trailing behind. Codi was the star quarterback this year. He'd come down here from New York over the summer and was already all the hype around school these days among the girls. He was a tall, light-skinned guy with a nice athletic build to him. Had a neat, curly fade with a clean-cut baby face. He was definitely easy on the eyes, but he hadn't said two words to me this school year. However, that was fine with me, because for whatever reason I still couldn't get Dame out of my head.

"Sup, shawty, you're looking sexy today," Big Rob said to me with a wink.

I just looked over at him and gave him a slight smile in acknowledgment. I was used to Big Rob's flirtatious remarks. He had been hitting on me since junior high, and just like I never paid him any mind back then, I wasn't paying him any today, but he knew that. That was just our thing. Big Rob was a tall, heavyset guy with a big gap between his two front teeth. He played defensive tackle for the football team, standing at about six feet two and weighing around 285 pounds. He always sported a big, bushy afro on his head. He was cool peeps, just not my type.

"You gon' finally let me take you out, Raina?" he asked sweetly.

I just shook my head and rolled my eyes a little, still giving him a smile though.

"Fuck that bitch, yo," Codi muttered under his breath.

My eyes instantly grew wide in shock as I was taken aback by his statement. Anyone who knew me and dealt with me in any capacity would know that I was far from a bitch. Even Big Rob shook his head and put his hand up to Codi's chest as if to say, "Nah, not with this one." But that wasn't good enough for me.

I walked over to him myself. With my chin held high, I wore the most disgusted look on my face that I could create in that moment. I stared him right in his dark, slanted brown eyes and cocked my head to the side, just like I'd seen Dame and his brothers do when they wanted to act like thugs, and I said, "No. Fuck you, bitch!"

"Ah, shit!" Big Rob erupted in laughter. "Bruh, Raina doesn't even cuss like that. You got shawty all fucked up right now," he said, still laughing and playfully hitting Codi on his arm.

Codi looked down at my small frame with the slightest malevolent grin forming on his pink mouth. His big, tall body towered over mine with intimidation. He dryly responded, "Yeah, a'ight."

My eyes stayed trained on him as I stared him down, almost daring him to say another derogatory word toward me. Seductively he scanned my body up and down, then slowly licked his lower lip before clasping his hands softly together. He again said, "Yeah, a'ight," before walking away.

About twenty minutes later, as I sat at my desk in the front row for first period, I heard the morning announcements chime through my classroom speakers.

"Good morning, students and staff. In just two weeks, we will have our annual homecoming game against the Hawks, followed by our homecoming dance on Saturday. If you have not purchased your tickets yet, please buy your tickets today at the bookstore. Just ten dollars per person or fifteen dollars for a couple. Also, the results of our 2016 homecoming court are finally in. Representing the freshman court, I am pleased to announce Melody Chambers and Aaron Cooper. For the sophomore court, I am pleased to announce KiKi Harper and Darius Williams. For our junior court, Aya Winters and Bernard Meeks. And now for the moment you've all been waiting for, our 2016 senior homecoming court will be Dutchess Perry, Ronald Hawkins, Kelli Brooks, Vince Daniel, Raina Brimmage, and Codi Taylor. Who will be our next king and queen?"

The entire class began to scream and congratulate me as I put my head down on my desk in disbelief. My face was completely buried in my arms, and my forehead was fully pressed against the cool surface. I was thinking about how I was going to have to be around this stupid Codi boy once again and how all of this led back to one person: Dame. Had it not been for him dating me at the end of last school year, no one would even know my name, let alone nominate me for homecoming queen.

After a long day of going from class to class and having people constantly stop me to congratulate me on my homecoming nomination or ask me questions like, "What are you going to wear?" "Are you nervous?" "Who's your date gonna be?" and so on, school was finally over. Walking out of the locker room in my red sequined unitard with a cutout in the back, I strutted my way into the gym. I made my way in there with the band and the rest of the girls for a quick rehearsal just before the buses arrived to take us all to the stadium.

When I entered, several band members were already sitting up in the bleachers with their drums and other instruments in hand. Suddenly, I could hear the sounds of Young Jeezy's "And Then What" starting to play. It was a song that Mr. Press, the band director, forbade them to play at the games, even though the band had it down pat.

They were murdering the beat with their drums while those in the gym were instantly up on their feet dancing. As they rapped the lyrics to the song, I began to high step sexily to the rhythm of the beat, making my way to the center of the gym. I flipped my hair from side to side majorette style before the beat dropped again. Everyone in the gym was on their feet, rapping in unison, "'Turn around, bend over, bring it back, bring it back.'"

I dropped my hips low and bent over, flipping my long hair back just before slowly bucking like my life depended on it. The small crowd cheered in excitement as I rocked my hips hard to the music. I stood up and began to prance a little more to the sound as my girls joined in unity. We all danced like we were one sexy mo-

tion, swaying to the beat of several drums. Out
the corner of my eye, I could see Big Rob standing by the door in his football uniform with his
mouth hung open, watching me dance with his
friend Codi right beside him. Both sets of eyes
were totally glued to me.

After the music concluded and the small
crowd had calmed, I immediately went back
to my shy, introverted self. It was almost like
someone cutting my switch back on, or maybe
it was cut off, I didn't know which. Dancing was
the only thing that allowed me to let go of all my
insecurities and feel free. It was the one place I
didn't care what people thought of me, because
I was in my own world.

As I gathered my things and started for the
bus, I could hear Codi yell out to me, "Raina!
Raina, hol' up, ma," he said.

I looked back, already annoyed by the sound
of his voice. My face was scrunched in a scowl
as he walked toward me in his football uniform.
It was a red and white uniform that was heavily
padded, giving him an even more muscular
appearance as he carried his helmet by his side.
That pretty baby face he had looked back at me
innocently with dark, slanted eyes.

"Can I help you?" I asked with my hands on
my hips. My voice was full of attitude as I stood
outside the bus.

"Look, ma, I apologize for what I called you this morning. A nigga from New York, na mean? I'on know how to act around y'all Southern belles and shit. Gotta teach me, ma," he said with a wink.

He was a little cute, but I still refused to smile. Instead, I just kept my hands on my hips and tapped my foot a little so that he could see I was growing impatient.

"Yo, you forgive me?" he asked, speaking with his hands in a way only a New Yorker could do.

I let out a hard sigh, because although I wanted to maintain this tough exterior, it wasn't like me to hold a grudge. I gave him a small smile, and I do mean a very small smile, before replying, "All right, I forgive you."

I extended my hand for him to shake, but instead, he gently turned it over and placed a soft, simple kiss on the back of it. I couldn't help but blush as I heard all the oohs and aahs coming from the girls on the bus.

"I guess we going to this homecoming dance together?" he asked.

"How do you figure that?" I retorted in confusion.

"Well, you know the king has to go with the queen," he stated matter-of-factly while slowly licking his lower lip and softly clasping his hands together. I was learning quickly that this was just his natural mannerism.

"Oh! I highly doubt I'll be queen, Codi," I said, shocked that he thought I'd actually be the homecoming queen.

"Well, you already a queen in my eyes, ma."

"So first I'm a bitch, and now I'm a queen, huh?" I said, letting out a small, sarcastic laugh.

"I thought you said you forgave me," he said, squinting his eyes curiously and licking his pink lips again. Okay, yes, he was sexy.

"I have. I'm just stating facts. That's all," I quipped with a laugh, holding my hands up in surrender.

"In all seriousness, though, will you go to the dance with me?"

"I don't know, Codi. I'm kinda in a relationship."

"Oh, my bad, ma. I ain't know you had a man. Shit," he said, scratching the top of his head.

"Well, I don't. Well . . . I don't know," I said with a confused chuckle. Shaking my head and covering my face with my hands, I just knew he thought I was crazy.

"Look, let me just get your number, and you can explain it to me a li'l later. You fucking my head up right now for this game, ma," he said with a wink.

"Sorry," I apologized.

We quickly exchanged numbers before going our separate ways. He ascended onto the bus with the rest of the football team, while I joined the band and the cheerleaders on a different bus, heading to the football stadium. That night we beat the Monarchs 24 to 7. Codi threw for 218 yards and had three touchdown passes. The band and I shut down the whole field during halftime. During the moments the game was underway, I sat quietly on the bleachers, thinking about Codi and wondering if what Dame and I had was truly over this time.

After catching a ride home from Keke later that night after the game, I made my way into the house. Still in my uniform, my makeup slightly smudged and hair puffed from sweat and the night's humidity, I heard soft chatter and laughter coming from the kitchen. I dropped my bags in the foyer and slipped off my flats before making my way inside.

"Hey, Ma," I said as both my mama and Ms. Calisa said, "Hey, baby," in unison. I laughed because I did always call Ms. Calisa Ma whenever I was visiting.

That night, right before I fell asleep, I sat up in my bed and cut the lamp on. I rubbed my eyes to adjust to the light and smoothed my hair back, which was in a loose French braid down my back. I grabbed my phone off the nightstand and decided to send Dame a quick text, just one text one last time before I'd agree to go to homecoming with Codi. It was a last, desperate attempt on my part.

Me: I haven't heard from you in over four weeks now, and I guess it's your way of telling me that it's over.

I lay back in my queen-size poster bed, staring up at the ceiling, humming to myself, and playing with my nails for the next fifteen minutes. I was anticipating a reply from Dame, but of course, I received nothing. I sat up to adjust the straps to my pink silk nightgown before deciding to send him one more.

Me: Well, Dame, I hope all is going well for you at school. I truly miss you, and I just want you to be happy. I was asked to go the homecoming dance today by this guy named Codi. IDK, I was going to talk to you about it, I suppose, but since you won't respond, I guess there really is nothing for us to discuss. Oh, and get this, I've actually been nominated for queen this year. Can you believe that? Crazy, right? LOL. Anyways, be happy, Dame, and take care. Love you always, Raina.

I immediately thumbed away a small tear that had formed at the corner of my eye before I cut the lamp off and sent out one last text message.

Me: Codi, or should I say Mr. Homecoming King, it's a date!

Codi: That's what's up, ma. Made my night. Sweet dreams.

Me: Sweet dreams.

Chapter 25

Damien

"Ughh! I'm cuumminn'!" Tina moaned as beads of sweat dripped down onto her face from mine.

Slowly pumping in and out of her, I could feel my nut start to rise when the bright light glowed from my vibrating cell phone on the nightstand. It was the only source of light in my dorm room other than small slits of light from the street seeping in through the cracks of the blinds.

"Keep going! Don't stop!" Tina said, thrusting her hips back up at me to keep me from slowing down.

I grabbed the backs of her knees and lifted them up before going in deeper and faster, still feeling that sensation that I knew was shortly coming. "Aaargh! Fuck!" I groaned, releasing into the condom as my cell phone vibrated again. I rolled off of Tina and instantly grabbed my phone to see who it was. Unlocking the screen and silently reading, I quickly learned who it was.

Beautiful: I haven't heard from you in over four weeks now, and I guess it's your way of telling me that it's over.

I just let my head fall back on the headboard, and I released a heavy sigh, rubbing my hand down my sweaty face out of frustration. I had been wanting to call Raina, but I was too wrapped up in this college life and doing too much dirt. I was ashamed to say that I'd been home twice in the last month and not once did I go see about my girl, which was totally fucked up on my part because of everything that she was going through with Romi still in the hospital. With both me and Raquel away at college, that left her home alone.

"Dame, what's wrong?" Tina asked, sitting up in my makeshift king-size bed. I wasn't about to share a dorm room with another nigga, so I'd pushed the two extra-long twin beds together and made me a king-size.

And yes, that's right, I was still fucking around with Tina. She followed me to Clark, and what could I say other than the pussy was convenient? I'm not going to lie though, I did care for her, but she knew where my heart was. Never once did I lie to her or any other girl for that matter about that.

"It's my girl," I said, tossing my phone back onto the nightstand before heading to the bathroom to clean myself off.

Tina immediately got up out of the bed and was right on my heels. "Your girl?" Tina quizzed, looking confused as if she didn't know about Raina.

"Yeah, nigga! Raina," I snapped, looking back, irritated at just the naked sight of her standing in the bathroom doorway.

"You still thinking about that high school girl?" she questioned, sucking her teeth and slightly rolling her eyes.

"You act like you weren't just in high school a few months ago. Chill out, Tina!" I said, pushing her and making my way back into bed.

Suddenly there was another text message coming across my phone. I picked it up and began reading.

Beautiful: Well, Dame, I hope all is going well for you at school. I truly miss you, and I just want you to be happy. I was asked to go the homecoming dance today by this guy named Codi. IDK, I was going to talk to you about it, I suppose, but since you won't respond, I guess there really is nothing for us to discuss. Oh, and get this, I've actually been nominated for queen this year. Can you believe that? Crazy, right?

LOL. Anyways, be happy, Dame, and take care. Love you always, Raina.

"The fuck? Codi?" I muttered, looking down at my phone in bewilderment.

I was glad that my shawty finally made the homecoming court and all, but I would be damned if she was about to go to a dance with another nigga. It was no secret that I was a selfish nigga, especially when it came to her, but I just couldn't help myself.

Looking down at the glowing screen and rereading her text messages, I thought about how no matter what I did to her, she was still the sweetest person I'd ever met. That was one of the things I loved the most about her. Some people would call her weak, but I found that to be her strength. Everything in this last text was telling me that she was letting me go but she still loved me, that I was free and clear with no hard feelings, only her love.

Nevertheless, shawty had me all the way fucked up if she thought I was going to willingly sit back and allow another nigga to take what I truly felt in my heart to be mine. There was no doubt in my mind that I wanted to be with Raina. I just wasn't ready to be fully committed. I mean, a nigga was only 18 years old. Plus I knew Raina wasn't having sex just yet. I didn't want to be the one to pressure her, but I also wanted to be her first and last.

It was eight days later, on a Saturday morning, after Dre and I came home from Atlanta the night before. We were sitting downstairs in the kitchen with my mother and Brandi, about to eat breakfast. Large plated portions of bacon, sausage, cheese eggs, home fries, and buttermilk biscuits were laid before us when the front door chimed.

"Ma!" I could hear Raquel yell throughout the house before entering the kitchen. Her long, pretty hair was back in a simple French braid while she wore khaki shorts and a white collared shirt. Her outfit was nothing short of a nerdy schoolgirl uniform with the exception of the flip-flops on her feet.

"You know that's ghetto as shit, right?" I asked, looking back at her with a smirk on my face.

"Shut up, Dame!" she said, mushing me in the back of the head before walking over to hug my mother.

Playfully, I jumped at her like I was going to hit her back, and I shook my head at her scaredy-cat self when she flinched.

"Where's Melo at? And why didn't y'all tell me that y'all were coming home this weekend? You know I could've used a ride," she said while shoving a piece of bacon in her mouth.

"He's upstairs, still asleep I think, but why do you care? Don't you hate that nigga?" Dre asked with a yawn and a scratch to his head.

Raquel scrunched her nose at Dre and rolled her hazel eyes. She didn't care to see him these days with Romi still being in the hospital and all, especially not with Brandi by his side.

"Why didn't y'all give that girl a ride?" Ma asked.

I shrugged to respond while Dre cut his eyes at me with a smirk on his face. "Didn't you just get a new whip?" I asked. She just rolled her eyes in response, the usual everyone got from her.

"Well, have you talked to Raina? Is she coming over today?" my mother asked, eyeing me intently.

"Nah, I ain't talked to her, Ma," I replied with a sigh.

"I heard she got nominated for homecoming queen. Isn't that something, Dame?" she boasted.

I let out a small, sarcastic laugh through my nose, thinking about how Raina actually thought she was going to go to some dance with another nigga.

"Yeah, that's why I came home this weekend. To help her get ready and all," Raquel interrupted me just before her eyes landed on Melo, who was walking in the kitchen.

He was yawning and stretching wide with his bare chest, sporting only black basketball shorts, the same as Dre and myself. He sat at the table next to her, just to annoy her, I was sure.

"Ughh!" she whined. I knew she was fronting, though. She was feeling my brother, and it would reveal itself in time.

"Ernie invited me over too. Just to help her get ready and to see her off," my mother said as she began to clean the counters.

"Did she also tell you that she was going to the dance with some fuck nigga named Codi?" I asked harshly, looking my mother in the eyes. She and Micah killed me with their disloyalty. Truth be told, I was the baby of my family in every sense of the word, and I was used to always getting my way. Ever since we started getting close with the Brimmage family, Raina seemed to be taking my position slowly but surely. Although I wanted her to be close to my side of the family, I found myself getting jealous every now and again.

"Don't make me slap the piss out you, boy, using that language in my goddamn house," my mother scolded me, shaking her finger.

"How come you didn't tell me, Ma?"

"Tell you what? I just found out that she had a date, but I honestly don't think it's that serious, Dame."

I just sighed, lying back in my chair with my arms folded across my chest.

"And from what Ernie tells me, you haven't even talked to the girl since you went up to Clark. So even if I did know, even if I did, why on God's green earth would I tell your li'l ass?" she asked, shaking her head at me in disappointment while going back to cover up the food.

"Well, we finna roll over there and shut that shit down anyway," I said, looking over at Dre as he sat on the barstool, playing in that curly mass on top of Brandi's head.

"We? Nigga, who the fuck is *we*?" Melo snapped, looking back at me with a raised eyebrow.

"Pssh! Niggas don't have my back for nothing," I muttered under my breath, shoving a forkful of home fries into my mouth.

"So how are you doing, baby?" my mother asked Raquel, changing the subject.

"Doing good. I'm getting A's in all of my classes so far, and I've been staying clear of boys and partying."

"You better," Melo mumbled.

"Whatever," Raquel retorted.

"Well, good. I went to see Romi yesterday. I'm hoping she wakes up soon, 'cause I . . . I gotta meet my grandbaby," she sadly said.

"Romi's strong, Ma. She's gonna pull through. Just wait, you'll see," Raquel said.

Dre got down from his barstool and gently tugged at Brandi's arm, motioning her to leave the kitchen with him.

"Well, if you can't stand the heat, get the hell up out the kitchen," Raquel muttered softly in sarcasm.

"He's still having a hard time with it all. He feels guilty, Raquel," my mother said in his defense.

"Obviously not, Ma, if he's still kicking it with that Brandi girl."

"Now you know I love Romi like a daughter, but I won't take anything away from Brandi. She's a nice girl and has been very supportive of Dre throughout this whole ordeal."

"Mmmph," Raquel muttered, rolling her eyes.

Later that evening, just before seven o'clock, my brothers and I were all headed over to Raina's house in Micah's black Range. My mother had left a few hours earlier with Raquel while Brandi left shortly after breakfast that morning. As Dre and Melo sat quietly in the back seat, sharing a blunt, Micah drove coolly with the music on low while I rode shotgun. Quietly resting my fist underneath my chin, I stared out the window, deep in thought, merely watching the green highway signs pass us by.

"What's the plan?" Micah asked, cutting the radio off completely and looking over at me.

"I don't know yet," I said low, still staring out the window and thinking.

"Why haven't you called her?"

"I don't know, Micah, damn! Let me think," I snapped.

"Are you really trying to be with her, or are you just pissed about her going with somebody else?" Micah asked, refusing to let up.

"Nigga being selfish as fuck is what it is," Dre said low from the back seat, blowing smoke out of his mouth.

"Nah, nigga, you being selfish. Pass that shit, bruh," Melo said, referring to the blunt.

"I know you not talking about nobody being selfish. You put your baby mama in the hospital while she's carrying your seed. And you're still smashing Brandi."

"That's not being selfish. It was an accident and Brandi is my girl," Dre explained, taking another pull before passing it over to Melo.

"What if Romi comes out of the coma and the baby is yours? Then what?" I asked, turning around in my seat.

"I'll deal with it when it happens. If it happens."

"And we not talking about Dre right now, li'l nigga. We talking about you and how you hurting Baby Girl," Micah said.

"She knows I love her ass, shit," I countered angrily. I felt the frustration of the whole situation take over my mood after realizing for the first time that those three little words had mistakenly escaped my lips. *I love her.*

"Love her? She won't know shit unless you show her, bruh. If you not calling, not texting, or even making a way to see her, then she probably thinks you don't give a fuck about her," Micah enlightened me.

I sat there and sighed at the reality of his words, feeling the contact high slowly take over my mental before I slightly cracked my window for some of the smoke to be emitted.

"I mean, I check in on Baby Girl at least once a week, and she always asks about you," he continued.

"Why you tryin'a make me feel like shit right now, Micah?"

He let out a light chuckle because he knew what he was doing. "I'm not," he said. "I just want you to realize that you got a beautiful girl who really cares for you. She's sweet, smart in school, and damn near perfect if you ask me, but you fucking up. I just don't want you to miss out on your blessing, bruh. That's all I'm saying. Shiidd, you already see how I'm locking down Risa's ass. Ain't no shame in my game either, bruh. At all!" he said, using his hands for emphasis.

"When was the last time you seen Mr. and Mrs. B?" I asked Dre, trying to change the subject once again.

"I usually see them about once a week or so when I come home and visit Ro at the hospital. Why?"

"Just asking. Figured they wouldn't wanna see yo' ugly ass after how you treated Romi and all."

"Stop worrying about Dre and just focus on how you gon' get ol' girl back," Melo said low but sternly as he blew smoke through his nostrils. Melo never really said shit, but the fact that he was weighing in on my situation let me know how much I was really fucking up.

"You still fucking with Tina?" Micah asked.

I sighed and ran my hand down my face before melting back into the leather seat. Micah snorted in response, already knowing the answer to the question.

"I mean, if you still dealing with Tina, then why not just let Raina go?" Dre asked from the back seat.

"That's not going to happen," I snapped, looking down and pulling the hangnail from my finger.

It was a quarter past seven that evening when we finally pulled up to the Brimmage family residence. Night had already taken over the sky as I observed their two-story brick home that appeared to have every light turned on in the house. As I hesitantly walked up the steps, I could hear the faint sounds of conversation and amusement from inside while Al Green's "Love and Happiness" played in the background. Micah was the first one to the door with the three of us trailing behind, smelling like weed and Gucci cologne.

After Micah rang the doorbell twice for good measure, we could hear Risa's voice getting louder as she approached the door.

"Oh, it's just the boys," she hollered back as she opened the door.

She gave Micah a quick peck on the lips, then turned back to walk into the house. However, that must not have been acceptable to him, because he quickly yanked her arm, forcing her to face him again. He pulled her into a tight embrace and tongued her down right there in front of us, letting his hands slide down to her backside for a firm grip. He ended with a hard yet playful slap on her ass before she broke away.

"Micah, stop!" she fussed with a flirty smile, exposing her deep dimples before turning around to lead us into the house.

"Nasty ass," Dre mumbled, shaking his head at Micah's vulgar display of affection. He pushed the back of my head, causing me to clumsily enter the house.

"Nigga, shut up. You just wish you had an ass that fine to grab a hol' of," Micah told Dre as he took off his army fatigue jacket.

"I do. Her name is Brandi, nigga," Dre retorted.

"Ha! Yeah, a'ight. If you would've said Romi, I might've let that one slide 'cause she is fine, but Brandi compared to my baby . . . Nah, bruh," Micah countered with a little chuckle.

"Whateva, nigga," Dre said.

The five of us walked into the back of the house and entered their formal living room, which was lavishly decorated with cream and gold accents. Raquel's baby grand piano was stylishly displayed in the corner. As I stopped in the doorway, I could see Raina posing by the fireplace in a sexy red knee-length dress that clung to her curvy frame. Her long, silky hair hung well past her shoulders in big, loose curls that were outlining her pretty face as she smiled for the pictures. Taking in every inch of her beauty, I silently stood in the entryway until she finally noticed me.

Her light brown eyes grew wide in surprise with a peculiar smile forming on her lips just before she exclaimed, "Dame, what are you doing here?"

arm of the chair on the other side of Melo like I
know her mama ass would.

I...here tried to ask you to your dance," Dame
said with a pink corsage in his hand, reaching
out to hug her.

but nigga did not move, with her red
the to

"I came here for the dance, Dre I... I've been
calling and texting you the whole couple of
weeks. Why are you here?" she argued with her

Chapter 26

Dre

This little nigga had us over at Mr. and Mrs.
B's house looking crazy. Melo and I were high
out of our minds, and Micah was running around
low-key trying to get freaky with Risa right up
under her parents' nose. Meanwhile, Dame stood
there in a three-piece Armani suit, wearing the
dumbest expression on his face.

"Dame, what are you doing here?" Raina repeated as she walked toward him. Her heels
clicked loudly against the hardwood floors with
each stride she took as she hunched her shoulders.

Ready to be fully entertained, I squeezed
right in between Melo and Raquel on the formal
loveseat.

"Uhh! Really, Dre!" Raquel groaned. "You
know I don't fool with you like that," she muttered. She got up and made her way onto the

arm of the chair on the other side of Melo like I knew her mean ass would.

"I'm here to take you to your dance," Dame said with a pink corsage in his hand, reaching out to hug her.

Li'l nigga didn't even coordinate with her red dress.

"I have a date for the dance, Dame. I've been calling and texting you for the past couple of weeks. Why are you here?" she argued with her hands now planted firmly on her hips.

"You ain't about to go to no dance with another nigga. Fuck outta here with that bullshit, Raina."

"Watch your mouth, li'l nigga," Mr. B spat, giving Dame a cold glare.

I couldn't help but snicker. Both Melo and I let out multiple snorts of laughter from being both high and highly entertained.

"You're my girl, Raina. Why would you think it was okay to go to the dance with someone other than me?" Dame questioned, trying to flip the script.

"What?" Raina shrieked in disbelief from the bullshit coming out of Dame's mouth. "Are you serious right now? Raquel told me that you've been out partying, seeing other girls, and—"

"The fuck?" Dame spat, whipping his head in Raquel's direction with his face scrunched up.

"Hol' up! Don't be putting Raquel's name in this shit, bruh," Melo let out as Raquel silently mouthed, "Sorry," to Dame.

I didn't care what Raquel and Melo say, they were both feeling each other.

"Well, she has a date, Dame. You can't expect my daughter to change her plans just because you wouldn't answer the phone for her," Mrs. B scolded, with my mother nodding in agreement. She sat quietly in the single cream chair, taking in the whole scene from the corner of the room.

Ding-dong.

"Mama! That must be him," Raina whined with panic in her voice.

"I got the door," Dame said.

Raina rolled her eyes and turned back to her mother for help.

"Hol' up! Hol' up! Lemme go get me some popcorn for this shit, bruh," I said, getting up from the couch.

"Bring me back some shit too. Anything, 'cause a nigga got the munchies," Melo said with red, swollen eyes while stroking Raquel's long pony-tail in the process just to fuck with her.

She repeatedly swatted his hand away and, of course, rolled her eyes. As I made my way into the kitchen, I saw Risa and Micah sneaking into the hall bathroom together. She was giggling, with him playfully smacking her on the ass just before they entered. I just shook my head because too much was happening at once.

"Ay! Ay! Mrs. Ernie, where all the snacks and shi . . . and stuff at?" I yelled out before opening their pantry door.

I discovered all the Cheetos, Doritos, Rold Gold, and Chips Ahoy that any high nigga would want at a time like this. I grabbed every last bag of them in my arms after popping two chocolate chip cookies in my mouth. As I headed back toward the living room where everyone was, I passed by Dame, who was now face-to-face with this tall, light-skinned nigga dressed in all-black Versace. He carried a red corsage in a clear box and two individually wrapped bouquets of red roses in his hands. Nigga was on his shit.

"Yo, you fucking up, bruh. Nigga came color coordinated and all. Roses in his hand and shit," I said, shaking my head and laughing with a mouthful of cookies.

"Fuck you, Dre," Dame muttered behind me as I made my way back into the formal living room.

Raquel was back in my seat with her legs crossed when I passed Melo the bag of Doritos. Nonverbally with a nod and my lips twisted up in a scowl, I let her know that she needed to move.

"Excuse you?" she said, rolling her hazel eyes.

"C'mere, bae," Melo said, motioning for her to sit in his lap.

After scrunching her face, she got up and sat in a single chair across the room from us. I proceeded to plop back down in my rightful seat and instantly tore into the bag of Cheetos.

"Greedy ass," she mumbled under her breath and rolled her eyes again.

"Yo, Raina, who is this, ma?" The tall, light-skinned nigga asked, walking into the living room with his thumb pointed back toward Dame.

"This is, um, my friend, um, my . . . Damien," she stuttered. Her light face was flushed with embarrassment.

"Friend? Nah, tell him the real, shawty," Dame said with a smirk.

My mother, Mr. B, and Mrs. B had already left and gone into the kitchen because they didn't want to watch the foolery that was about to take place.

"This is my situationship that I was telling you about, Codi," Baby Girl said.

"The fuck? Situationship?" Dame questioned, wearing a fully pissed expression on his face.

"You heard her, son. Situationship! How you gon' have a girl looking like this"—Codi pointed at Raina—"and not call her for weeks at a time.

Not respond to her texts or come through to see her?" he quizzed, moving in closer to Dame's personal space.

"You been telling this nigga my business, shawty?" Dame asked, looking over at Raina.

She held her head down in shame.

"Bruh, don't come at me talking about me and mine. This my girl, so you don't need to worry yo' ugly ass about my situationship, nigga," Dame spat, now inching closer to Codi. I could see him tightening his fists by his sides and that vein popping out of the side of his neck. That vein was usually a key indicator that he was about to get some shit popping.

"Look, we going to the dance or nah, ma?" Codi asked impatiently while still glaring at Dame.

"Don't address her. Talk to me, bruh. Her man is right here," Dame spat, beating on his own chest before pushing Codi hard in his.

Raina instantly got in between the two of them, but they both towered over her small frame. Codi was first to land a clear punch on Dame's face. It was a hard hit that made a cracking sound when it connected to that nigga's jawbone.

"Damnnn!" Me and Melo shouted out in unison.

"Mama!" Raquel yelled out, getting up to go get her parents.

By the time they entered the room, Codi and Dame were on the floor in a full-out fight. Dame was on top, getting the best of Codi now. His light face was covered in blood, but he was still fighting my brother back. He wasn't no bitch nigga, that was for sure. That's when Mr. B and Micah pulled Dame up off Codi and got in between them. Both of their faces had already begun to swell from the beating they put on one another.

"Y'all just sitting here letting this shit happen?" Micah fussed.

Me and Melo snorted again in laughter. Higher than a muthafucka!

Raina had taken Codi to clean his bloody face while Dame was still seething in a chair in the corner.

Moments later, Mrs. Ernie's iPhone vibrated. "Hello," she answered. "She what?" she shouted in shock, stepping back into the quiet hallway to hear better.

I could see her put her hand to her chest, followed by a series of nods while tears began streaming her face. My mother immediately walked up to her out of concern and placed a gentle hand on her right shoulder just before she hung up on the caller.

"Y'all, we gotta go! We gotta go now! Romi woke up!" she hollered.

My high was instantly gone when I heard those three words, "Romi woke up." My eyes stretched wide as I sat up straight in my seat, making sure that I'd heard Mrs. Ernie correctly. When our eyes met, that was all the confirmation I needed. My fast-beating heart instantly sank to my stomach, and my throat began to close. I wanted to move, but I was frozen in my seat.

"Dre, let's go, bruh," Melo said, reaching his hand down to help me up from the sofa.

It was eight thirty, and the moon was full that night when everyone rushed over to the hospital. Codi must have headed over to the homecoming dance by himself, because Raina was in the car with Risa and Raquel. My heart hadn't stopped racing since we received the call, and now there I was, sitting in the front passenger seat of Micah's Range. No music, chatter, nor laughter could be heard. Only silence. The only thoughts in mind were silent prayers. Prayers that she was okay and that the baby was still healthy.

When we pulled into the hospital parking lot, I hopped out of the car before it could even fully come to a stop. I ran in, full speed and ahead of everyone else, anxious to see those green eyes that I hadn't seen in months. When I reached the elevator, my hand automatically went to push the number three button as it had done for many weeks prior. I could hear my mother and Mrs. B calling out for me in the distance as the elevator doors closed, but I couldn't wait for them. I couldn't wait for anyone in this moment.

Finally arriving on the third floor, I took a hard and deep breath just before stepping off. I ran down the hallway, bumping into an old lady in a wheelchair.

"My bad, ma'am," I said out of breath.

Continuing down the hall still at full speed, I bumped into a pretty nurse wearing green scrubs. I knocked her entire tray of medical utensils out of her hands. With my hands held high up in surrender, I said, "My bad," but quickly spun around and continued on my way until I finally reached room 304.

Standing outside of the door, I kneeled over, resting my hands on my knees, trying to catch my breath. I wanted to rush in and see her, make some grand entrance and let her know how sorry I was. I wanted to show her that I hadn't forgotten about her after all this time. Instead, I suddenly found myself immobilized. My feet felt like they each weighed a ton and I just couldn't walk in the room. I could hear the monitors from inside. One was slow and steady, matching the thumps within my chest, while the other was fast and rhythmic. The television was on, and I could hear the voice of Alex Trebek on *Jeopardy!* while the smell of disinfectant permeated the air just as the janitor mopped the linoleum floor outside her door.

"Dre, are you going to go in or what?" Mrs. Ernie asked, giving me a confused look before walking into the room herself.

Everyone was walking toward me and then passing me by as they entered her room. I could hear gasps and laughter in between bouts of "Praise God," and "Thank you, Jesus," before I heard her soft voice.

"Where's Dre?" she asked.

I slowly walked into the crowded room. Everyone was surrounding her bed with Romi sitting up directly in the middle. She was fully alert, her black hair wet and hanging down around her beautiful face while those bright green eyes stared directly at me. Silence instantly fell upon the room, and all gazes were turned toward me. The only sounds that could be heard were those same rhythmic beats in the background. With sweaty palms, I slowly walked toward her in disbelief. I had dreamed of this day, but in the back of my mind, I really didn't think I'd ever hear her voice or see her beautiful eyes again. Taking a hard swallow, I let out the only words I could think of at the moment.

"Sup, stranger," I said just above a whisper, finding my place in the room right there next to her.

"Hi, Dre," she said with her eyes still locked on mine as though we were the only two people in the room.

"I'm so, so sorry, Ro," I said with a trembling voice, choking back the bitch-ass tears that were threatening to fall.

I didn't even realize that a lone tear had already escaped and had begun to fall down my face until she reached up to thumb it away. I grabbed her soft hand and gently kissed it while quietly whispering over and over to her again, "So sorry, Ro," with pleading eyes. I wanted her to instantly forgive all my actions and finally take me out of my misery.

"It was an accident, Dre. It's not your fault," she said, taking both of my hands in hers then gently taking one and placing it on her pregnant belly.

"What is the doctor saying, Romi?" Mrs. Ernie asked, interrupting our intimate moment.

I looked back, and Dame was standing behind Raina with his arms wrapped tightly around her while she rested her head on his chest. *Convenient time for him,* I thought and smirked.

"He said that everything looks normal. He's gonna run a few more tests in the morning and go from there," Romi replied with a shrug.

"Is the doctor coming back to talk with us tonight?"

"Yeah, he'll be back soon," she said.

"We're having . . . I mean, you're having a boy," I blurted, wearing a confused expression.

Romi's face instantly saddened at my comment. It was like I had put us back at square one all over again. It was a reminder that we still didn't know if the baby was mine, but I was praying that it was. I was really beginning to care a lot for Brandi, but for some reason, I couldn't stomach the thought of Romi actually having a baby by another nigga.

As soon as that thought ran through my mind, I felt my phone vibrate. I looked down at the screen, and it was Brandi. I quickly sent her to voicemail and tucked the phone back into my pocket, but Romi had already seen it. I looked at her face, and she just gave me a half smile.

"Don't worry about me, Dre. You can answer her call," she said, staring at me with her green eyes.

"Nah, I'm here for you right now. Anything else is gon' have to wait," I said, rubbing my hand down her long, wet hair.

After everyone filled Romi in on current events and talked to the doctor to learn that she would be discharged in the next three days, I left with a lot on my mind. I realized that I still had love for Romi regardless of whether the baby she was carrying was mine. I was determined to at least get my friendship with her back. After everything we'd been through, she deserved that much from me. Besides, I truly missed laughing, smoking, and playing poker with my friend.

Chapter 27

Raquel

It had been three weeks since Romi woke up from her coma and was released from the hospital. Now here I was, back at school in my dorm room getting ready for my first college party right before the Thanksgiving break. It was no secret that I was somewhat of a weird girl. I didn't care to party or have any friends, but my roommate, Candice, had begged me to go with her out tonight. She said that the frats were throwing a party at Club Nixx, plus Risa said that she and Sabrina would meet us there, which instantly made me feel better.

The alarm clock on the nightstand we shared read eight thirty. After being lazy all day, I finally got up from my bed and made my way over to my armoire, which housed some of my clothes. I hated living in the dorms because for one, I didn't like people enough to be sharing all of my

personal space with them, and two, there wasn't
enough storage for all my belongings in these
teeny rooms. All we had were a few drawers underneath our twin-sized beds and an armoire to
hang a few items in. Luckily, I lived only an hour
away from home, so I could often get additional
things as needed.

"Girl, what are you wearing tonight?" Candice
asked, sitting up Indian-style on her bed. I knew
she thought that just because I stayed dressed in
sweats and sneakers all day, every day, I didn't
know how to dress for the club, but that was
where she was mistaken. Both Risa and Romi
were highly into fashion, and they made sure to
always keep me and Raina on point.

"I think I'm going to wear this," I said, pulling out a new long-sleeved navy blue Pia lace-up
dress from Guess. It was a form-fitting dress
that stopped right above the knee. There were
gold laces that crisscrossed horizontally at the
tops of my breasts and over my stomach, exposing the skin underneath. Then there was my favorite part of the dress, which was a subtle but
sexy long gold zipper that went all the way down
the back.

"Wow! That's hot," she complimented me as
she eyed my dress.

"What are you wearing?" I asked with my dress
on its hanger, still in my hand.

"I don't know yet," she replied, looking down at her acrylic nails.

I bet her ass was second-guessing herself after seeing what I was wearing, but I didn't care about any of that. I just wanted to get out and see Risa. It had been almost two weeks since I last saw her, and I had really missed my sister.

After undressing and wrapping my soft towel around me, I grabbed my shower caddy off the shelf and said, "Well, I'm going to go hop in the shower."

Later that night, when we pulled up to the club in my BMW, the parking lot was packed, so I had no choice to but do valet. Quickly, I gave my face a check in the rearview mirror, smoothed my hair, which was simply parted down the middle, then pressed my lips together to seal my nude MAC lip gloss. After stepping out and handing over my keys, I saw that the line was wrapped halfway around the building. I opened up my clutch and pulled out my cell to call Risa just as she had instructed. Apparently, her dating Micah had its perks, and we were able to get in without waiting in line. There was this tall, ugly *The Green Mile*–looking dude at the door who waved me and Candice over.

"Raquel Brimmage?" he questioned.

"Yes, sir, that's me."

He nodded and opened the door to let us in. When we entered the club, it was packed and almost steaming hot. I could hear "Black Beatles" by Rae Sremmurd being played while strobe lights bounced throughout the smoke-filled dance floor.

"Ayyee!" Candice sang, swaying her hands and hips to the beat. I looked up and saw Risa on the steps waving for me and Candice to come upstairs to VIP. As we made our way through the thick crowd, several guys were trying to cop a feel, and I could hear every catcall in the book like, "Damn, shawty, wassup," "Can I buy you a drink, li'l mama?" and "C'mere, lemme holla atchu for a minute."

I ignored all of that and pushed my way through until I was directly in front of Risa.

"Okay, I see you. You're gonna have to let me borrow this dress," she approved, looking me over before giving me a hug.

"You look pretty too," I said.

Risa always looked like she was stepping off the runway. She wore a cream crisscross halter bodycon dress and nude pumps. With her long, flowing hair tossed to one side, she wore dangling gold earrings and complementary gold bangles on her wrists.

"Oh, Candice, this is my sister Risa. Risa, this is Candice," I said.

"Hi," Risa said before grabbing my hand to lead the way upstairs.

As soon as we got up to the second floor and through the VIP rope, the first person my eyes landed on was Melo, who had a pretty Latina chick sitting in his lap. Although I couldn't stand him, I couldn't ignore that I was low-key jealous. Plus he was looking handsome in his black Balmain jeans, a long-sleeved black fitted T-shirt, and all-black Balmain boots. He wore a gold Jesus piece around his neck and diamonds in each ear. Seated in that area was also Micah, Dre, and his girlfriend Brandi. I hated that he was still with her after everything that he and Romi had been through, but I finally concluded that it wasn't any of my business.

"Hey, y'all," I said before sitting next to Micah. Risa sat down in his lap and took the glass of brown liquor out of his hand before taking a small sip.

"I told her not to wear this little shit tonight. Got all these fuck niggas in here looking at her ass, and now I got to keep my eyes on you too," Micah said to me, shaking his head.

"Nobody is worried about me but you, babe," she said.

"Yeah, whatever," he said before pecking her lips.

They were the cutest couple ever, and when I thought of relationship goals, I instantly thought of them.

"What y'all want to drink?" Dre came over and asked.

"I'll take a cranberry juice," I said, crossing my legs. Dre laughed at me.

"Cranberry juice?" Candice asked with her nose scrunched up. "Well, let me get a Long Island Iced Tea."

"A'ight, I got y'all," he said before going over to the cocktail waitress.

Even though the cocktail waitress was talking to Dre, I couldn't help but notice that she kept her eyes on Micah. However, Micah and Risa were so into each other that I didn't think either of them noticed. When I looked back, my eyes instantly met Melo's. He was staring at me while the girl in his lap appeared to be sucking a hole in his neck. I just shook my head and rolled my eyes in disgust. Of course he blew me a kiss just to get under my skin. Then he reached for a blunt that Dre was passing him and whispered something in his ear before they both looked at me and fell out laughing. My face instantly got hot from embarrassment because I was certain they were talking about me.

Cyko and Rich Homie Quan's "So Much Money" began to play, and Risa immediately pulled me up to dance. For me to be as square as I was, I actually liked to dance. I seductively swayed my hips from side to side while singing, "'So much money on me, so much money on me.'" I looked over at my sister, and she was rocking her hips to the beat as well. With my hands in the air, I dropped my hips down low and began slowly bucking to the hook of the song just like Raina showed me. Risa and I fell out laughing because she knew that I was stealing Raina's signature move.

Suddenly, I felt someone come up behind me and place strong hands around my waist. I turned around to see a nice-looking brown-skinned guy. He had a low, curly fade and was probably about five foot ten or eleven. Instantly, he got into the rhythm of the song and was dancing close up on my ass. I didn't mind because he smelled really good and it was all in fun.

After a few moments, I was really getting into it. I began to snake my body on him, which instantly got him hard. I could feel his dick pressed up against my backside before he leaned down in my ear and said, "Damn, shawty, what are you trying to do to a nigga?"

I shook my head and laughed it off before I could feel him being jerked away from behind me. When I turned around, I was met with Melo's cold stare.

"Fuck is you doing?" he spat, mushing the guy in the face.

"Oh, my bad, Mr. Borrego, is this you?" the brown-skinned guy asked as though he hadn't been blatantly disrespected.

"No," I answered, shaking my head.

"She's off-limits," Melo interrupted, walking closer to the guy.

"I didn't know, man. My bad, bruh," the guy said, holding his hands up before walking off in a hurry.

"Why did you do that?" I yelled over the music.

Melo leaned in real close to me and glared at me with his hazel eyes. He knew he was intimidating standing at six foot three inches tall as he towered over my small frame. His body was pressed against mine before he bent down to my ear and whispered, "Don't make me fuck you up in here."

"What?" I shouted in his ear.

I was so mad that Melo thought he could control me. He wasn't my boyfriend, and he damn sure wasn't my daddy.

Suddenly, we were interrupted by his Latina friend when she grabbed Melo's arm to turn him away from me. "*Papi*, whatchu doing ova' here with dis bitch for?" she asked, popping on her chewing gum all ghetto-like with her hand on her hip.

"Bitch?" I questioned with my face scrunched up.

Risa must have heard her too, because she came in close to the commotion. Neither one of us took disrespect lightly.

"I'm talking to you, bitch," she had the nerve to say, and she started taking off her earrings. Well, she only got one earring off before I punched her hard in the face. Crack.

She never even got the chance to get the other one off. She fell back onto the floor, and I immediately jumped on top of her. Yes, in my good dress and all. I pounded her pretty face over and over until I could feel somebody pulling me up off her. It was Melo. I kicked, punched, and screamed as he threw me over his shoulder and began walking out of the club with me.

When we got to his car, he threw me in the passenger seat and slammed the door in my face. My body was still pumping with adrenaline, and my chest was heaving up and down from all the rage that I had inside.

"Calm the fuck down, Raquel," he spat, turning on the engine.

"Where are you taking me?" I asked, still fuming.

He ignored me. I immediately reached for my phone, but then I remembered that I had left my clutch purse with Candice. "I need to call Candice. I left my purse and phone at the club. And what about my car?"

He called Micah on Bluetooth in the car.

"What's good?"

"Yo, tell Risa to get Raquel's purse and cell. And make sure ol' girl get home safe, too, if she's driving back with Raquel's car."

"We already on it, bruh."

"Good looking out," he said before disconnecting the call and turning up the music.

"And where are you taking me?" I asked again after turning the music back down.

"Don't touch my shit," he said, looking at me with a scowl on his face. He turned the volume up once again and cranked the heat up a notch.

I folded my arms across my chest with an attitude and stared out of the passenger window. After fifteen minutes, I could clearly see that we were headed toward Clark Atlanta, so I felt a sudden sense of relief.

"I live in Wright Hall," I said.

He ignored me and continued driving. After he passed the turn toward my residence hall, I grew more irritated.

"Melo! Where are we going? You know this is considered kidnapping, right?" I snapped.

After being ignored once more, I rolled my eyes and laid my head back on the leather headrest. When the car finally slowed, I could see that we were approaching an older neighborhood just a few streets over from campus. He pulled his car into the driveway of a large two-story brick house with a large porch and big white Greek letters on the front. I looked over at Melo after he cut the engine off and got out the car. I stayed put because I really only wanted to go home.

"Bring ya ass," he hollered over his shoulder before walking off toward the house.

"Ughh!" I sighed dramatically before getting out of the car.

There were two lone trees in the front yard. They were bare, the lawn covered in fallen leaves. I could hear neighboring dogs barking in the distance mixed with sounds of cars passing by. When I finally reached the top of the porch and approached the glass storm door, I could hear music coming from inside, along with people laughing and talking. I knocked on the door even though it was apparent that Melo had left it opened for me. Upon waiting, I looked back and noticing the flickering streetlight in front of the house.

Then I heard a couple of male voices yell out, "Yo, come in." When I entered the house, the strong smell of weed hit me in the face. There were several long plaid couches that lined the walls of the front living room. Several guys and half-naked girls were seated about with red cups in their hands. There were dominoes scattered on a large coffee table in the center of the room that was also littered with beer cans, bongs, and incense ashes.

"Ay, Melo upstairs," the big, fat one said with a nod toward the staircase. He was on the couch shirtless with a Jesus piece around his neck and a blunt hanging from his lips. I put my hands across my chest to hide the exposed skin from the crisscrosses on my dress. Don't ask me why I was shy all of a sudden.

"Her pretty ass looks like she scared, yo," another guy commented with a laugh. He was dark skinned and had a pretty baby face. No mustache or beard, just a dimple in his left cheek.

"Yo, she should be. That nigga's straight-up crazy, bruh," another one said, causing the room to erupt in laughter.

"Shit, I'll trade places with her," a brown-skinned girl with bright red hair uttered as I started making my way to the steps.

Melo appeared at the top of the old wooden staircase. "Y'all stop fucking with her. Come on up here," he said, motioning for me to come with him while wearing his usual mean expression on his face.

When I made my way up the stairs, Melo grabbed my hand and led me to a bedroom. To my surprise, the room was neat and clean. There was a blue and green plaid comforter neatly made on the bed, which was positioned between two wooden nightstands. A navy blue lamp was placed on each. In the corner was a large wooden desk with a laptop and a few neatly stacked textbooks on it. There were a few pictures of Melo and his brothers wearing their fraternity jackets and another of Mr. and Mrs. Borrego. In another corner of the floor was an old computer and several laptops arranged up against the wall with a large flat-screen television mounted above. And in the last corner was a long dresser and an old, faded blue tufted chair with a book bag in the seat. Next to the chair, I could see a door that led to an adjoining Jack and Jill bathroom.

"You can sit down," he said before taking off his necklace and placing it on his dresser.

I picked up his book bag and nervously sat down on the blue tufted chair. *So this is where he stays.* I had never been inside a boy's bedroom before, but I was kind of impressed, considering how much of a pigsty downstairs was.

Interrupting the silence in the room, he grabbed the remote control off the nightstand and cut the TV on. He slowly removed his shirt, exposing his caramel muscular physique. My eyes automatically scanned his smooth body, taking in his abs, which were chiseled to perfection, and that V that led down inside his Versace boxers, which were visible due to his pants slightly sagging. He had a large tattoo across his stomach that read "Borrego" in black capital letters and a few other tattoos on each of his arms.

"See som' you like?" he asked with a smirk.

I quickly looked away, embarrassed that he saw me staring at his cocky ass.

"It's all good, shawty," he laughed. "Take your shoes off and get comfortable. I'm about to jump in the shower."

"When are you taking me home?" I asked in an irritated tone.

He only ignored me as he walked into the bathroom and shut the door.

Chapter 28

Melo

After taking my shower, I walked into the room with nothing but my towel wrapped around my waist. Raquel was still sitting in the chair in the corner of my room with her heels still on her feet. It was now two in the morning, and I had no plans on taking her little mean ass home. I was tired as fuck and just wanted to go to bed after all the drama that went down at the club tonight.

I walked over to my bed and reached over to cut the lamp off so that the only source of light in the room was the glow of the TV mounted on the wall. After removing the towel from my waist, I pulled back the covers and got my naked ass in the bed. To be honest, I really didn't give a fuck. If she wanted to keep her ass over there in that chair all damn night, that would be just fine by me.

When she finally got up from the chair, I saw her walk over to the side of the bed with her arms crossed over her chest. I could see that she was rolling those pretty eyes of hers again.

"You're really not gonna take me home?" she asked. Her tone was softer than before, and it had a lot less attitude in it.

"I'll take you in the morning," I said, keeping my eyes trained on the television.

"Where am I going to sleep?" she whined.

"You can lie down with me. I'll get you a T-shirt," I said, getting out of the bed to get her a shirt out of my dresser drawer.

"But you're naked!" she squealed.

I looked back to see her childish ass actually had her hands up to cover up her eyes. I couldn't help but chuckle to myself.

"I won't touch you, Raquel. Just put this on and lay ya ass down," I fussed, tossing the T-shirt at her.

"Gawd, you're so mean," she said as she made her way into the bathroom.

After grabbing up a clean towel and washcloth, I knocked on the door. "I got you a towel if you want to take a shower," I said.

She cracked the door open and grabbed them out of my hand. I could tell that she was naked behind the door because I saw her bare shoulder and her naked hip exposed through the crack. Raquel was beautiful in every sense of the word. Even with her little attitude and eye rolling, she made me feel some type of way. I liked the fact that she didn't want to be like everyone else or had to do what everyone else did just to fit in. She was her own person, and I could definitely fuck with that. Plus her ass had talent out of this world. Her voice was nothing short of magical.

Shortly after I heard the shower stop, the door opened, and I saw her place her belongings in my chair. She cut the bathroom light out and began making her way over to the bed. Her long, silky hair was tossed to one side, and her flawless brown face was bare. Since she wore nothing but my oversized white T-shirt, it allowed me to take in her smooth legs and pretty feet. I felt myself instantly getting hard, so I quickly turned away, putting my back toward her.

"What, saw som' you like?" she asked sarcastically as I snorted in response, hearing the smile in her voice.

I could feel her peel back the covers and ease her way into the bed with me. I always slept naked, so tonight would be no different. To my surprise, she didn't mention it again.

"Can I at least call Risa and let her know that I'm here?" she asked.

I sat up in the bed and grabbed my cell off the nightstand. I texted Micah and Risa together.

Me: Raquel is with me tonight.

Micah: A'ight. Risa said to tell her to call her tomorrow.

"Risa must be with Micah but she said to call her tomorrow," I said.

Micah: Risa got her purse.

Me: One Love Borrego.

Micah: One Love.

"Oh, and she's got your purse, too," I said, looking over at Raquel.

She nodded. I could see that she had a sad expression written on her face before I cut the TV off.

"What, you sad for Floyd?"

"Floyd?" she questioned.

"Yeah, Mayweather," I said with a light chuckle.

"Oh, you got jokes," she said.

"I ain't know you had hands like that, shawty."

"Yeah, I don't play disrespect. You have to get your girlfriend in check," she snapped.

"Nah, that ain't my girlfriend."

"I couldn't tell by the way she was sucking all the blood out your neck like a gotdamn vampire."

"What, you jealous?"

"No. Were you jealous when you pulled that guy off me tonight?" she retorted, probably rolling those hazel eyes of hers.

"Hell yeah, I was jealous."

From the streetlights peeking through the cracks of the blinds, I could see a smile beginning to form on her face. She then quickly tucked her lips inward to hide it. It was cute.

"Why were you jealous?" she probed, rolling over on her side to face me. When she propped her head up with her hand, I found myself smiling at the bracelet I bought for her sparkling on her wrist.

"Did you see the way you looked in that damn dress? Had every nigga's attention in there, shawty," I said, pushing her soft hair out of her face and tucking it behind her ear.

"You don't even like me," she said just above a whisper.

"Well, you don't like me either."

Suddenly, there was brief silence between us as we stared into each other's eyes. I didn't know if it was her heartbeat or the sound of her breathing picking up speed, but all of a sudden, there was this intensity between us. Slowly, I reached my hand over to place it on her chest, right above her fast-beating heart, and to my surprise, she let me. She continued to stare into my eyes. Gradually, I moved my hand up to caress the side of her neck and to softly swipe the flank of her cheek with my thumb before gently pulling her in for a kiss.

At first, it was a soft peck followed by another one. The sound of our fast breathing could now be heard in anticipation just before I slipped my tongue into her mouth. My other hand finally found its way up the T-shirt she wore to caress her soft thigh. As if my hand had a mind of its own, it began to slowly travel up to her smooth stomach and then to her supple breast. Our mouths still intertwined as each kiss grew more intense than the last.

"You want me to stop?" I pulled away and asked low.

She shook her head and allowed me to pull the T-shirt over her head, exposing her beautiful naked body. Her legs instinctively fell open, allowing me to lie between them, resting on top of her as we kissed some more. My kisses began to deliberately travel down her neck and onto her breasts, first teasing her nipple with the tip of my tongue before sucking on each one entirely.

"Ahh," she moaned before covering her mouth in shame.

"You want me to stop?" I asked again, just above a whisper.

She shook her head again.

"Lemme hear you say it," I demanded.

"No, don't stop," she whispered.

My tongue gently journeyed down her abdomen until finally reaching the front of her clit. I softly latched on and began planting soft kisses on it.

"Mmmm," she moaned through labored breath, squirming beneath me.

Dancing my tongue all around her warm, wet center, I could feel her legs began to tense up. I inserted a single finger inside of her before rapidly flicking her clit with the tip of my tongue.

"Wait! Ahh ughhh!" she wailed, having her first orgasm.

I sucked each of her inner thighs before coming up to kiss her lips. "You taste good," I whispered with my mouth still covering hers.

Her eyes were still closed, and her hands were delicately crossed over the center of her breasts.

"Do you want me to stop?" I asked.

"No," she said quietly with her eyes still closed.

"You know what this means right?" I asked.

She opened her eyes up one at a time, and I could see that she was smiling.

"What? That I'm yours and I bet' not give your pussy away?" she mocked in a deep voice.

We both fell out laughing.

"You been reading too many of them damn books. But nah, it means you won't be a virgin anymore," I said in all seriousness.

My body was still hovering over hers with my weight resting on my forearms.

"I know. I said I was waiting for love," she said with a sigh before staring to the side as though she was deep in thought.

"You love me, you just don't know it yet," I teased with a chuckle.

"So cocky, I swear," she said, shaking her head. "Well, do you love me?" she asked, turning her gaze directly into my eyes and catching me completely off guard.

There was a pregnant pause in the room before I responded. "Probably. I just don't know it yet," I whispered before sucking on her bottom lip, then slipping my tongue into her mouth again.

After reaching down between us to stroke myself, I began sliding up and down the outside of her wetness. I stretched over to the nightstand and grabbed a condom before kissing her lips some more and gently running my fingers through her hair. Easing just the tip of the head in, I immediately felt her body tense up.

"Ssh, just relax," I whispered in her ear. I pushed a little more in and began trying to work the head of my dick in and out of her.

"It hurts," she cried.

"It'll only hurt for a minute. You just have to relax," I whispered.

She nodded, and I could feel her body begin to relax beneath me. After gradually working my way inside of her, I felt like I was going to instantly burst. She was so tight, yet her body felt like it was created just for me. I grabbed her hips and steadily began picking up speed. Her pain-filled cries were starting to turn into pleasure-filled moans with each thrust.

"Feel good?" I whispered. She nodded. "Say it!" I commanded.

"Yes."

"Yes, what?" I commanded, thrusting deeper inside of her.

"Yesss, it . . . it feels good," she cried out in pleasure.

Pumping in and out of her, I began to hear the headboard rhythmically pound up against the wall. Both of our sweaty bodies were in sync, moving in unison. With one hand, I gripped her right hip, and with the other, I grasped firmly on to her hair, going in as deep as I could.

"Open up for me," I hissed.

"Ahhh," she moaned, opening her legs wider for me.

I began to pound in and out of her, repeatedly, until I could no longer take it.

"Ungghh!" she moaned with her body trembling underneath me.

After she unknowingly granted me the permission I needed, I began to release into the condom.

"Ugh, shhiittt!" I groaned before collapsing on top of her.

I rose up and looked to see that she had tears coming down from the corners of her eyes. In all these months, I had never seen her so vulnerable. Suddenly I felt like shit. Raquel was a good girl with a tough exterior, and I was a creep nigga, but whatever apprehension she was feeling at the moment, all I wanted to do was take it away.

"You okay?" I asked. She just nodded.

"Talk to me, shawty. What's wrong?" I asked, wiping the tears from her wet face and hair.

"Just don't hurt me," she whispered.

I bit my bottom lip and nodded in agreement.

After getting up to throw away the condom, I got a warm, soapy cloth for Raquel, but when I returned to the bed, she had already fallen asleep. I got into bed and snuggled up behind her, softly kissing the back of her neck. As I listen to her lightly snoring, I couldn't help but think that I hadn't had a girlfriend in all my 21 years of living, and now finally I had this girl whose heart I definitely didn't want to break.

Chapter 29

Romi

"Twenty-seven weeks and his heartbeat is still strong. That's wonderful!" Dr. Mahoney said, putting away the fetal doppler.

While lying on the table, I glanced over at Dre, who was texting away on his phone.

"How have you been feeling?" she asked, pulling up the stirrups beneath me.

"So far, so good. He's been really active in there," I said, skimming my belly with my fingers before scooting down to the bottom of the table, spreading my legs, and putting my feet up into position.

"After the pelvic exam, I'll send you two over to the lab for the prenatal paternity test, okay?" she asked, looking at Dre for confirmation.

He nodded while his eyes and attention remained on his cell phone. Although he previously apologized for his actions, we still didn't communicate much other than a text here or there. When Dr. Mahoney told me that I didn't have to wait until the baby was born to get a paternity test, I immediately called Dre. At this point, I just wanted to know. After everything I had been through, I made a vow to myself that from here on out, my only focus would be my unborn child. Whether Dre wanted to be with me or be a father was no longer my concern.

After I got my pelvic exam, we headed down the hall to the lab with Dre lagging behind me, still texting on his cell phone. Once I sat down, the lab technician immediately tied my arm up tight and made me squeeze a blue squishy ball in my hand because she said she was having trouble finding a good vein.

"Ah, there we go," she said, smoothing her hand down the front of my forearm where a greenish vein appeared beneath my pale skin.

I squeezed my eyes tight in anticipation of the pain because I absolutely hated needles.

"Just breathe. Can you hold her hand, sir?" the lab technician asked Dre.

He put his phone in his pocket and took the seat next to me before extending his hand. I was almost too stubborn to hold it, but I really needed something to distract me. I placed my hand in his and squeezed it, closing my eyes tightly once more before I felt a piercing sting in my arm.

"All done. You did good," she said before I opened my eyes.

Dre had a slick grin on his face and was shaking his head.

"What?" I asked him.

"You's a big-ass scaredy-cat, shawty," he teased.

"I just don't like needles," I said, removing my hand from his.

After putting a piece of gauze and tape on my arm, the lab technician prepped to take Dre's blood sample next. After she tied his arm and cleaned it with an alcohol pad, he squeezed his eyes closed and clenched his teeth as if he were bracing himself for the needle.

"You trying to be funny?" I said with a laugh.

"You not gon' hold my hand, shawty? That's not cool," he whined in a joking manner.

I placed my hand in his and held it as he acted like a fool.

"Sss, ouuuu . . . ouch!" he joked as she drew his blood.

"All done. You should get the results within seventy-two hours," the lab tech said while taking off her latex gloves.

After the appointment was over, we headed outside to our cars in the gusting wind. It was two days before Thanksgiving, and the late fall air was full on display. Just as I had clicked the button to unlock my car, Dre gently grabbed my arm.

I turned around to look at him, and he asked, "You hungry?"

"I guess I can eat," I simply replied with a shrug before pushing back my hair that was blowing into my face.

"Leave your car here and I'll bring you back," he said, zipping his letterman jacket all the way up.

I hesitantly got into his car, not knowing what to make of the whole situation. I didn't want to get my hopes up high thinking that Dre was finally coming around or draw any conclusions that we were getting back together to be one big, happy family. When he got in on the driver's side, he turned on the ignition and instantly reached to hold my hand. I still loved Dre, and I didn't want to resist his affection, so I gave him my hand to hold on the center console. There was an awkward silence between us. Only the sounds of the radio could be heard on our way over to the Cheesecake Factory, which was close by.

When we got to the restaurant, he was a complete gentleman, opening doors for me and pulling out my chair. Before I knew it, we were eating and enjoying each other's company like old times. He and I always did have a friendship beneath it all, and I was glad to see that nothing had changed on that front.

"You look beautiful today, by the way," he complimented me.

I stretched my eyes out wide before taking a big swallow of my lemonade. "Thank you."

"This pregnancy is making your ass fatter."

"Geez, thanks," I said, rolling my eyes.

He laughed in response. "Nah, it looks good on you, shawty. Real good."

He licked his lower lip and gazed at me lustfully, causing me to turn my head and blush. I really didn't know how to respond because Dre hadn't given me any compliments or shown me any type of affection in months.

"You know I miss yo' ass, right?" he asked while cutting into his steak.

"Hmmm, and what would Miss Brandi have to say about that?" I replied with a bounce of my eyebrows.

He just snorted and scratched his head, not really knowing how to answer the question.

After Dre paid for our meal, he helped me up out of my seat and placed his hand on my belly. I could feel the baby instantly starting to kick, and I couldn't help but think it was because of his touch.

"Did you feel that?" I asked.

"Hell yeah, that's crazy." Smiling, he pulled his hand away and stared at me in amazement.

The baby began to really move like crazy then, so I grabbed his hand and placed it back on my belly to hold it there. He grinned so wide and looked at me before running his hand down the back of my hair and all the way down to small of my back. He then started to lean in real close, and I instinctively closed my eyes, inhaling his scent before I felt his lips on mine. It was just a peck, but our mouths stayed softly connected for what seemed like minutes before I opened my eyes and stared into his.

"What you looking at me for, girl?" he joked as we both fell out laughing.

"You two make such a beautiful couple," the hostess said as we were finally making our way out of the restaurant.

An hour later, we found ourselves naked in his bed. I was on all fours while Dre drilled me from behind. Truth was, my body actually needed this release since I hadn't had sex in months.

"Ahhh, Dreeee!" I moaned as he gripped one of my breasts and pumped in and out of me.

"Shit, bae, pregnant pussy is the truth," he muttered, steadily working his hips. He reached down between my legs and softly played with my clit while he continued to stroke me from behind.

"Ughhh fuuucckk," I moaned again on the verge of my orgasm.

"Throw that shit back, Ro."

"I can't, Dre."

"Throw it back," he commanded again, slapping me on the ass.

I began throwing my ass back to match his stroke as best I could with my pregnant belly hanging beneath me.

"Aaahhhh, Dreeee, I'm cummiinn'!" I wailed out in pleasure as he came inside of me.

"Shhiiittt," he hissed with a slight tremble before placing several soft kisses on my shoulder, neck, and back.

That night I stayed with Dre at Mr. and Mrs. Borrego's house. We played several games of Uno and ate snacks all night in bed, laughing and carrying on like the oldest of friends until sleep finally took us over around 2:00 a.m. Our naked bodies stayed merged under the covers until late that next morning. Suddenly, I found myself completely happy and in love all over again.

***

It was finally Thanksgiving morning, and we had dinner plans later that evening at the Borrego family home around four. My grandmother, Lisa Mae, was in town from New Orleans, and all of us girls were in the kitchen, listening to Mama's favorite Motown CD and cooking our assigned dishes for the night. I was making the baked macaroni and cheese while Mama was making her famous shrimp, collards, and sweet potato pies. Risa and Raina shared the duty of making candied yams while Raquel, who was the worst cook of us all, got assigned the cranberry sauce and yeast rolls. Mama bought her a few cans of cranberry sauce and a few packs of frozen yeast rolls to take over.

"How much longer on the macaroni and cheese?" Mama asked, reaching up high into the cabinet for some cinnamon.

"It still has about thirty minutes, and then you can put your pies in the oven," I replied, looking down at my phone to see if I had any missed calls or text from Dre. To my surprise, there was nothing. I hadn't heard anything from him since yesterday afternoon when he took me back to the doctor's office to get my car.

"I'm gonna have to see all these fine Borrego men y'all children keep hollin' 'bout," Grandma

Lisa Mae said while fanning herself with the "Dollar Saver" paper Mama had lying on the table.

I just shook my head. Mawmaw was a mess, and she didn't hold her tongue for anybody. At 68 years young, she made sure to keep it real at all times, so I could only imagine the things she'd be saying tonight at dinner.

"Oh, you're gonna love Micah, Mawmaw," Risa said with a wide grin. She was madly in love with Micah, and it revealed itself on her face every time she mentioned his name. It was funny to see because I loved Dre that exact way.

"So now if you dating Micah, then which one is you dating?" she asked, pointing to Raquel.

"I'm not dating anyone, Mawmaw," she said, keeping her eyes on the sweet potatoes she was slicing up.

"Mmmhmm," I muttered under my breath while rolling my eyes. Raquel thought none of us knew about her spending the night with Melo, but Risa had let the cat of the bag with that one. She had Raina and me on a three-way call the same night it went down. I just hadn't gotten around to mentioning it to her, but I was sure Raina did.

"Oooh, turn that up, turn that up. The Supremes, 1964," Mama squealed. "'Baby love, my baby love,

I need you oh how I need you,'" she sang while moving her hands back and forth like windshield wipers as she danced.

Mama could definitely sing, but Raquel's voice outshined everyone's in the family, and she knew it. Raquel quickly grabbed the wooden spoon off the counter and began singing into it as if it were a microphone.

They started singing together in harmony, "'But all you do is treat me bad, break my heart and leave me sad.'"

"'Tell me what did I do wrong to make you stay away so long,'" we all sang in unison, laughing.

Suddenly I felt my phone vibrating in my lap. I looked down in hopes of seeing Dre's number, but instead, it was my doctor's office. I quietly slipped out of the kitchen and into the hallway to better hear since everyone was still singing.

"Hello," I answered.

"Yes, may I please speak with Romi Brimmage?"

"This is she."

"Yes, we have the results of the paternity test you've requested."

"Okay," I said before taking a deep breath. After the night Dre and I shared, realizing that our connection was still there, I silently prayed that this baby was his.

"There is a 99.9 percent match with the alleged father we tested against. We will send you a copy of the results in the mail, but since you requested a courtesy call . . ."

"Oh, thank you. Thank you so much," I said, smiling ear to ear.

I was so happy, and I couldn't wait to tell Dre. After hanging up the phone, I made up my mind that Dre would be the first one I'd tell tonight before dinner, and then we would tell the whole family together. I envisioned that we would all be sitting down at the table, eating dinner together. Dre and I would be seated next to one another, and he'd glance over at me and grab my hand to confirm that I was ready. Then we would stand up proudly together and tell everybody our good news. The family would be so happy for us, and then Dre and I would seal our union with a kiss right there in front of everyone on Thanksgiving Day. I had it all planned.

Later that afternoon, we pulled into the large, circular driveway of the Borrego home. I sat in the back of Raquel's car about to bubble over with excitement as I kept replaying how I would share the news with Dre in my mind. As we walked up to the front door with our prepared dishes in hand, I had to keep hiding my smile. I was just that happy about carrying Dre's child.

"Hell, you over there grinning to yourself for, chile? Is ya high?" Mawmaw asked, genuinely concerned.

I laughed and shook my head.

Suddenly, the door opened, and Mrs. Calisa greeted us. She stood there looking flawless as usual with her neatly twisted locks pulled up high, exposing her strong bone structure. She looked just like Micah with that damn beauty mark.

"Come on in, ladies. Where's Brad?" she asked.

"He's bringing in the rest of the food," Mama replied.

We all went into the kitchen and started sorting out the food. My back was killing me from standing on my feet all morning, so I sat down at the kitchen table and rolled up some dinner napkins for us while everyone started preparing the dining room table. Unexpectedly, the baby started kicking something serious, and that got me excited all over again about telling Dre the news. I tried my best to hide the smile that was threatening to spread across my face, but I was unsuccessful.

"You still smiling, I see," Grandma Lisa Mae said when she came back into the kitchen to grab a few bottles of wine.

"Yes, ma'am. I'm just happy about this baby."

"Hmmm, well, I'm happy too. My first great-grandchild," she said, making her way back into the dining room with me trailing behind her.

"Well, it looks like we're ready," Mrs. Calisa said while looking at her watch to confirm the time.

"Now, where are the boys at?" Mama asked.

"I told them all to be here by four, but here it is a quarter after, and I haven't heard from not a one of them."

"Micah should be pulling up any minute now, Ma," Risa said while looking down at her phone. She must have texted Micah, asking where he was.

Twenty minutes later, we were all sitting around the extra-long dining room table with a huge feast laid before us. Daddy took one head of the table while Mr. Borrego took the other with Mama and Mrs. Calisa sitting next to them. Micah had finally shown up with Zaria and was seated beside Risa. I watched Dame and Baby Girl as they sat directly across from me at the table, sharing laughs together in between soft pecks that he delivered to her cheeks while whispering in her ear every so often. They were on again off again, but whatever they were, they were in love, and it was a joy to watch. Melo sat to the right next to me, and I noticed that he kept staring at Raquel, who was seated across from us next to Baby Girl. I could tell that she knew he was gawking at her, but for some reason, she kept avoiding his stare. I'd have to ask her about that later.

Dre was the only person missing from the table. I had left him an open seat in between me and Mawmaw. I had texted him a few more times, and when he didn't respond, Mrs. Calisa asked that we get Thanksgiving dinner started with a prayer. I instantly felt a sense of disappointment wash over me, but there was nothing I could do. We all held hands and bowed our heads when Mr. Borrego began.

"Heads bowed and eyes closed. Lord, we thank you for allowing us to come together and share this day. We thank you for the food—"

Before Mr. Borrego could complete his next sentence, we all heard Dre's voice echoing from the front of the house. My eyes lit up, and excitement took over my mood from the anticipation of seeing him again.

"Ay! Where y'all at?" he called out before reaching the dining room.

I felt the biggest smile spread across my face when he entered the room, but it quickly faded when I saw Brandi trailing behind him with her hand interlaced with his. My heart instantly sank to the bottom of my stomach, and when he looked at me, I could tell with just one look in his eyes that he was silently pleading with me not to let our secret out.

Wasn't this some shit. I was the one dating him first. I was the one carrying his unborn child. Yet here I was having to keep quiet about my love for him and the passion-filled night we shared less than forty-eight hours ago. All because he wanted to protect her and her little feelings.

His eyes darted to the lone seat that was next to me before he said, "We gon' just eat in the kitchen, Ma."

"Hi, Brandi. No, just grab a chair for her from the kitchen, Dre," Ms. Calisa said as Brandi waved to everyone.

She looked at me and offered a half smile, which I returned.

The entire dinner was awkward for me, and I could tell it was for Dre too. He sat right between me and Brandi and didn't say a word to either of us the entire time. Even though the food looked delicious, I couldn't eat a thing. I just kept pushing my food from one side of my plate to the other with my fork, hoping that this night would quickly come to an end.

After dinner, I went into the kitchen and helped Risa, Raina, and Raquel clean up. Even though my sisters protested, I still rinsed the dishes before Raina loaded them into the dishwasher while Risa and Raquel cleared the dining room table. Our parents were all down in the bar, drinking and listening to music, having a good ol' time. Zaria was upstairs sleeping while Micah, Melo, and Dame all played dominos at the kitchen table.

"Yo, how y'all gon' play bones without me?" Dre said, entering the kitchen.

I looked back at him from where I stood in front of the kitchen sink before looking over at Baby Girl. She looked back at me and smirked, then rolled her eyes at the sight of him. My sisters and I could have a whole conversation without saying a word. We were just that close. She knew that I wasn't pleased with him, and she could sense how uncomfortable I was at dinner seeing him with Brandi.

"Where your girl at?" Micah asked in his deep, raspy baritone.

"In the bathroom," Dre answered, making his way up behind me.

Feeling the warm presence of his being pressed up against my back instantly had my center throbbing. I hated how my body would always betray me like this when it came to him. It was the scent of his Prada cologne, the memories of our last lovemaking session, and just the simple fact that I was in love with this man, all in one. He placed his hands on the counter on each side of me as I stood at the kitchen sink. Then he positioned his face next to mine.

"You mad at me?" he whispered.

"What do you think?" I snapped.

"Yo, I planned Thanksgiving dinner with her months ago, shawty. Her family is from Cali, so this is so she wouldn't have to spend the holidays alone and shit," he explained.

I turned around to face him, creating some space between us with my pregnant belly, and looked him in the eye. "Don't do this to me right now, Dre."

"What you talking 'bout, girl?" he asked.

"Who's it going to be? Her, or me?" I asked bluntly while drying off my hands with the dish-towel.

I spoke loud enough that everyone in the kitchen's attention had turned to us. He ran his hand down his face and let out a deep sigh as if it were the toughest decision in the world. That was all the answer I needed. Nigga didn't need to say another word. I moved one of his hands that was trapping me between him and the counter, and I started to walk away. He instantly grabbed my arm to bring me back to him.

"Don't worry about it, Dre. The baby ain't yours anyway," I said before pulling myself out of his firm grasp and storming out of the kitchen with tears in my eyes.

Chapter 30

Risa

It was four days before Christmas, and I found myself staring out of the living room window of Micah's apartment, merely watching the snow flurries fall. It was a beautiful sight to see from twenty stories high as delicate white snow dusted the entire city of Atlanta. I could see the bumper-to-bumper traffic below and hear horns randomly honking as people drove in panic, not knowing what to really make of the weather. Then there were the pedestrians who walked hastily up and down the streets of downtown, wrapped tightly in their hats, gloves, and scarves. It was an unusual sight to see, but beautiful nonetheless.

Suddenly, I heard the apartment door slam shut. I turned around, leaving a frosted outline of my nose and mouth, which were previously pressed up against the cold glass window. My eyes instantly fell on Micah, who was layered down in a long black Triple F.A.T. Goose jacket, black leather gloves, black skull cap, jeans, and black Nike boots.

"You supposed to be getting ready, bae," Micah said, cocking his head to the side and giving me a knowing look.

I walked over to greet him with a tight hug and a simple peck on his cold lips. I could feel the wetness from the snow on his jacket, and when he embraced me, I could smell the wintery city on him.

"We have another three hours before we are supposed to be at the club, Micah. I have time," I whined.

"Nah, I know how you do. You take all day getting ready, and I'm telling you now I cannot be late. Pops will have a nigga's head if we are late to this grand opening."

"I know it's your big night, Micah. I would never ruin that for you," I said, putting my hands on the sides of his cool face to bring him in for a deeper kiss.

His hands automatically gripped my lower back and slid down to my backside before he pressed himself into me. "Umm," he groaned mid-kiss.

"We don't have time for that," I teased, knowing that he probably wanted a quickie.

"Let's make a deal. We can jump in the shower and—"

"No, Micah, because it's not going to end there with you. It never does. It starts in the shower, then on the bed, then in the kitchen, and before you know it, we'll be running late," I said, pulling away from him with a laugh.

As I started to walk toward the bedroom, I turned around and noticed that Micah wasn't following me. In fact, he was just standing there in the same spot, staring at me with his coat still on.

"What? Why are you just looking at me like that?" I asked, confused.

"I love you, woman," he said with his deep, raspy baritone voice.

I could feel the biggest smile begin to form on my face. All of these months Micah and I had been madly in love, I knew it, and he knew it too, but today, today was the first time he'd ever said it. My heart instantly skipped a beat.

"I know you do," I simply said with a smile before turning around to make my way back to his bedroom.

"That's all you got to say?" he called out behind me.

Smiling to myself, I ignored him and headed for the closet to pick out my dress for the evening. It was comical because just seven months ago, I was in a similar situation, living with my man in his downtown apartment while I still had a dorm room on campus. The difference this time around was I actually felt safe and loved, something I hadn't felt with Zo in years.

It was now eight thirty on the dot when we pulled up to Club Luxure, which was a part of their newest hotel. When Micah opened my door for me to step out of the black Bentley limousine we rode in, I was greeted with a red carpet and a bunch of cameras and flashing lights in my face. I fought back any nervousness I felt, and I stepped out while placing my arm in Micah's. After I pulled my shoulders back and slightly lifted my chin, we proceeded to walk in.

"Don't be nervous. You're the most beautiful woman here," he whispered in my ear.

With just those words, any anxiety I felt instantly disappeared. "Oh, and Micah," I said, looking over at him.

"Yeah, bae."

"I love you too."

He pulled my hand up to his mouth to place a kiss on the back of it before we continued walking together hand in hand. We were looking and feeling like celebrities as we smiled for the cameras and waved to everyone. He wore an all-black Armani tuxedo, with diamonds in each of his ears, while I wore a strapless silver sequined gown that had a high split down my thigh, and my makeup was flawless. My hair was in a simple up-do, which I complemented by wearing a pair of five-karat diamond drop earrings that Micah bought me for our six-month anniversary. We were definitely the couple to be in that moment, and I had to acknowledge that I liked who we were together. I had finally found my Mr. Right.

When we entered the club, I was impressed. It was a lot more upscale than Club Nixx. Everything was elegantly decorated in white with silver accents, between the white floors that had just a sparkle of silver in them, the white marble countertops on the bar tops, and the white leather stools that sat on chrome feet. There were also several shimmering chandeliers that hung from the ceiling throughout. It was a grand sight to see.

Already a few hundred people were in the building dressed in their best formal attire, champagne flutes in their hands, while soft dinner music played in the background. As I quickly scanned the crowd to see if I could find my parents and sisters, my eyes locked with a young woman whose face looked almost identical to mine. She had beautiful, flawless chocolate skin and silky, shoulder-length black hair. When she noticed me, she instantly hid her face and ducked behind a crowd of people.

"Did you see that?" I asked Micah, pointing to where I saw the young woman.

"No, what are you talking about?"

"There was a girl over there who looked just like me." I pointed.

Before I could go into it any further, my sisters all walked up to us.

"Wow, you guys all look gorgeous," I said.

Romi wore a bright red off-the-shoulder maternity gown that was sequined at the top and had chiffon at the bottom. She wore red lipstick to match, and I had to admit the color played beautifully against her buttery skin and bright green eyes. She was seven months pregnant and the loveliest I had ever seen her look. Raquel, on the other hand, wore a long black gown with silver beading. The sleeves and chest of the dress were sheer, and she wore her hair in an elegant side bun while keeping her makeup soft and pink. Well, all but her eye makeup that was. She rocked a dark, smoky eye, making her bright hazel eyes pop even more. Lastly, there was Baby Girl, who wore a satin mermaid gown with a sweetheart top that was the shade of money green. Her hair was in a loose fishtail braid, which flowed into a low bun resting on the back of her neck. Her figure looked amazing as I took in the sight of her. I had to confess that my Baby Girl was all woman now. She was no longer our little girl.

"No, you two look amazing," Raquel said, giving me and Micah a hug.

"Yeah, I love that dress. You look like a royal princess or some shit," Romi chimed in with a laugh.

"The Brimmage sisters are the most beautiful women in all of Atlanta. Y'all are shutting it down tonight," Micah said with a wink.

"Lemme go find my pops and Melody. I'll be back in just a li'l bit," he said before kissing me on the lips. I couldn't help but watch his fine ass walk away from me as he headed toward the elevator doors.

"Awww. Y'all are so cute, Risa," Romi cooed.

I must admit that after Romi came out and told us that Dre wasn't the baby's father, she had been much happier. She just let all that craziness go and started focusing on herself and the baby. Even in that short amount of time, I could already see her maturing. I was definitely proud of her.

"Girl, it's beautiful in here. Have you seen the inside of the hotel?" she asked.

"No, not yet," I replied, still looking around the crowded room for this girl who was wearing my face.

"What up, sis?" Dame walked up and said before giving me a hug. He was all decked out in his black Burberry Millbank tuxedo and black Louboutins on his feet. He even wore his Gucci shades for effect.

"Hey, Dame."

"Beautiful looking beautiful tonight, right?" he said with a chuckle, proudly looking back at Raina, who was obviously blushing.

"She definitely is a beauty," I said, smiling at her.

"Whatever," she humbly said with a shrug.

"Oh, I see Mama and Daddy over there, so I'm gonna go say hi," I said before walking away.

After grabbing a champagne flute off the tray one of the men passing me by was carrying, I continued to where I could see my mother and father seated with Mrs. Calisa. That's when suddenly I felt my phone vibrate from within my silver clutch purse.

"Hello," I answered.

"Nah, I can't do this with you tonight, Melody," Micah said.

"Micah? Hello," I said again.

"I do this for you every week, Mr. Borrego. Why not tonight? Please don't tell me it's because of that bitch downstairs."

That's when I suddenly realized that Micah must have butt dialed me by accident. I was now listening in on a conversation between him and his assistant Melody. Instead of walking over toward my parents, I decided to duck off to a more private area so that I could hear better.

"You being mad disrespectful right now, shawty. That's my wife."

"Micah, she's not your wife. She's just your girlfriend. And given that you've been sleeping with me these past few months, I hardly think even that title qualifies."

"Nah, let's keep it real, shawty. We only slept together once. I mean, yeah, I let you top me off, but other than that there's nothing more between us. I love my girl, and whether you want to believe it or not, she will be my wife one day," he said.

"Yeah, yeah. I'll believe it when I see it," she said.

I was so sick to my stomach, hearing that my entire relationship with Micah had been a lie. There I was wondering why the bitch was giving me all kinds of evil death stares and funny looks when he had been cheating on me this entire time with her. With my phone still to my ear, I immediately began making my way upstairs on the elevator. Although I had no idea where they were or how to find them, nothing was going to stop me from looking for them.

There was a long pause on the phone before I heard Micah say, "Stop, Melody."

"Just relax," she cooed seductively.

"Stop playing, girl," he whispered.

I figured that by this point, Micah was losing the battle, because his once-strong and demanding voice was growing weak.

A few more seconds went past before I heard, "Ahhh, shit. Just like that," followed by his all-familiar groan. I could hear sounds of her slobbering and sucking the skin off of my man's dick. By this point, I was furious, and my hands were trembling. My stomach was so queasy, and my body was literally shaking all over. *How could Micah do this to me, and even more importantly, with me right here in the same building?* I wondered.

"Michahhh!" I wailed into the phone, but he didn't respond.

When the elevator stopped and I had reached the second floor, I began opening every door that looked like it could have been an office. That's when I ran into Mr. Borrego. He was with Dre and Brandi. I quickly tried wiping away my tears, but I knew they could see that I was upset.

"Mr. Borrego, do you happen to know where Micah is?" I asked in a shaky tone.

"I left him and Melody in the office two doors down, dear. Is everything all right?" he asked, concerned.

"Yes, sir. I just really need to see him, that's all."

After walking down the hall where Mr. Borrego instructed me to go, I found myself standing directly outside of the office door. I closed my eyes and took one last deep breath before knocking. Yeah, there was a part of me that just wanted to say forget knocking and kick that bitch in to bust in on them, but then there was also this part of me that was purely scared. I didn't want to catch my man in the act with some other woman. Hearing it was one thing, but seeing it was another, and I truly didn't know if my heart could take that.

"One minute," he shouted from behind the door.

When he finally came to the door and opened it, I could tell that he had just gotten finished fixing his clothes. He just stood there looking at me with a sad yet guilty expression written on his face while my chest heaved up and down. He knew that I knew, but he damn sure wasn't going to be the one to speak on it first. That's just how men are.

I looked directly at him, and my silent tears willingly fell while I watched his body language became more and more defeated. There was so much I wanted to say, but I just couldn't find my voice in the moment. That's when I looked over his shoulder and saw Melody sitting there in the office with her legs crossed, reapplying her cherry-colored lipstick like this was nothing out of the norm. That's what drove me over the edge.

I reached back far and smacked Micah's face as hard as I could. Whap! "How could you?"

"Baby, lemme explain," he said with one hand up and the other holding the side of his face I had just slapped.

"This is how you do me? Someone who loves you with all her heart and someone who loves your daughter. Really, Micah?"

"I fucked up, bae. I—"

"You're right, you fucked up. I told you back then that you only get one chance with me. Didn't I?" I yelled.

"Yeah, but—" he stuttered.

"Didn't I?" I screamed.

Micah was speechless. I wasn't sure if it was because he had never seen me that mad or because he just couldn't find any words in the moment.

"You know what? Fuck you and fuck that bitch over there," I spat. I looked over his shoulder again and saw that she had the nerve to be smirking. "Is something funny to you, bitch?" I yelled.

I never even gave her a chance to respond. Before I knew it, I pushed past Micah and slapped the piss out of Melody. After getting her to the ground, I began punching her in the face while she tried grabbing for my hair. The two of us were tussling on the floor using whatever we could to hurt one another when I was suddenly lifted into the air.

"Get the fuck off me!" I yelled while trying to kick and fight from Micah's grasp.

"Calm down, Risa, please. I know I fucked up. I'm sorry," he pleaded, placing me on my feet.

"It's over! Don't call me, don't text me, don't even look my way, nigga!" I yelled through labored breath before leaving the office with tears coming down my face.

Micah was following me, but I wasn't hearing anything he had to say. All I wanted to do was get out of there. I hit the elevator button a few times but grew impatient and decided to head for the stairwell instead.

When I finally made it downstairs, Romi and Raquel rushed over to me.

"What's wrong? What happened?" Romi asked, concerned.

I knew my makeup was ruined from crying and fighting. My once-elegant up-do was now hanging halfway down, and my dress was slightly torn. "I just gotta get out of here," I said.

"Risa, hol' up. Just talk to me first," I could hear Micah say as he trailed behind me.

I stormed past my sisters and was headed for the front door when, unexpectedly, two men in jeans and black wind jackets with badges on the front approached me.

"Ma'am, are you Risa Brimmage?"

"Yes, sir, I am," I replied, scrunching my eyebrows in confusion.

"You are under arrest for the murder of Zo'mire Johnson."

"What? This is a mistake. I didn't kill Zo. You have to believe me," I cried.

They immediately began putting me in handcuffs right there in front of everyone. As they were hauling me out of the building, I looked back, and my eyes met Timo's. He had a confused scowl on his face. I knew he was now thinking that I killed his brother, but that was far from the truth. I just shook my head at him to let him know that it was not what it had appeared.

"Officer, this is a mistake. I didn't kill anyone," I begged.

Then I heard my father say, "I'll handle it, baby. Don't worry, and don't say anything."

After they took me outside in handcuffs and put me in the back seat of the police car, I stared out of the window in disbelief. This was the worst night of my life. Not only had the man I'd fallen deeply in love with broken my heart, but now I was being accused of a crime I didn't actually commit.

As the police car pulled off, I could see Micah standing there on the sidewalk with his hands in his pockets and a worried expression on his face. He mouthed to me that it would be okay. I cried because in my gut, I felt that it wouldn't be.

That's when I saw her again, the girl wearing my face as her own. I stared at her as she stood on the sidewalk becoming smaller and smaller until I could no longer see her from a distance. I knew then that everything would not be okay, that this was only the beginning of what was yet to come.

To Be Continued . . .